PROMISE OF FAMILY

Also by Anne Schroeder

PROMISE OF FAMILY
FIELD OF PROMISE
BOOK III

ANNE SCHROEDER

Promise of Family
Paperback Edition
Copyright © 2024 Anne Schroeder

CKN Christian Publishing
An Imprint of Wolfpack Publishing
701 S. Howard Ave. 106-324
Tampa, Florida 33609

cknchristianpublishing.com

Paperback ISBN 978-1-63977-494-4
eBook ISBN 978-1-63977-493-7
LCCN 2023952244

PROMISE OF FAMILY

Chapter One

❧

Levi Ruth's familiar black buggy glided toward the house, pulled by a high-stepping thoroughbred, its reins threaded between the fingers of a middle-aged, graying man hunched over in a scowl, his eyes focused on the country road. He wore the garb of his Amish community, a blue shirt, suspenders and a newly purchased straw hat to replace the black felt one he'd worn through the winter months. Amanda raised her hand and waved. He was abreast when he glanced over and gave her a wary smile barely visible under his untrimmed beard. *"Wie ghets? Gott gives us a blessed gute morning, this is for sure."*

"We're fine, thank God. Yes, a wonderful morning." Amanda's hand fell to her side as she waited for the whirring wheels to slow.

From behind, her three-year-old son made a panicked plea. "Mama, it's Granddawdy! Ask him, pleeeease!"

A slight flick of the driver's wrists brought the horse to a halt.

She leaned across her yard gate and tried to keep her voice from carrying back to where Noah waited. "Levi, would it be possible to take the child with you today? Take his mind off his leg wound? He would be so grateful."

Her father-in-law hesitated, indecision furrowing his snowy brows until he glanced over to where Noah sat dressed in a fleecy red sweatshirt with a fluffy green cap that nearly covered the eyes. His mouth tightened in a tight scowl, and he shook his head. "*Nei. Gmayna* business I'm on. No time for *rutsching* around." He turned back with a barely perceptible tilt of his straw hat and called to the horse as he gathered the reins. A second later, he was back on the road.

Amanda's heart plummeted when Noah's chin dipped in disappointment and his eyes filled with tears. "Granddawdy doesn't like me."

She hesitated, unwilling to dash the light from his bright, expectant eyes. "Granddawdy has church business. 'No time for fooling around,' he said. See, even his horse is hurrying." She shaded her eyes and watched the buggy disappear around the bend. "Maybe another day."

"Aunt Lorie said I could ride with her."

Amanda followed his glance to the smoke rising from a woodstove chimney in the farmhouse down the road. "Aunt Lorie's nice, isn't she? And she bakes the best cookies. Which ones do you like best? I love the snickerdoodles."

"I like moon pies. But I always have to share mine with Cousin Silas, 'cause Aunt Lorie says one is too much for little boys." Noah whipped his head up at a sudden movement in the pasture across the road, where his uncle John was leading the harness team to work. "I wanted to ride the horse, but it's too late, Mama," he wailed. "You waited too late. The horses are already in the field."

Amanda heard the disappointment in his voice and the accusation. "Maybe Lorie will let us ride to market with her on Tuesday."

"That's what you said last week. But Uncle John said he needed the horses. Remember?"

"We need to respect their beliefs, Noah. Even if it's hard sometimes. Lorie loves you, I know." Amanda turned from the direction of her in-laws' neat Amish farm and grimaced at the lingering remnants of winter decay that filled her own yard. A burlap sack of iris bulbs and winter-starts lay waiting to be planted. Nearby, her abandoned hoe and shovel taunted her. All she needed to get started was motivation. But first, her son needed a distraction.

As if on cue, a massive female cat with a matted scar on its face leaped from a tangle of winter-worn hollyhocks.

"Timberly, you raggedy little monster. Where have you been?" Amanda stretched her arms as forty-five pounds of Maine coon cat launched against her, pitching her backward onto the stoop. She buried her nose in the mottled gray fur while a huge, black-ringed tail whipped the air like a serpent. "You big, goofy, gentle giant. Where have you been hiding all these weeks? Did you miss me?"

"Mama, what is *that*?" Noah stared at the oversized, beat-up cat.

"That, buddy, is Timberly. She was my roommate here before I met your daddy. And she's come back to meet you and Jules. Come over and say 'hello.'" She ruffled the cat's silky hair, matted with burrs. "Timberly, meet my son Noah, another member of the Miller family."

Noah timidly ran his finger across a fan-shaped ear while Timberly eyed him inquisitively. After tolerating a dozen tentative strokes, the cat hopped down to sniff out the cast on Noah's leg.

"Old friends, new friends. Just like the book we're reading," Amanda reminded her son as the cat made a wary circle across the yard before returning to stand over its empty food dish. "She likes you, Noah. Do you want to be her feeder?" When her son responded with an enthusiastic nod, she added, "But she stays outside, understand?"

"Okay." Noah glanced toward his uncle's farm down the road. "Cousin Silas has barn cats. They no come in the house, either."

"That's right. On a farm, every animal has its job. Cats catch mice. Timberly's proud of her hunting ability and we don't want to spoil her, do we?"

In the house, the baby monitor erupted with a child's crying. Amanda rose with the familiar quickening in her breast that happened each time she heard her infant daughter stirring. "Mama's coming, Jules."

She made a nest for them on the sofa and smiled as Julie rooted at her breast, her fingers clenching spasmodically as she sucked. With eyes closed, she inhaled the essence of her baby's unique smell, a combination of herbal shampoo and stale milk and a scent that had imprinted itself in her brain until she knew she could pick her child out of a thousand newborns, blindfolded. Already she dreaded the day the baby scents would disappear, replaced by childhood scrapes. Babyhood forever gone. A sharp pang of guilt reverberated when she remembered her reaction to a hasty pregnancy test she'd stressed over a year earlier. *I was an idiot. How could I have not imagined such joy?*

When Jules was sated and burped, Amanda carried her into the kitchen and strapped her into a baby carrier while she made a cucumber sandwich for Noah on special low-protein bread, and sliced carrot sticks to dip into cashew yogurt with cinnamon. She dumped a scoop of protein substitute into a cup of fruit juice and added a few crushed strawberries to tempt a three-year-old into drinking something he dreaded. With the baby carrier crooked over one arm, she carried everything to the front porch where Noah sat on his bean bag chair with his broken leg propped against a makeshift banister.

"Noah, here's your lunch. Better drink up before Timberly gets it. I have it on good authority that kitty loves strawberry swifties."

Noah glanced warily at the cat and reluctantly drained his glass. *Another meal down. Thank you, Jesus.* She chuckled without bothering to correct him as he fed part of his sandwich to the cat. Time enough tomorrow for setting limits. He was happy and occupied and obviously fascinated with his new friend.

"Let's get a picture for Daddy. He'll want to see your new friend."

"When is he coming back?"

"Soon. Before your birthday." Soon? Three weeks was an eternity for a little boy, but she needed every one of those twenty-one days if she expected to form a relationship with Jacob's family. No matter that they lived just up the road their Amish beliefs would forever make her the outsider, the *Englischer* who had lured their son from their faith community.

As if they read her thoughts, the peal of women's laughter echoed from behind the white farmhouse. Jacob's mother and sister-in-law were preparing their garden for spring planting. Amanda closed her eyes and imagined what it might be like to have her own mother and her aunt Lydia helping her plant a garden. When she opened them again, Noah was feeding Timberly the last of his scraps while Jules contentedly chewed on a teething ring she'd dragged through the cat's matted fur. Amanda shook the cobwebs from her head and reached to wipe the ring with her apron. *What am I complaining about? I have a perfect life.* When another peal of laughter interrupted the silence, she made a spur-of-the-moment decision. "Let's go visit Grossmummi."

"Yeah!" Noah clapped his hands and tried to struggle to his feet.

"Not yet. Remember what the doctor said, 'no walking on a broken bone'?"

She bundled him into a jacket and helped him into a child-sized wheelchair the hospital had loaned them. With Jules transferred to a backpack, they started down the same road she'd walked on a similar day, five years earlier. *My shameless ploy to meet a handsome Amish neighbor! Praise God it worked.*

Chapter Two

꧁꧂

From a distance, the lofty barn and silo stood sentry over the entire yard, giving the farm an air of authority in the crisp, bright morning, and a thin plume of smoke promised freshly made pastries or cookies. They rounded the corner just as Noah's cousin, Silas, came running to meet them, his baby-fine blonde hair and beaming smile so identical to Noah's that the two could be twins.

Her in-laws looked up from where they were bent over in the long rows of freshly tilled loam, conferring about what they should plant in the garden. Jacob's mother Emma and her daughter-in-law Lorie were dressed identically in plain blue dresses with white aprons and white *kapps* perched on their tightly coiled hair.

"*Guder nammidaag. Willkumm!*" Emma offered a smile and wiped her hands on her apron before she swiped a stray strand of graying hair and reached to take the baby. "*Ach du lieva.* Look who comes ta visit

Grossmummi this fine day. We are deep in dirt, for sure and certain. Spring planting waits for no one."

Noah arrived from the henhouse he'd dashed off to and set his egg on the ground next to a mechanical planter before he followed his cousin Silas to pick up a spool of garden twine. When the two boys began unwinding it, their grandmother stilled their efforts with a "tsh tsh" that cowered Noah in his tracks. "Look at you two! Three-year-olds with more energy than a pressure cooker, yet." Emma smiled as she salvaged the matted twine.

"I'm almost four, Grandma," Noah protested.

The boys' uncle Samuel rounded the corner and added to the chaos, teasing the little boys in a tone that indicated he'd recently entered the uncertain range of puberty. Amanda hid her smile behind her hand as Samuel's voice thundered and cracked. "Save that twine for the bean stringing, *kinder*. Unless you plan to hold the vines above your heads until harvest day. You will make scrawny scarecrows, for certain." He swung Noah onto his shoulders and galloped across the planted rows.

His younger brother tagged behind. Nicknamed Young Levi to differentiate him from his father, this youngest Ruth sibling seemed older than Samuel, even though he was fifteen months younger. His mother's change-of-life-baby, Emma teased. Unlike Samuel, whose peach fuzz covered his cheeks while he waited his turn for *rumspringa,* Young Levi had traded childhood for quiet efficiency. A son an Amish father would be proud of. He looked up to notice her gaze on him and blushed crimson before he ducked his head. His untrimmed sandy brown hair beneath a straw hat was identical to every Amish boy's she'd seen. It was as though she were seeing a younger version of Jacob.

He looked around, clearly searching for something to focus his embarrassment on rather than his strange new English sister-in-law who had remained behind when his brother Jacob saw fit to return to Oregon alone. Seeing the hens that were invading the tilled garden, he scowled and called to the little boys. "Chase the hens to the pasture before they undo my tilling."

Emma flapped her hands at her youngest son. "Ach, no need to become techy, Young Levi. Get about the task yourself and the little boys will follow."

Samuel trotted past with Noah still perched on his shoulders, whooping with laughter as they shooed the chickens away. Amanda glanced down at the rich, loamy soil with its wealth of plump earthworms wiggling about. *Amish farmland lives up to Jacob's boast.* The hens joined a dozen free-ranging turkeys in the pasture already pecking the grass. A handful of Emma's ducks swam in the pond. She glanced around at the farm, unchanged from the first time she'd seen it. Further along the path sat the henhouse when she'd looked for an excuse to spend a few minutes with Jacob the first time she visited, out of sight of the parents. *Noah is almost the age that Young Levi was, back then. Time flies.*

Her sister-in-law Lorie approached, easing her muscles with a one-shouldered shrug as she wiped loose dirt from her fingers. "Forgive us our *Deitschi wege,* our Dutch ways. We are delighted to see you and the *kinder.* Welcome to our *gaarde,* such as it is." She chuckled. "We hurry to get the root crops planted in the waning of the moon. Although the Lord may send us another sprinkling of winter yet. It is not unheard of, a late storm. We accept whatever comes. But we prepare the soil, just in case."

Amanda heard the happy, lilting acceptance in Lorie's tone and turned to hide her surprise. How is it that this happy girl could have chosen Jacob's older brother for a husband? Grumpy John always finding the sour lining. *Lorie is the sister I'd have chosen, if I could have one.* "What can I do to help? Truly, give me something to do."

Lorrie laughed. "You miss your Jacob already, and he gone to attend to his affairs only a few days now. You need good, honest toil to keep yourself occupied until he returns?"

Amanda swept her gaze around at the battered fence that circled three sides of the garden, their patched wooden slats freshly whitewashed. Here and there, newly emerging perennials had begun to climb back onto the fence. By summer, the garden would be filled with sunflowers, asters, lavender, rosemary, and thyme, alongside a dozen long rows of vegetables needed to feed their large family. The earth smelled glorious. Fecund, the aromas filled the air with the promise of life and vitality. "I enjoyed many fine meals from this garden in my year here. I would like my children to do the same. I'm only sad we won't be here long enough to enjoy the bounty this summer." She looked around for Jacob's sister, the sibling closest to him in age. "Where's Sarah? She's usually in the middle of things, helping you."

"Our Sarah makes busy working for an Englischer these days. At a shop in town. She comes home late, sometimes after supper. And she works even some

Saturdays. Levi has laid down the law that she is not to miss family prayer in the evening."

"What is she now, sixteen? She isn't needed here on the farm?"

Emma chortled and glanced down at her hands, embarrassed. "Near to seventeen. A *maedel*, near enough," she teased. "A maiden. That means, for us, marriage age. She now wears her black kapp to signify to the boys that she is not yet married. Anyway, a woman's job is never done. When she joins us in baptism and has her own family, she will learn this for herself. Time now for her to spread her wings, some little bit. She is a good, sensible girl. We expect no trouble from her."

Unlike Jacob. The words didn't need saying. Emma was holding a bright smile, clearly trying her best to be a good mother-in-law. Amanda's heart skipped in gratitude at the acceptance she saw in Emma's beautiful, open manner. No matter what Jacob felt, she wanted a mother for a lifetime. "You two have been busy preparing your garden," she said, changing the subject.

"Ja. Young Levi saw to the tilling with one of the smaller horses. It saves our backs, for sure. We grow seedlings in the covered porch until it is time ta set them into the ground for the *frieyaahr gaarde*, the spring garden. This way we get an early start. Until then, we rely on the canned goods we put away last summer to tide us over."

Amanda smiled. "I'm spoiled with my trips to Costco, I suppose. But I freeze a lot of my orchard when it's ripe. My aunt Lydia and I canned every summer. She wanted me to keep the traditions alive."

Emma nodded approvingly as she dragged a

planting stick across the top of the furrow. Her control was unerring, her long, straight lines as true as the rows her oldest son was digging in the far field behind his heavy team of Belgian draft horses. "It is good to keep the old ways. We believe it is not good to rely on a government. Only ourselves."

Amanda paused to study her stern father-in-law, who was hoeing out the lumpy soil in a far corner of his wife's garden. He had aged in the past five years. His stern countenance had given way to a softness. Not gentleness. She could never consider such an emotion in a man of such deeply held convictions. For Levi, life was black and white, either good or bad. Nothing in between, not even a son whose opinion differed from his own. But he was more willing to allow his English daughter-in-law to visit, and she was grateful. That he didn't walk forward to greet her was not necessarily a bad thing; he was kind to Noah, and that was enough.

Amanda shifted her glance from Jacob's father Levi back to the rows where Emma waited for her to follow along behind. She picked up a salt shaker to shake salt on each radish seed as Emma had shown her. "What's that coming up through the soil?"

Emma pointed to the closest rows. "The butter lettuce will be ready soon. And the early greens. We provide you with those, even if the other vegetables aren't ripe yet. And drippy eggs for the boy. One a week won't harm him." When the boys came running back with their hands filled with eggs, she chided, "Use the basket, *kinder*. Lest you waste Gott's provision."

Amanda's heart sank in sympathy for Noah as his lip curled downward in embarrassment, but when he saw that his grandmother's stern words had no effect on his cousin, he added his eggs to her basket and ran back to find more. Emma noticed her watching. "Gentle, steady guidance from the time they are small, not praise."

So different from the methods I am allowed to use on my students.

Lorie danced Jules around in a circle, letting her play with her kapp strings. "Once and always a mother," she mused. "Even when my own *kinder* require much, I enjoy to play with other of Gott's wonders."

"Your children are beautiful. You're a great mom." Amanda glanced where Lorie's children, Leah and Silas, were trying to help with the planting.

Lorie kept her head lowered. "I don't take credit for the gifts Gott gives me. Only His work. No other."

Amanda heard the reprove in her sister-in-law's soft reproach. "Let me grab a rake. It's the least I can do since I've disrupted your morning."

"One task as important as another." Lorie smiled. "But I don't turn down the offer. Many hands make light work." She loaded the hand planter with carrot seeds and began rolling the wheels along furrows laid out in the raked soil.

"Everything is so orderly," Amanda said.

Emma returned from the kitchen in time to hear her comment. "Ja. We plant the fine seeds in the middle of the garden, where the soil is better mixed. The lumpy edges are saved for beans and corn. Squash as well, with a handful of wood ash on the mounds for the root maggots." She handed Amanda an ancient rake and showed her how to smooth the furrows. The handle was burnished to a satin sheen from years of use, and a layer of linseed oil and polishing during the winter months. "We plant the same way each year, teaching it to our children. If our methods work, we don't make ta change it." Emma glanced up to be sure Amanda was listening. "Tradition makes for a bountiful garden. We rotate the crops and make sure ta prepare the *felt,* the soil. It is a living thing, the soil. It needs feeding."

"Do you make already, an appointment to see the specialist doctor for your Noah?" Lorie asked. "It would be a good thing while you are still here in Ohio, to visit our clinic that specializes in the blood disorders."

Amanda nodded over the top of her rake. "I've printed out everything I found online. It's been helpful." She noticed Lorie's children running their dirty fingers along the cast on Noah's leg. "I can print you out the information."

Lorie hesitated. "We do not be so concerned with the 'why' of the infirmity, but only how we might treat the child so that he better serves Gott." She paused to correct her children. When Silas turned to play with Noah without including his sister, she picked up Leah, and wiped the dirt from her tiny hands. "Gott has sent the Ruth family few girl babies. Mostly boys. Time will tell if that makes a difference. It is possible that the mothers carry the blood gene," she admitted. "Some of the Englisch doctors suggest that we take precaution so that we no longer have children. This is a sin for us. We must trust in the Lord's plan." Lorie's daughter reached for her kapp strings, and she wiped the child's face with her apron.

Not sure if she should press the conversation, Amanda inhaled the earthy aroma of dark, loamy soil bursting with promise. She imagined it in another month, bursting with color and teeming with helpful insects.

After a moment, Lorie continued. "So yes, we welcome your information. But it will make no difference for us." At a noise from the porch, she turned to watch Emma rocking Jules. "We are prayerful that you and Jacob have more children. Often, the doctors tell us we should avoid a big family. But for us, this is not true faith." She shifted to ease the strain on her back. "We will bear children according to Gott's plan. Only He determines life and death for us."

Amanda thought back to the day they found they were pregnant with Jules. It was Jacob who calmed her nerves. Granted, she was still nursing Jules as a degree of safety against another pregnancy. But she'd panicked at the idea of another child with special needs. She continued raking the row of carrots without admitting that the doctors had talked to Jacob about a vasectomy. *Better to leave sleeping dogs lie.* Even though Jacob refused the doctor's suggestion.

"We plant the string beans next," Lorie explained. "We will need to put up plenty in jars to get us through the winter. We sell what we don't need." She carried a tin can filled with small, kidney-shaped runner beans, which she handed to Amanda. "We begin on the end near the chicken house. And pray to finish before the *kinder* get cranky."

Amanda set the rake aside, grateful for the change of conversation. Best to stick with the things they had in common: food and babies.

Emma joined them to string twine over the posts the men had set along the rows. "We do not believe in modern medicine," she said. "Doctors can quick-part an honest farmer from his hard-earned money. So much trickery. Plain folks ignore the virus fears spreading among the Englisch. No one of our faith received an injection, even though we had the lockdown, same as others. We had deaths, same as with the outside community, but it was Gott's will, who lived and who died. We are comforted in our decision."

"Do your children get immunized from childhood diseases, Lorie?"

Lorie glanced toward her mother-in-law before she admitted, "We pray as a family on this. So ja, we decide for it. Some do. It is an individual thing. Most don't. But our doctor made the argument that Silas's body is already compromised. Illness will make his body weaker, so we allow the immunization. And of course, our other children will have the same." She glanced up to see Amanda's reaction and continued. "But most mothers do not feel the need. It is not something we talk about. Our ordnung allows a personal decision for each." She shrugged. "Come, let us return to the house and not speak of serious matters."

Chapter Three

E mma looked up from the kitchen where she was heating coffee with Jules on her hip. "Who is ready for some *kaffi* and a bite?"

Amanda reached for her daughter. A strange, sweet odor on her baby's skin caused her heart to dip in sudden terror. *Not maple syrup.* She gave a silent prayer that the scent didn't seem connected to Noah's Maple Syrup Urinary Disease, that ran in the family bloodline, but it wasn't a normal scent of olive oil and baby, either. "What do I smell?"

Emma smiled. "Bentonite. Shampoo clay. I change the *windle,* the diaper. She had a touch of diaper rash, and I used what I had on hand. It will cure the rash in no time."

"Clay?"

Emma nodded. "Some mothers use their own breast milk. It is very useful. Or calendula flowers and aloe vera." She smiled. "We do not spend money on store-bought products when nature provides us with everything we need. I will send you home with some."

At the reminder of home, Amanda glanced at her phone. "It is time for Noah's swiftie."

"Swiftie? What is this?"

"His supplement. He doesn't like to drink it, so we try to make a game of it. Four times a day can be a bit much for a boy." She glanced down at her dirt-stained shoes, suddenly embarrassed. "Sometimes I feel overwhelmed by his condition," she admitted.

Emma exchanged an understanding glance with Lorie. "It is easier when your community can support you. Come, you take a seat, and I show you some of the ways we find ta ease the child." She poured a portion of vanilla-flavored supplement into two pottery cups and set them next to two apple muffins warming in the oven. She drizzled honey on each and instructed the two little boys to sit. "It is better ta share the burden with a friend."

Silas drank his supplement without complaint. When it was his turn, Noah followed his cousin's example without his usual fuss. When the cup was empty, he nibbled the muffin until the last crumb disappeared before looking around for more.

"Apple juice for thirsty boys," Emma offered as she poured each a scant amount. Without waiting to see that they drank, she reached to pour coffee for the women.

"How did you manage that?" Amanda whispered.

Emma gave her a wise, knowing look as she set a jug of thick cream and a plate of muffins on the blue checkered oilcloth. "It does no good ta allow a child to decide for himself. The parent knows what must be done, it is so since the beginning of time. The child is comforted by structure. Gott taught us that rules and boundaries are for our own good, and a child is no different. Noah is happier because his body is nourished. Now he can return to his play without a thought to himself." She paused as her son Samuel stuffed what remained of his own muffin into his mouth and lifted Noah onto his shoulders before starting for the barn.

"Does the doctor think the break in the leg is made worse by the blood disease?" Emma asked.

Amanda felt her heart skip. "He didn't say. Why?"

Emma shrugged. "Weak bones make an unfortunate side effect of this disease. But this is out of our control."

"We mothers do what we can. It is all Gott asks of us." Lorie rose and reached for a recipe box overflowing with odd bits of papers, 3x5 cards, and clippings. "Let us share our recipes for the special low-protein breads we bake. Send you home a loaf for later." She rummaged through the box and pulled out several well-used recipes before she handed Amanda a blank tablet and a pencil. "Here yet are some recipes flavored with fruits and honey. I call this one *Silas Bread*. When his sister begs for some, my son feels he has something of his own." She smiled. "We don't encourage selfishness, but it is perhaps a small sin for the many things he must do without."

"Do you send in samples of the monthly blood draws?" Amanda looked up. "That is the hardest on us. Noah hates having it done."

Lorie flushed. "We are not always diligent in this. We pay cash for everything. And sometimes the fuss and bother..." She paused to take a sip from her mug. "For us, such fear demonstrates a lack of faith. But we want to be fair to the child."

"We have a routine when it is time for the blood draw. Noah makes windmills with his arms. Whips them around and around until his blood is circulating and his hands warm. I draw blood from the side of his finger, whichever finger he chooses. He can also decide whether it be heel or finger. And which color Band-Aid he wants afterward."

Lorie nodded politely. "Does this make Noah feel his illness is the most important thing? That he is first a sick boy and only afterward an ordinary child?"

Amanda flinched at the feelings of inadequacy ranging through her head. Apparently she hadn't learned anything from the books and articles she'd read. Just once, she'd like to have something to offer Jacob's family to prove she wasn't a useless Englischer. "In truth, Jacob and I have discussed this. He thinks I coddle our son. That I should let Noah be a boy, not a patient." She laughed. "That's how Jacob puts it."

Emma smiled and nodded. "This is how he was raised...ta trust in providence, not live in fear." She glanced intently at Amanda, her eyes grave. "Your husband will not change in this, no matter how much you argue the matter. It will be better to understand and ta submit to his wisdom for the sake of your marriage and for the boy. No good will come of coddling."

Amanda opened her mouth to protest, but their advice made more sense than her own pitiful excuses. She missed her mother's quiet counsel and her father's. She allowed herself a deep breath before she spoke. "Maybe you're right. I hadn't considered it from his side." She managed a weak laugh. "Noah has a pediatrician, a metabolic specialist, a nutritionist...he's so used to going to the doctor that he thinks it's normal."

Emma nodded, her eyes bright with compassion. "Let the boy live and prosper. Do not smother him. Offer him the supplement he needs. Add it to a bit of *kaffi* if he likes the taste of coffee. Let him add honey, or fresh peaches, or even maple syrup, but do not fuss over it at each meal. He is not special because of his blood; he is special because he is a child of Gott."

Amanda's heart fell as she considered the advice. She opened her mouth to protest, but heard her mother in Emma's words. "I've allowed the doctors to define my child."

Lorie exchanged an uncertain glance with Emma and extended her arms in a stiff, unfamiliar hug that softened into a lingering embrace as the grandfather clock ticked off the seconds in the great room.

Emma's throat clearing broke the silence. "Noah may live a long life. Or he may soon go home to be with the Lord. The same with Silas. This is not up ta us. But what use is he to Gott if he is crippled with doubt? He will live an empty life."

Lorie released her grip on Amanda. "Let us pray for peace in this matter. Thank you, Gott, for all your help. Forgive us our sins, help us with the land."

"And the children," Amanda added. After the prayer ended, she slumped back into her chair and picked up her empty coffee cup, unnerved by the enormity of the moment they'd just shared. Emma leaned in and gave her an awkward pat on her shoulder. The gesture surprised her. Jacob had told her his mother didn't hug anyone but her husband.

Without warning, the gesture opened the floodgates

for her. "I'm so sorry. But your touch...I miss this so terribly. All the years my mother was paralyzed..." Her sobs deepened, and she opened her heart to a secret she'd been carrying. "On some level I blamed Jacob for our son's blood disease," she confessed. "I tried not to, but..."

"*Zeugnis* is good for the soul," Emma said. "Search out your failings and confess publicly. It is our way."

"I wanted my family to be perfect. Happy and healthy. Smart and successful." She heard her bucket list spoken aloud to two women who smiled non-committedly, politeness covering their expressions like a masque. Until she wasn't sure if they were agreeing with her or pitying her. When she realized that it didn't matter, she straightened and wiped her tears.

A moment later she was unable to hold back a chuckle. "I'm clearly in need of some motherly advice. So go ahead. I need to hear it!"

"You are wonderfully made, sister. Pray to Gott. Listen for His answer in the silence. Do not worry about tomorrow. Be at peace today. That is all you need." Lorie waited a moment before she reached to refill their mugs.

In the silence, the ticking clock and the snap of the woodstove lent a camaraderie that filled the cracks of her heart. Small, ordinary sounds, the cooing of babies in their laps, the creak of stiff leather shoes, the click of her wedding ring against the handle of a mug seemed to harmonize with the sounds of their breathing, until the sound of children's laughter pierced the silence.

Outside, Noah and his cousin were perched in the hay pile, throwing handfuls of hay at their uncle Samuel—who didn't seem concerned that Noah's cast might get soiled. A dozen consequences played in her mind, diseases that her son could contract. She started to rise, but she caught her mother-in-law's wry smile and settled back on her chair.

"The coffee hits the spot," Emma murmured.

She toyed with the handle of her mug while childish laughter continued in the background, her son's seemingly louder than the rest. When Samuel drove his buggy past, a few minutes later, pulling the boys down the driveway with the wheelchair tied on the end of a rope, she clenched her coffee cup and fought an anxiety attack. She took comfort that neither Emma nor Lorie seemed concerned. The buggy slowed and returned to the barn with the little boys unscathed. She released her grip and took another sip of coffee.

Emma smiled. "Little boys have grown up on farms for thousands of years. Our Jacob would agree."

Small steps, Amanda reminded herself when she collected Noah in the wheelchair for their walk home, with all his limbs still intact and his enthusiasm at fever pitch.

"Do you see me, Mama? I love Uncle Samuel. He's my bestest friend next to Silas."

The changes in Noah's behavior began with his next meal. He insisted on spooning his supplement into his father's favorite coffee cup, with a generous dollop of honey that he stirred until it was smooth. "Silas says girls can't drink swifties. Only boys."

"Is that so?" Amanda smiled as she prepared a plate of oven roasted vegetables and a dip of ranch dressing for him.

Noah glanced around. "I want Grossmummi's muffins for supper. Two." He held up two fingers.

She retrieved a muffin from the batch Emma had sent home. "One's enough."

"Okay."

She phoned Jacob as soon as the children were asleep, from her side of the bed they would share again once he returned. She slid her leg along the rumpled sheet. "I miss you, sweetie. Everything reminds me of you. You're driving me crazy, wanting you and then remembering you're not here. We spend a lot of time at your mama's, talking about what a great guy you are."

"Is that right?"

She wiggled her toes in delight over the wariness in his voice. He was actually worried that the two of them were comparing notes! "Your mother's a genius with the boys. She has all the bases covered. She gave me some clay for that pesky diaper rash of Jules's that keeps flaring up. And—"

Jacob laughed through the speaker. "You are filled with praise for a woman I know pretty good."

Amanda squeezed her eyes shut to contain the goodness in his honeyed voice while contentment flooded her veins, soft and sweet in the warmth of bedding that still held his essence. She was filled with gratitude for the blessings of this day. "Jacob, I love her as a mother."

"She is kind and loving. I'm glad for you. But don't let yourself in for disappointment. You are not one of them."

She felt reality reassert itself into the bliss of her imagination and she nodded. "Yeah, there's a lot we don't talk about. But it was nice. I'm thrilled for Noah. He loves his cousin."

"John's kid?" His tone held a trace of sarcasm that he didn't try to mask. "Ja, right."

"Jacob...don't start!" She heard herself make a quick nervous laugh before she changed the subject. "Hey, I'm thinking to run down to the Mercantile in Kidron. You need anything?"

"In truth, I could use a pair of suspenders like Amos Byler wears. No laughing now. I'm serious. I haven't gotten the knack of a belt yet. I prefer the suspenders."

Amanda burst out laughing. "Now you've ruined my surprise. I was planning to get you a pair for your birthday. In bright red."

"Well, okay then. I'll wait to be surprised." His voice broke into huskiness. "What else you giving me? You miss me?"

"More than you can imagine. Only today I was remembering..."

She hung up the phone when Jules's crying brought their call to an end. Her heart was light as she lifted her daughter from the crib.

Chapter Four

❦

"Lorie, I need to drive down to Lehman's Mercantile. Jacob needs something from there. Maybe you'd like to ride along?" When Lorie hesitated, Amanda added, "We could leave after lunch and be back before you need to start John's supper." She glanced up in time to see Lorie's face flood with color. When Lorie glanced at the floor to avoid looking directly at her, she thought she understood the hesitation. "Maybe Emma could watch the children for us?"

Lorie's gaze flickered to meet hers. "Amanda, we are not like other people. It is no secret we are called 'peculiar.' It is true. I am so sorry, but my husband demands that I tell you the truth. People would see me, and they would report my transgressions to the deacons. My husband...even Emma would be put in a difficult position, do you not see?" She pressed her hands together, embarrassed.

Reality hit with the force of a hammer. Every day she saw Amish people riding in cars driven by stern-faced Mennonite drivers or women of a certain age. Surely some of them were going shopping. Not everyone could be headed to the doctor's office. "Of course. I just thought..." It was her turn to be embarrassed. "I should be going, anyway. I'll collect Noah and see myself out. I didn't mean to—"

Lorie swiped at her hands with a dishtowel from the counter, a quick, nervous motion that betrayed her. "Amanda, it is fine that Noah spends time with my son. You will only be here a short time and they are friends, cousins. They are not yet concerned with the rules that bind us adults. Leave them to enjoy their childhood." She stood pleading, with tears in her eyes. "I enjoy your company, Amanda. I love hearing about your mother, and the things you have suffered in your love of her. And your love of Jacob." Her voice thickened and her tone lowered to a whisper. "But my husband warns me that we cannot be friends. And I know this even without his telling. We are linked by circumstance, but we cannot be friends. I am sorry."

Amanda leaned to pick Jules up from where she was playing on the hardwood floor, glad for the distraction while she blinked away tears of humiliation. When the moment passed and she could look up without embarrassing herself, she straightened and made her way to the door while she tried to think of something that would ease the awkwardness. "Thank you for watching my son. I promise I won't take advantage of you again. It's just that he and Silas play so well together. He gets so bored with the cast on, having to sit on a cushion and play with his trucks. He's always asking to come up and see all the animals and everything...and he loves the chickens...and—"

"Stop, Amanda, please!" Lorie advanced until she was standing in the small area where the door needed to swing if Amanda was to make her escape without tears. "You do not be *deerich* to me, foolish. If you lived Plain, we would be inseparable, our lives intertwined. As would our sons'. But you are not." She brushed her fingers across Amanda's loose-flowing hair and smiled. "You have a beautiful heart. A loving spirit. And I will miss you when you return home to Oregon." Lorie stepped quickly back when she heard footsteps approaching. Her husband entered and frowned at Amanda before he disappeared into the kitchen. Lorie gave a short, sharp laugh. "Look at the time. My John is in for his noon dinner...and me dawdling with a customer. Thank you for the purchase of the eggs, Amanda. I will have Noah fed when you come for him this afternoon. Do not have a care for his cast. Silas will play gently with him. Have a blessed day."

Amanda stepped out of the door and heard it close behind her as she carried Jules to her car seat. She leaned in, grateful for the excuse of strapping her in. She managed to straighten and wave to Noah without betraying the fact that her brain felt numb with the shock of the last five minutes. She drove home and parked before she allowed herself to cry.

After a few minutes, she talked herself out of making a call to Jacob. He had enough on his plate. After all, he'd warned her that things might be difficult. Instead, she made a call to her best friend in Ohio, her guide to all things Amish, *faux pas* soother and general all-round good listener. "Carol, gotta minute?" When the phone projected her face on the screen, Amanda saw Carol's curly disarray and her wide-set brown eyes that dripped with warmth and compassion.

"Oh-oh, I know that face. What's up?" Carol's voice brought a smile without her even trying.

Amanda hesitated. They'd been fast friends since the day Carol offered her a cup of coffee and a piece of pie at the diner to curb her homesickness. *Best friend in Ohio* had gradually yielded to *best friend, period.* Matron of Honor, Godmother to her first-born, they were racking up some serious best-friend mileage. Carol's presence was one of the reasons she'd stayed behind in Ohio instead of driving home when Jacob needed to return for the family business. *Girl time.* They made late-night wine toasts to each other; sisters that neither of them had ever had.

On the other end, Carol sounded concerned. "What's up? You sound like you're ready for some company. You can come over here. Rennie's home, but maybe we can find a quiet corner."

"No thanks. Tell your husband I'm sorry, but I have four hours to myself. I was thinking of making a shopping run. Something to make me feel normal again." She hesitated. "That's why I'm calling. I need someone to snivel to."

"I'm on. Let's do this."

In the car, Amanda wasted no time in explaining why her makeup was smeared and her eyes swollen. "I'm so ashamed, Carol. What was I thinking? That we were going to be besties? But then, why not? Look at us, our kids the same age. We're sisters-in-law. Even neighbors. I never had a sister. I thought..." She swallowed before she admitted, "Lorie as much as told me to leave." She braked for a slow-moving Amish family buggy that she nearly didn't notice until she made a last-minute pull-around to pass.

Carol gripped the passenger's door handle. "Watch it, sistah. We got precious cargo in the back seat. Something happens to you, your son might end up being reared by his uncle John. When he's old enough he'll grow out his beard and marry Plain." Her tone was joking, but her face had paled.

"Seriously." Amanda whacked the steering wheel with her palm. "I thought I could...that she and I were going to be friends."

Carol's eyebrows lifted in surprise. "Haven't we been down this road?"

Amanda glanced up at an exit sign and eased her foot on the accelerator. "I changed my mind. No wallowing in a Plain store today. We're going to the Galleria Mall in Cleveland. I've wanted to see it since I was a little girl. My aunt Lydia was going to take me to see the glass tower."

"Oh-oh. Too late. Curse of the online shoppers, another brick and mortar hit the dust. But I know just the place. Let's check out the wharf then do the Rock and Roll Hall of Fame." She glanced at the baby and frowned. "The wind comes off the lake like crazy this time of year. Jules will get an earache."

"Jackets in the trunk, always. And we'll stay indoors. No more sniveling, I promise." Amanda felt her tension headache easing as she drove past neat rural farms and industrial yards, past road signs that directed them to the airport. "Cleveland Hopkins Airport," she read aloud. "I was just here two weeks ago. Noah waved his daddy off." She waited as a jet raced down the runway and roared overhead. "Noah's an airport nut. He'll be upset if he hears he missed this."

"Your kiddo's better off at the farm. He'd hate our shopping trip." Carol glanced over her shoulder at the baby seat. "Jules is out like a light. That baby's a self-soother, for sure."

"Wow! Someone's been reading her parenting book. Anything you want to tell me?" Amanda intended it as a joke until she saw the happy look on Carol's face. "So you're having a baby! When were you going to tell me? Their laughter filled the car, happy noise that woke Jules from her nap. If there'd been any chance of her falling back asleep, an overhead plane jinxed the plan.

They pulled into a parking spot just as a spring shower began. They raced along the waterfront, inhaling the aromas of ozone and restaurant food while they ducked in and out of shops. When Jules gave her hungry cry, they found an indoor seat at one of the cozy bistros that offered fresh fish tacos with cilantro lime cabbage.

As soon as the young waitress brought their order, Carol spooned a bit into Jules's mouth while Amanda watched her daughter laugh and reach for more. "I missed this with Noah. Ordinary things. Ice cream cones. Quesadillas, hotdogs. I hope he never discovers how much he's missed."

Carol glanced up with a taco halfway to her mouth. "Do you ever feel tempted to blame...I mean, feel like it's Jacob...after all, it's an Amish genetic disease."

"Mennonite. No. We don't go there. Ever. My dad taught me that blame never helps anything. In all the years, he never blamed Mom once. Or even the other driver. And that lesson stuck."

"Hey, my bad. I shouldn't have—"

Amanda handed her daughter a cracker and watched as she made a gummy mess. "Jacob heaps enough blame on himself, he doesn't need me to."

"Touché!" Carol wiped her fingers on a growing collection of used napkins and reached for her phone. "Let's hit the R&R Museum next. Nothing like a little culture to wipe the egg off Auntie's face." She leaned over the table and drained the last drop from Amanda's glass of chardonnay. "Last drink for me until baby arrives. Unless I opt to go French and allow myself a nip every night. Haven't made up my mind yet."

"I opted for no alcohol. Glad I did. When Noah was born with his problem, it was one less guilt trip for me, I guess."

"Point taken!" Carol glanced at her phone. "We better hit the museum if you wanna get back home before four."

Chapter Five

A manda pulled up at the Ruth farm as the boys were driving the cows into the barn for their evening milking. Noah rode on Samuel's shoulders, holding an oversized staff with a look of such self-importance that she had to scramble for her phone camera. She snapped two shots from inside the car, hopefully without anyone noticing. Afterward, she remained rooted in her seat, dreading the moment that she'd need to knock on the door and see John's scowling face.

A moment later, Lorie emerged from the door, wiping her hands on her apron. "A successful market day for you, Amanda?"

"I...my friend Carol and I went shopping. I needed a pair of suspenders for Jacob. He prefers them to a belt."

"Try Wiser Good's Mercantile. He carries a serviceable pair. Or you can sew them from strong fabric as we do. No reason to spend well-earned cash on such a basic need. I will show you how."

Her vision of John's scowl was enough to discourage the idea. "I don't want to trouble you. I'll try the Mercantile."

Lorie's smile softened her face. "Amanda, come by on sewing day, and let me show you how we make them. Jacob will appreciate the familiar feel. It is the least I can do. Between us, we will find a path that offends neither our beliefs nor our husbands."

Noah came riding up, grinning from ear to ear. "I got eggs in a basket. I help Uncle Samuel push cows. And I shut the gate. And cows gave milk. And I wear his hat. My leg has an ouchie, but I am a farmer. Uncle Samuel sez I beat the pants off him."

Amanda flashed a grateful look at Samuel. Noah's cheeks blazed with pride, and his fists held enough grime to fill the bathtub when he got home, but the fragile little boy had disappeared. "That's wonderful, Noah. Wait until we tell your daddy! Now thank your Aunt Lorie for allowing you to stay and hop in your car seat. Time for your swiftie before your favorite cup decides to run away with the spoon."

"Nu-huh. It's the dish, not the cup, Mama. You're silly."

Contentment flooded through her like warm sand as she glanced around at Jacob's family. She smiled at Lorie and saw the feeling reflected. "Thank you for keeping him. Noah loves this place." *Just like his father did.*

Lorie's plain face was wreathed in kindness. "No need for *denki*, Amanda. He is welcome here to learn our values. It is our duty. And he is a *wunderbarr gute* helper."

At home, Amanda assembled Noah's dinner while

he talked non-stop about his day. She ran a bath and sponged his leg, avoiding the cast while the water grew dark with dirt. "You like farming?"

"Ja."

She laughed. "What did you just say?"

"Ja. Like Daddy. And Uncle Samuel. It means, 'sure, I do.'"

"Ja, I know it does. Do you want to dry off and call Daddy? Tell him about your day?"

"Ja."

When he finished sharing his news, Amanda took the phone. "I miss you guys," Jacob said. "This house is quiet without the small voices and the mother hollering at her brood."

"I don't holler. I'm balanced and reasonable. Logical and caring."

The sound of his laughter soothed the ragged edges of her soul. "I miss you, too." She reluctantly conceded the morning's dust-up with Lorie. "I guess I thought that since I'm a good person, she'd welcome me with open arms." Jacob's slow, measured breathing aimed a hammer blow to the guilt she felt. "You're not saying it, but I can hear 'I told you so' in your voice," she admitted.

"Nah. None of that. You'll figure it out. You always do. And what does it matter if they don't want to be your best friend? That's my job."

Her throat clogged with tears. "I guess I wanted a sister, you know? Cousins for the kids. A bigger family." She hesitated. "Your brother Samuel is so good with Noah. He carries him on his shoulder so Noah isn't as confined. Our son's going to miss this so much."

"We knew where this path led when we started on

it, liebchen." His voice thickened with emotion, and he gave a low chuckle. "We'll just have to make our own brood. Do you think Gott gives us six or seven?"

She heard his suggestion, spoken in the low, seductive voice he used when they were alone. She closed her eyes and imagined him lying in their bed, his eyes dusky gray with passion. Her heart fluttered with a need to be held, even if the distance made it impossible. "My life begins and ends with you, Jacob. Sometimes I get selfish for more. And then I remember how much I have." She paused to swallow the lump in her throat. "With you and the kids."

His voice sounded rusty with passion. "I feel it, too. I returned to an empty house, and I realize how much I love this place, and the fellows working for us. And walking just a few steps home to my family at the end of the day. So many things the same as an Amishman enjoys. I have the best of both ways. I am a happy man."

After a moment of silence, Amanda remembered her news. "Carol and Rennie are expecting. My kids will have cousins, after all."

"Good friends...close enough to family, anyway. And who knows what the future brings? Difficulty is a miracle in its first stage."

"Jacob, I heard your mother say that very same thing this morning." She laughed. "When we get home, I'm going to write Lorie once a month. Send her pictures of the children as they grow. We may not be best friends, but we're still family."

"Ja, this will be a good thing. You will follow your conscience and no matter, the shame will not be on you if they reject your efforts. *Ich lieba dich, liebchen.*"

"I love you, too, sweetheart."

Chapter Six

❦

Amanda peered from behind the curtain, certain she saw a car parked near the creek behind her house. Dusk had fallen and the evening was already growing brisk. "It can't be one of the Ruths. And I don't know anyone else."

With a glance at her sleeping children, she grabbed a flashlight from the kitchen drawer and closed the door behind her. The corn stubble crunched under her feet as she made her way across the field to a tangle of willow at the creek's edge. She was almost ready to retreat when she heard giggles and terse whispers, mostly English with some scattered phrases in the Pennsylvania dialect. Amish. Obviously, they were no threat. She flicked her flashlight on and swept it across the cab of the pickup.

A couple of teenagers peered out of the open window. She recognized the girl, one of the teenagers who had welcomed Jacob home when he ran into them at Wiser Good's Mercantile. Rose Hottenbach. While the others chatted with Jacob, she'd stood silently staring as though she wanted to ask a question of them, but in the end she'd left without speaking. Tonight, Rose was huddled against the driver, clutching her jacket against her unbuttoned front.

Amanda jerked her light away and stood holding the flashlight against her leg. "Look, I'm going back to the house. I'm sorry I bothered you."

Inside her kitchen, she ran a basin of water and finished her dishes. While they drained, she made a batch of popcorn. A few minutes later she heard a knock at the back door. The Hottenbach girl stood alongside a very red-faced young man dressed in town clothing while the three of them stared at each other while Timberly brushed past from outside to rub against her leg.

Amanda tried to break the tension. "I see you met Timberly. She was my aunt Lydia's cat. Lydia used to say that dogs have masters, but Timberly has staff. I guess I'm the staff."

Rose and the boy managed weak smiles, but neither spoke.

"Come in, please. Would you like something to drink? Some popcorn?"

"N...nei."

"No thanks."

She gestured toward the empty chairs at her kitchen table. When the boy nodded for her to do so, Rose took a seat, but he remained standing—pacing actually, with his fists punched into his trouser pockets. Finally, he came to a halt. "You can't tell Rose's dad."

Amanda tried and failed to erase her smile. They looked so serious, both of them watching her. "I don't know Rose's dad."

This time Rose spoke. "You know Levi Ruth. And you are married to his son. That makes for trouble if you talk to him. Will you give us your promise?"

Amanda crushed a tea bag between her thumb and forefinger, unaware until the leaves spilled through her hand. "I won't tell Jacob. He's not here, anyway. He flew home to Oregon. But he'd understand." She ran water over her hands and wiped them on a towel while she waited for one of them to respond. When they remained tongue-tied, she blurted, "Hey, I'm sorry I disturbed you. I thought you were a trespasser."

The young man seemed more concerned than embarrassed. "It's not how it looks. Those Amish can be real uptight."

Amanda smiled. "I take it you're not Amish?"

"No way. I'm Tom Reynolds. I work over in Akron, and I've been seeing Rose for a while. We plan on getting married when she turns eighteen. Then she's going to get her high school diploma. Right, Rose?"

"Ja. We have settled everything between us. My daed, he would be for whipping me if he finds out what plans Tom and I make. Daed wants me to promise I do not see him anymore. This promise I can't make, so I run away."

Amanda looked for something to occupy her while she tried to think of a response, found a box of tissues and handed it to the girl. She waited until Rose finished wiping her eyes and stuffed the crumpled tissue into her pocket. "What can I do to help?"

"Can she stay here with you?"

Rose stood with her fists balled up at her sides, her swollen eyes fixed on the table while her cheeks flooded with embarrassment. Tom obviously noticed, because he moved to stand beside her with his hand on her shoulder like a mother bear protecting her cub.

"Here?" The question sounded lame, even to her ears. "For how long? What if her father finds out?" She remembered her promise not to tell the Ruths. What excuse could she give if one of them knocked on her door? With a start, she realized Rose was talking.

"Daed will find out, but my leaving will make him realize I am serious. There makes no use reasoning with him—he is only for talking and giving orders. That is how it is with him ever since my sister Lorina runs off in the middle of the night to go to the big city to work as a model. She writes me sometimes, with news of her travels. I keep the letters secret, but they give me the idea that I can leave, too, if it suits me. But Daed is furious. It makes him seem lax in front of the others, to have a *dochder* behave so. He comes down even harder on the *kinder* who remain at home. Mamm makes no help for me. She takes orders too."

In the muted kitchen light, Amanda took a closer look. It was as though she was watching herself on the day she arrived at Lydia's house, filled with the same fierce determination. She had run away, too, but with Aunt Lydia's cooperation.

Tom's confidence left little room to doubt that the two of them had formed a plan. "Maybe you could help Rose with her schooling," he said. "I hear you're a teacher. She could be your student."

She looked around her big house and wondered how she could plead off. Jacob would be returning in a couple of weeks and they would be returning to Oregon. She had the children. But judging from the determined look on the boy's face, the scared and brave eyes of the girl, she had no choice. "You plan on getting married?" She tried not to be obvious as she checked the window for a lantern light on the road.

Tom nodded and squeezed Rose's hand. "We're not kids." He looked to be about twenty-two. Rose was younger, but she seemed to know what she was doing. Tom's serious brown eyes shone with concern for his girl. Tall and well-built, he looked to be a man who knew how to work. He might surprise Rose's father if given a chance.

Amanda glanced from one to the other and realized she had little choice—at least for tonight. It was too late for an Amish girl to be driven home in the pickup Tom had parked in her driveway. She shrugged. "My father used to tell me, 'Better to face trouble on the morning sun.'" It sounded lame, even to her ears. "I'd be happy to have Rose stay tonight."

Tom nodded and the vein pulsing near his throat seemed to ease. He swallowed, reached for the cup of coffee she'd set in front of him and drained it without releasing his white-knuckle grip on the mug.

Rose blushed, the faint color making her seem fragile and delicate next to her sturdy boyfriend. "*Denki*. I don't make for trouble." She glanced at Tom with a look of trust that seemed to seal their fates. Whatever the future might bring, they would face it together.

Suddenly the room seemed crowded. Amanda nodded toward the living room. "Look, I'm going to leave you two alone now. There's soda in the fridge, and popcorn. Take your time. I'll be upstairs." She started into the living room and hesitated. "I have two children. My son is sleeping downstairs. He has a cast."

She made her excuses, climbed the stairs and stripped her sheets. When the bed was remade, she brushed her hair and tried to read. An hour later, when the words blurred, she flipped the book shut. Downstairs, Tom was still talking in a hushed tone that hinted of secret plans and lovers' dreams. Stifling a yawn, she called down the stairs, "Rose, maybe I better show you around before I turn in."

A few minutes later, she heard the door shut and the pickup drive off.

Rose appeared at her doorway, looking small and overwhelmed. Amanda felt like an older sister. "You can sleep in here, Rose. I'll take the sofa."

"Oh, I do not wish to be a bother. At home we share. If you don't mind, I do not."

Amanda nodded. She'd shared her bed with Lydia, but she'd always wanted to share a bed with a sister. "Would you like a bath first? With bubbles?"

Rose's voice was soft and hesitant. "I do not wish to be—"

"I know—a bother." Amanda meant her smile to be encouraging and was relieved to see Rose relax. Across the hall, Jules stirred and called for her feeding.

Rose smiled timidly. "A hot bath sounds *wunderbaar*. If it is okay."

"Absolutely. It will be soothing. I'll feed the baby and then make some tea."

While Rose bathed, Amanda carried the teapot upstairs with two fresh cups and a selection of herbal tea bags. She found one of Lydia's nightgowns and set it at the bathroom door as she had done with Jacob's newly washed clothing the night of his father's barn fire.

Rose appeared, shyly wearing the borrowed night-
gown, her hair gathered in a messy bun on the back of
her head. Amanda handed her a cup of tea, and after a
few minutes of awkwardness, reached for the lamp next
to her and clicked it off. She was exhausted by the late
hour. In five hours, Noah would be up, and another day
would begin. She closed her eyes and waited for sleep.

In the dark, Rose hesitated. "I am *glickleck*, lucky,
to have you and Tom on my side. Can we talk a bit?
Before we sleep?"

"Sure." Amanda reached for the switch before
deciding that darkness was preferable. "Tell me how
you met Tom."

"At the pizza shop in Springdale. Some of us
stopped by on our way home from the movies. We girls
had loosened our hair and removed our kapps like we
do when we are among the English. He didn't know
right off I was Amish." Rose laughed softly. "He says he
did, but I don't think so. He asked me if I would dance
with him, and I said I would. My friends were watching, but they didn't care because they were dancing, too.
Then he said I was the prettiest girl he'd ever seen and
one day I'd be marrying him. I knew then he was a
terrible liar. Imagine a fellow wanting only for a girl to
be pretty and nothing else." Her laughter made a strangled sound in her throat, and she covered her giggles in
her pillow.

Amanda joined her, and their laughter seemed to
ease the awkwardness in the room. "I think men are the
most unpredictable creatures on earth. Don't you,
Rose?"

"Ja. Sometimes I am sure it would be easier to
remain a little *kind*."

"I know what you mean. I had so many decisions to make when I moved here. But it's not easy being an only child. I grew up under the weight of responsibility. It suffocated me, or at least I thought so at the time. I needed to see what I was capable of."

"Me too. That is why I must leave. With my community, I have only the decision of who I will marry. After that, not so many choices." She gave a contented sigh in the darkness. "Tom shows me that the Lord intends a different life for me than my mother's. I have attended services at outside churches, and I believe Gott is more forgiving than harsh. It would drive me *narrish*, crazy, wondering up to the hour of my death whether Gott has saved a place for me. Especially after living all of life under tough restrictions. This is why I must change. Does this make sense?"

"Hey, don't ask me. I'm the last person to give you advice. You'll have to find your answers for yourself."

"Is it hard for you, married to someone from our faith? Are there ever doubts or misunderstandings?"

Amanda swallowed. "Maybe we should leave this for another time and catch some sleep."

Rose was already up, preparing pancakes, when Amanda made her way downstairs the next morning. The girl stood with a bowl in her hands, the batter whipped to an eggy yellow. "I do not know how the stove works. I would make coffee, but I do not see the coffee pot that sits on the stove." She laughed nervously. "I hold the *kind* while you prepare the meal. Babies I know about."

"Gladly. This is Jules. She's six months already. She's hungry for some rice cereal with pureed peaches. Her favorite." Noah stood at the doorway with a puzzled look. "Noah, come meet our guest. This is Rose. She will be eating with us. Can you show her how you make your swiftie? She doesn't know how you like it."

Rose rescued the container of supplement when Noah pulled it off the counter and struggled to open the lid. She bent to Noah's height and watched him as if his method of putting a spoonful of powder into the blender was the most fascinating thing she'd ever seen. Filled with importance, he pulled a frozen bag of peaches from the freezer and added a few to the mixing cup. When he was ready, he pressed the button, and the sound of whirring filled the kitchen. He offered Rose the first sip.

She smiled and declined with an assurance that it must taste wonderful, but she needed to leave room for her pancakes. While Noah finished his drink, she turned to the baby chasing Cheerios across the tray of her highchair. "What beautiful children. I hope Gott blesses me with such *wunderbaar kinder*. What manner of name is Jules?"

"Short for Julie. We started using it, and it sort of caught on."

"Oh." Rose looked over mischievously. "I thought maybe named for Jewel, the singer that I like. My sister let me listen to her tape and I like her songs."

Amanda nodded without showing surprise. An Amish girl's taste in modern music was none of her business; besides, she loved Jewel. "Here, you're welcome to the first pancakes." She quickly mixed a pancake for Noah made with his special flour and almond milk. While they cooked, she broke off a bit for Jules. When she sat to eat her own breakfast, her first bite was a revelation. "Wow. These are fluffy. What's your secret?"

"No secret. Just fresh eggs and John Ruth's fresh milk. And lots of baking powder. Mamm says to stir with love."

Amanda glanced over at Noah. "Remember your *Silas Bread*? Now you have *Noah Cakes* for breakfast." Her son nodded and continued eating. *A week ago, he would have whined about his pancake and refused to eat it. Thank you, Lorie. Thank you Rose.*

After breakfast, she bundled the children into the car and drove Rose to the library to borrow a copy of *On Walden Pond.* That evening, she found herself explaining Thoreau to a girl who understood him without trying. In the days that followed, they finished Steinbeck and started on Hemingway, but Rose gave up after a few pages. One night she read a chapter of *The Catcher in the Rye* while Amanda heated frozen vegetable lasagna for supper. "What makes this boy Holden so angry? What kind of life has he lived that such filth comes out of his mouth?"

Amanda looked up from the counter where she was chopping broccoli for a salad and felt a wave of pleasure at being a teacher once more. She loved being a mother, but this moment was a bonus. Helping young people find parallels in their own lives was priceless. "Oh, he's supposed to be a poster child for modern society, I guess. There are a lot of random concepts floating around in our society. Maybe you're not ready for Salinger."

"Huh! I doubt I will ever feel like that spoiled boy. He lacks purpose and would rather remain a child."

Rose insisted on doing all the laundry. She was

fascinated by the washing machine and dryer. After gathering dirty clothes for a load, she selected her wash setting and sat reading while the machine accomplished work that took her an entire day at home. The two of them folded clothes and laughed while Amanda taught her the words to Frank Sinatra's "I Did It My Way" from the radio. But the surprising questions came at night after the light was off.

"Amanda, can I ask you something? I don't know who else to ask. It's about...babies."

The stark, uncarpeted room echoed with the girl's hesitation, but she pressed on fearlessly. Amanda smiled in the darkness. "You seem to be a natural mother. You take such good care of Jules. And—"

"No. About making babies."

"Oh." Amanda swallowed. "Well, okay."

"How do I keep from having babies? Mamm makes so many. I know they are precious. And I want a bunch. But why do the Englisch have so few? Is it a sin to use the condoms that some of the girls talk about? Mamm says that Gott doesn't bless the Englisch as fully."

"Hey, that's more than one question. Let's see..." Amanda considered where to begin. "How much do you know about sex?"

"Sex? You mean about making babies? Not much. Why do you outsiders concern yourselves so much about...sex if you don't try to make a baby?"

"Ummm."

"It is the girl's place to say 'no.'" But it seems to us that Englisch girls say 'yes' only. Never 'no.'"

Amanda laughed. "It might seem like that. Especially if you spend any time watching TV or the internet. But not all of us are like that. A lot of us walk a narrow path. Not all 'Englischers' are sinful in the way you mean.".

"I read only *Family Life* and the *Budget*. Nothing there about life," Rose admitted.

Once she got started, Rose probably would have talked all night. She wanted the names of the reproductive parts that she knew about, both hers and Tom's. Amanda felt like an anatomy instructor, describing a process she had started learning in fifth grade.

"My older sister Lorina lives on the outside now. She could answer my questions, but we don't hear much from her. Someone tells her she is beautiful, and she gets the idea to be a fashion model. She goes to Cleveland. She is very pretty, and she works very hard. Now she lives in New York. She gets a boyfriend. More than one, I think...but she doesn't get married. She wrote me a letter, but she don't come home anymore to visit Daed and Mamm. It's too hard."

A faint stab of recollection connected the name to a girl that she first saw flirting with Jacob, when he offered them a snack of moon pies to tide them over while they waited for the meal to be served. "I remember her. I met her at your Sunday service. She was with her cousin Martha. We talked. She was very pretty." *I put the idea of modeling in her head. What was I thinking? Maybe I ruined her life. I should have kept my mouth shut and she'd still be here in Ohio, married and raising a family.* Guilt thickened her tongue, making explanations too difficult. Finally, she said, "Let's get some sleep. We can continue this tomorrow."

The next night, Rose scarcely waited for the lamp to be shut off before she began discussing the plans she and Tom had been whispering about when they returned from a drive in his pickup. "When Tom and I marry, I want to make him pleased with me—in bed, I mean. I know how it looked out there, but we never do very much. Some of the girls use rumspringa for the excuse to make wild, but Tom and I have better sense. We don't...you know...try to make a baby yet."

Amanda was glad the dark hid her smile. "I'll tell you what. You teach me how Amish men think, and I'll teach you everything I know about the rest of it. Deal?"

That night they talked until their voices woke Jules for her late-night feeding. Amanda slept in the next morning while Rose kept the children entertained. When she came downstairs, she found Rose reading a story to Noah on his bed, with Jules cozied under the covers dressed in a fresh diaper and a light sweater against the chill.

She gave Rose a hug on her way into the kitchen for coffee. "I could get used to this. You sure you don't want to be an *au pair*? You could earn serious money. Travel to Europe with the host parents. Seriously." *Amanda, you're meddling again. Leave these people be.*

"*Nei*, I have no wish to be like my *schwester* Lorina. I want only to marry Tom and make our own family. I have no need to travel to Europe. Everything I need is here. But maybe one day, after I am a teacher and my children have left home, then ja, I would like to travel."

"Smart girl. Keep your options open. Say *yes* to life unless there's a reason to say *no*. That's what my mother used to say."

"She was a good teacher, your mother?" Rose handed Noah the book and shook her head when he begged her to read it again.

"She was the best. Although I didn't realize it at the

time. But her lessons follow me around. I see her, hear her all the time." Amanda sipped her coffee and contemplated her own words, surprised that she no longer felt bereft at the mention of her mother. Still, having another woman around, being close like Emma and Lorie, gave her a momentary twinge of envy. "Rose, one piece of advice. And this is important. Whatever you decide to do, don't part from your mom in anger. It's not worth it. Make peace with your family. You won't get another one, you know. A mother, I mean. Some of us don't have that choice."

"Ja, this is what Tom says, also. He wants us to be close, my family. At first, I tell him it makes no matter, but he convinces me otherwise."

Amanda smiled. "You picked a good man."

Chapter Seven

❧

A horse twitched its tail in Amanda's driveway, waiting on a tall, stern man with crooked teeth and a big belly who sat unmoving in a buggy.

"Rose, your father's here." Amanda stood with the screen door half-opened and hoped her voice carried upstairs.

"*Ach du lieva.* Daed?" By the sound of her footsteps, Rose had halted midway down the stairs then retreated to the bedroom. A moment later she appeared, smoothing her kapp over her tight coil of brown hair. She stood behind Amanda and peered at her father through the screen while the sun caught the glint of her new nose piercing.

"Won't you come in?" Amanda pulled the door open.

The frowning Amishman remained in his buggy seat and glared at his daughter while Amanda listened from inside the door. "What goes with this foolishness? Your home is no longer good enough that you decide to take up with the Englisch?" Amanda could understand only the word English, but she had a father of her own; the conversation wasn't hard to imagine, especially with the man's gruff, commanding tone. "Come, we go home." He gestured toward the wagon.

Rose glanced in her direction and blushed. "No," she said. Instead of backing off, she walked across the lawn and stood in front of her father. "I don't come home. My mind remains made up. In one month, I will be eighteen, and I will marry."

"An Englischer?"

"A good man, I marry. One who will care for me and our *kinder*. You may meet him if you wish."

Rose's father scowled. He faced the universal dilemma of all fathers who realize they are dealing with a stubborn daughter. If he had not lost his oldest daughter to the English world, perhaps he would take care to keep the ties with this one. His frown eased so slightly that at first it was only the furrows on his forehead, until he shook his head in frustration. "We see about this. You come home with me, and on Saturday night you have this Englisch boy to supper." It seemed as though, for the moment, he would settle for having Rose return home.

Amanda let out a breath.

"First, I want your promise." Rose's words trembled, but she remained with her arms crossed and her spine stiff, as though she had rehearsed her stance in the full-length mirror that hung on the bathroom door.

Outmaneuvered, with no such mirror to practice in front of, her father flicked a glance at Amanda and nodded. Rose must have understood her father's compromise because she ran upstairs and returned with her things.

She was out of breath when she returned and offered Amanda a quick hug. "When Tom comes, tell him he should visit on Saturday night. Seven o'clock. Remember to tell him that we go by the Amish 'slow time.'" She waited for Amanda's nod before she mounted the buggy with her head held high.

Amanda watched until she was out of sight before she snapped the screen door shut.

Tom was less subdued when he arrived. She relayed Rose's message before he stalked back to his truck and grabbed the door handle as though he intended to race out to the Hottenbach farm and rescue Rose. "How could she just give up like that?" he fumed.

Amanda heard herself defending the decision as though she bore some responsibility. But she'd learned her lesson; no more meddling with things that didn't concern her. This sister had acted on her own volition. "She seemed determined, Tom. I think you have to let them work this out for themselves. They've been doing it this way for centuries. Girls run away, girls go home again. It's not like her dad's going to lock her in the shed, is he?"

"Nah. He won't go that far."

"So she made her point. She said to come at seven o'clock, *Slow time*. Whatever that means."

Tom nodded. "The Amish don't want to be in step with the outside world. They set their clocks a half hour ahead, so no matter what time of the year it is, the outsider is always off. That way it's harder for us to do business with them."

"I figured that out the first time I was late."

"They don't usually tell you. It's no concern to them."

Amanda glanced over to where Noah was playing with his wooden toys in the dirt. With Rose gone, Tom apparently had no pressing obligations; he stood beside the pickup with his hands in his pockets, in no hurry to leave.

She bounced Jules on her hip and tried to think of something to break the silence. "Do you worry about the adjustments the two of you'll need to make?"

He shook his head. "Nothing we can't handle. A lot of Amish kids go over. Towns around here are filled with them. Some have been excommunicated."

"Yeah. I saw some Amish people eating at the coffee shop. The waitress went over to serve them, and she wouldn't touch their menus or their plates. It looked pretty strange."

"It's done all the time. Technically, that waitress wasn't serving them."

"My friend Carol explained it to me later. According to her, if she works a shift with a shunned waitress, and someone from her community comes in, she takes the table."

"Less embarrassment for everybody that way."

She considered. "What happens if it's a family member?"

"Sometimes the rules get side-stepped. Depends on the type of rule they broke, I guess. And how long it's been."

"Is it forever?" She knew the answer, but Tom seemed to need to talk.

"Sometimes. Sometimes not. I think they call it

being put on the Bann. Sometimes it's only for a few months."

"I saw this with my friend Carol."

Tom smiled. "We're used to it. A good portion of the Mennonite Church in town is made up of disgruntled Amish. Sometimes the Mennonite ministers tell a potential member to go on home and try to work out a compromise before they come back wanting to join a new church. Sometimes it works, too. Changes come about from time to time, usually because one of the members pushes it to a vote."

"You know a lot about them."

Tom shifted with a look of pride. "You work in the factories alongside them, and you have a chance to talk. I don't agree with everything, but I have a lot of respect for their ways. Sometimes they're just plain stubborn, but more often their way makes a lot more sense than ours does."

"Why not join them?"

His eyes flickered with a burst of frustration. "Heck, I could live and worship among them for a lifetime and I still wouldn't fit in. I never was a conformist. Don't suppose I could start now. Rose been wanting to go on to school and her father won't let her. She's sharp as a tack. Could be a good teacher if she set her mind to it.

"Think she'll get homesick?"

"We'll have our share of problems but keeping her from her folks won't be one of 'em. I have no argument with them. If they want to see her, she can visit as often as she wants. I'll go too, if they want to see me. Meantime, we'll find us a church where we'll be comfortable and raise a few kids."

"Nine? Rose comes from a big family."

"Nah. World's different, outside. Costs more. Besides, I don't have a farm to raise them on."

"What if her father won't let her get married?"

"I have a feeling he won't interfere. But I'll marry her, no matter what. She'll do fine, soon as she gets over her shyness."

"We talked some."

Tom grinned and his neck grew red, but he kept his head up except for a quick flicker to check out his boot laces before he met her eyes again. "She mentioned something to that effect. Reckon it did her a lot of good. There's no way those Amish girls can learn facts of life. Sex for them means making babies. They don't even have another word for it. They just call it 'making babies.'"

Amanda smiled.

"When they're sick, everyone in the countryside comes by to see them. They'll go to great lengths to find a new doctor. But they don't always stick to the medical advice they pay for. They'll start taking some 'Dr. Feel-good' remedy the peddler brings by. Have you read their newspaper, the *Budget*? It's filled with salves and remedies. Whether the stuff works is anyone's guess. Time they're old, the Amish are pretty well worn out. They put themselves through a lot more than we do, that's for sure."

She recalled the day Jacob's community had descended on his father's farm to rebuild their barn, after the lightning strike burned it to the ground. The entire town had been there, including a lot of outsiders. But no one had worked as hard as the Amish. "Were you at the barn raising? A lifetime of that kind of

punishment, and I'd buy liniment from a peddler, too."
A swallowtail butterfly landed on her rosebush. She
pointed it out to Jules, and they watched it together
until it floated off. "What if Rose is still needed at
home?"

Tom cracked his knuckles to relieve the stress. He'd
obviously had the same thought, but young love was
more powerful than doubt. "She probably is. Her
mother had the last baby two years ago. If we don't
move fast, there'll be another one on the way, and
Rose'll be expected to stay and help." He grappled with
his truck door. "Guess I better be going. Amanda,
thanks for all your help. I hope I don't seem too down
on the Amish. I just want better for Rose."

"You'll be perfect for each other." Amanda smiled
at the relief she saw in Tom's eyes from her simple reassurance, something that had been missing from her own
marriage to Jacob. "Invite me to the wedding."

"Will do. That's a promise. Well, I'm off. Got a lot
to do before Saturday." He spun out in the driveway
and made the dust roll as he headed toward town.

She heard his truck winding up, then shift, and she
felt a prick of homesickness for Jacob. "Timberly, I have
a feeling that life's not going to be dull with that boy."
The cat nosed the rosebush, hunting for a butterfly
until she distracted it with a twig. "Do you think it's
easier for an Amish girl to leave her family, Timbers?
Maybe it only seems easier because Rose has Tom."

Timberly arched her neck and leaped onto the
fence without responding.

❧

On Sunday, Tom and Rose stopped by. He stayed in the cab of his truck while Amanda and Rose visited just outside.

Tom had been right about one thing, but they hadn't hurried fast enough. "Mamm makes another baby. But me and Daed worked out a compromise; I can work in town as a hired girl for twenty-five hours a week until the baby is born—and I can save every penny I make. When the baby arrives, I help Mamm for three months. In return, they give me their blessing and attend my wedding."

"Rose, That's great!"

"I come to see if I can borrow a book. I can read in my spare time as long as I keep the book hidden from the *kinder*—so they don't get ideas. On this last point, Daed spends long hours meditating."

"And they'll come to the wedding?"

"As long as we marry in the Mennonite church." Her face glowed.

"Tom, what if Rose's mother has complications?"

He frowned, but his eyes remained steady. "We'll cross that bridge when we come to it. I'm happy enough to have a wedding date that I don't mind waiting."

Rose's eyes sparkled. "Daed says we can court. That means we can attend movies together. We can take rides and make plans."

Amanda glanced at him, and he shrugged. "I haven't been to any church in years, but I promised her dad I'd make amends before we married. He and I went out to the barn and looked over the year's tobacco crop. When he lit up his pipe, I pulled mine out, and we talked farm prices."

Rose's face glowed with contentment. "I knew

Daed would see things my way..." She pulled off her kapp. "But just in case, I cut my hair. Our community won't permit me to join the church now, even if I wanted. Not until my hair grows long enough to pin up. By then we'll be married."

Chapter Eight

❧

A manda cleaned up the kitchen with one eye on the clock while she waited for her Zoom meeting with Jacob. Finally, seven o'clock rolled around. She set Noah in front of the screen, freshly bathed and dressed for bed. He held up a bandaged finger and proudly announced that he'd smashed it on a gate when he helped Uncle Samuel drive the cows in for milking.

"Did Mama take you to the emergency room?" Jacob teased.

"No. Aunt Lorie washed it and wrapped it in a white rag. She tear up a scrap and tie it around my finger for...vacteria. Germs. Silas got one, too."

"I used to wear those bandages. My mama would pour mercurochrome on my ouchie. Did Aunt Lorie do that for you?"

Noah nodded. "It was brown. It hurt. And I cried. But Uncle John say it's okay. He say you cry too."

Jacob glanced down and nodded. "You're a brave

little farmer, son. I'll bet your mama never had that stinging medicine."

Noah regarded her seriously. "Did you, Mama?"

She smiled at his seriousness. "No. Never. And I would have cried the first time, too."

"Aunt Lorie don't give lollipops for ouchies. Only my doctor. She says molasses cookies are better medicine."

With held breath, Amanda studied Jacob's face as he grappled with this proof of his sister-in-law's kindness to his son. Clearly such a close family connection didn't match the tense disapproval he'd convinced himself his family would receive. To his credit, it took only a few seconds before he bounced back with a joke for Noah that had them both laughing.

"Time to say good night to Daddy, Noah." She waited for him to hop down before she whispered, "Call me back after I get the kids to bed, okay, Jacob?"

***

The next time Jacob called, Amanda handed the phone to Noah. "Give Daddy your news. Tell him what we did today."

"We go to the doctor. Guess what? No more cast. Mama says I can run. I got a lollipop." He lifted his foot in the zoom camera to show his leg.

Jacob gave him the "two thumbs-up" sign. "Now you can herd the cows proper. Have you shown your cousin yet?"

Noah shook his head. "Tomorrow. Silas will be surprised. We can play in the barn now as long as we don't get into mischief. Mama will stay at Aunt Lorie's and sew something for you that's a secret. So I can't tell."

So much for the suspender surprise. Amanda noticed that Jacob wisely refrained from asking if the leg hurt. They'd discussed the subject, and he was relieved that she'd stopped obsessing about every ouchie and scrape. Now, Noah was proudly explaining how the doctor cut off the cast with a loud electric saw. She didn't bother adding that she'd been cringing with fear that the saw would slip and slice Noah's little leg to the bone. But it didn't. Noah had watched stoically, and when the cast was off, asked to keep it.

"My birt-day is in ten days, Daddy. Mama says when you come, we can go to the zoo and take Silas. It has elephants and everything. And I get a cupcake and ice cream. Mama says only for birt-days."

"Wow, that's going to be some special day, son. Two milestones in one day." Jacob's joy was palpable, but she detected a hint of loneliness. She was counting the days, too.

"This has been good for us," she told Jacob later when Noah was asleep in his upstairs room. "His leg healed faster than the doctor expected, thanks to the fresh eggs and milk your brother sent home with us. And the winter greens from Lorie's garden. Lots of calcium and vitamin D, she claims. She's right. I'm not sure how I'm going to keep your son occupied now that he has his freedom again."

"Should he be running so quick?"

She laughed. "Now who's being fussy? Wait until you see him. He's brown as a berry, and his legs are getting muscles. He's lost his baby fat. He's a little warrior now, just like his daddy." She hesitated to say the thought that was freewheeling in her brain—*didn't I tell you this would be a good idea?* But to be fair, it was easier for Jacob's family to accept Noah and Jules. It was the adult Englischers that tested their beliefs.

Apparently, Jacob heard her thought. "I'm glad for our children's sakes that they have a place in the family. And you—even if my mother is just a pen pal." His chuckle was self-deprecating. On the computer screen, his slow smile spread across his bronze cheeks, and his brilliant blue eyes softened. "You are right about many things, liebchen. I married a wise woman."

"Back at you, my love. We're better together."

"Ja, this may be so. Like all *gute* marriages."

She took a deep breath and blurted out the thing that was keeping her awake at night. "Jacob, what happened that day you ran away? I thought you couldn't come home again. That you were shunned because you left after you were baptized. But your family has said nothing. In fact, your mother sounds as though you'd be welcome back."

Jacob's face flooded with color, and he ducked his head from the camera's view. "I didn't say I was baptized." When he could no longer ignore her incredulous stare, he expelled his breath. "I was close to standing the pledge. But at the last session, the bishop came round behind me. He shouted at me, and I thought to lose my hearing in that ear. 'What is this? Three!'"

Amanda waited, afraid to interrupt Jacob's confession. She'd waited a long time for the truth. Whatever *that* turned out to be, it had been a long time coming.

Jacob continued, his eyes far off, reliving the memory. "The bishop was looking at my hat. I explained it was a blustery day and I needed to use three pins to secure the hat. But he was not to be convinced. 'Leave my class,' he shouted. I tried again to soothe the criticism over, but he was stubborn as a fresh-broke mule. 'You are not worthy to be here among us. Leave!'"

Amanda's heart contracted with sympathy for him. She had married an honorable man who didn't deserve to be humiliated in front of his friends. "Why did the man kick you out?"

His eyes blazed with remembered humiliation. "Because the *ordnung* allows only two hat pins. Conformity in all matters. To do otherwise is to show vanity and disregard for our community. For our Gott." He lifted his gaze, and his eyes were filled with pain. "I prayed on the matter and decided that I could bend in this matter. After all, I was already like the willow, bending to the ground. It was in my mind that I needed to make *zeugress*. I make a plan also to confess my sin of loving an English girl. To give myself a fresh slate. In my mind, I planned that I will accept my community's forgiveness as I stand beside the girl I plan to marry and announce my marriage banns. But then my brother stands up and makes his public confession."

He paused and shook his head. "My bruder makes *zeugress* for liberties he takes with my girl. Sex and drugs, he admits. And I look over, and I see that even my father and hers know the truth of his confession. And she looks stunned, angry that he has shared their secret. But not once does she look at me for forgiveness. Nor my father, nor John. I am the laughingstock. The dark sheep that needs not be considered. In their minds, I deserve my humiliation. All must be done to bring

John back into the fold. But Jacob? He is not important. Not even to his betrothed."

His face looked mottled and angry. "I do not find it in my heart to forgive my bruder. I leave in such anger that even now it weighs on me like a festering sore. I try to be a good husband and father, a good provider and son-in-law, a good employer. But how do I do these things if I have failed the Commandment to be a good son and brother? My anger and guilt are destroying everything good in my life. I can hardly breathe sometimes, it hurts so much." He looked up into the cold, impersonal camera with a plea for understanding.

Amanda reached to touch the computer screen while her eyes overflowed. She pressed her fingers against his on the screen and tried to feel his warmth. "Oh, sweetie. I'm so sorry. I didn't know." As if her fingers could penetrate the screen, she traced the contours of his cheeks before pausing on the outline of his lips. Then she brought her fingers back to her own as her tears slipped down. "You've held this in for so long. I had no idea. I thought—"

He gave a strangled laugh and swiped at his eyes. "You thought I was just another stubborn Amish farmer with an axe to grind."

"Well, that too." She joined him until their laughter blended in the speakers. As suddenly as it began, the laughter died. "All this time, Jacob. How was I to know?"

"I could not share what I buried inside me. I thought it would die. But going back...seeing familiar people...places. The wound opened wide, and I knew I could not live without healing. You see why John's apology makes so important to me, yet? I don't know if I can let it go. I tried. Truth is, this business back home here could have waited another few weeks. But I could not stand to be among hypocrites. So I left, like a coward."

"Not a coward, Jacob. Never that. You left to get a different perspective. And everything is working out as it should. Noah's leg has healed. He needed the farm, just as you did at his age. He needed a cousin. A grandmother. He's learned to adapt to his challenge without letting it define him. He's not fragile anymore. He's a warrior like you."

"What am I fighting? My brother, like Cain and Abel? Is this what I do to redeem myself?"

His groan seemed reflective in the lateness of the hour. Amanda glanced at her clock. One o'clock. They'd been talking for hours. "What do you want to do, Jacob?"

His silence stretched into contemplation. Finally, he admitted, "All I know is to come back for you. Maybe something will turn up. I don't know. Something. I'm happy for my son that he has found a family. Maybe they will allow him to spend a few summers with them, until it is time for a decision. Maybe Silas can travel to visit us in his rumspringa. Something may be salvaged from all of this, who can say?"

They talked for another half hour until Amanda's eyelids were dragging themselves against her cheekbones. Her voice felt like it was coming from somewhere outside herself, woozy with exhaustion and his low, breathy pillow talk. Finally, when one of their silences stretched into a dangerous threat of falling asleep, she summoned her resolve and made the decision. "I can't wait to see you, love. But we need to get some sleep. It's late here. And the baby makes for a long day tomorrow."

Jacob's sigh resounded from the speaker. "Yeah, I'm being selfish. I wish I was there. Noah's off to herd cows, tomorrow. That would be something to witness."

"I watch him and imagine I'm seeing you at his age. He's so cocky and full of himself."

"So full of himself?" Jacob's laugh sounded good. "I never hear those words at his age. Not until a beautiful English girl tells me this about myself. But I let you go to sleep now, liebchen. *Ich lieba dich.*"

You always say it first. She gave him a drowsy, contented smile and felt her body flood with contentment, even though her words slurred with exhaustion. "I love you, too."

Chapter Nine

❧❦❧

The Ruth buggy drove past with Emma at the reins. Her white kapp bounced on her head like an aura of light against the rising sun. Amanda raised her hand to wave, but Emma stared straight ahead, her face pinched with the effort of concentration. Clearly she had a pressing need because she had a shopping basket on the seat beside her.

"There goes Grossmummi, Noah."

How odd the words sounded. She glanced over at her son and wondered if he found it as strange and amazing as she did, being part of this family, this culture. Never that, she reminded herself. *Among, but not of.* They stood watching at the doorway in silence until the buggy rolled another quarter mile past the school and disappeared.

On her way back from town, Emma drew her buggy to a halt at Amanda's gate and inquired whether Noah wanted to come to the farm for a visit. When he climbed up and took a seat, she admonished him to keep his hands clear, not to scare the horses, and to remain seated. He nodded solemnly as they started off.

A month ago, he would have been terrified. Amanda watched them disappear. When Jules struggled in her arms, begging to ride alongside her big brother, she looked around for something to capture the toddler's attention. Fortunately, Timberly had dragged something dead from the creek for them to discover. "We'll visit the farm later to collect your brother," she promised.

She spent the afternoon on the floor, playing with Jules who was learning to sit up on her own. "You just need a little help from Mama, sweet thing!" After several sit-ups, Jules batted her hand away and struggled to right herself. "You better save something to show Daddy when he gets here."

Amanda went into the kitchen for a drink and to collect her phone to check her emails. She returned to the living room, expecting to find Jules still on her blanket. Instead, she found her daughter across the room, trapped behind a chair on the far wall, with her legs flailing in frustration. "How did you get over there, missy?" She rescued her daughter and reversed her travel direction as Jules wriggled backward across the floor. "Look at you! Aren't you the clever little baby. Let's post a video for Daddy."

By the time she scooped her up for a snack break, Jules was worn out from exploring the room backward. After she woke from her nap, they started for the farm with Jules bundled in her jacket and fuzzy hat like an Eskimo child. They stopped to watch Noah proudly stomping his rainboots through the pasture as he helped his uncles push the cows. He'd done the same several times on his uncle's shoulders, but today he marched on his own, through clumps of manure that looked from a distance like huge mushrooms. He was holding his stick overhead while he beat time on the grass to some vague tune he was singing. He'd explained that it kept the cows calm.

The overhead clouds promised rain for the newly planted garden. *Everything has its season here.* There, the beans were still germinating. Rows of kale, onions, broccoli, and peas lined the ground, already an inch high, the seeds properly soaked before planting and the rows mulched with straw against a late frost. The neat, well-tended garden with its loamy black soil seemed to support a zillion contented earthworms. A pile of children's toys near a discarded hoe provided the only sign of disarray in the garden and hinted that Noah and his cousin had been helping with the chores, which probably explained the uprooted tomato plant at the end of the row. "Someone has some 'splainin to do, Jules."

Noah emerged from the barn, looked over and frowned when he saw his mother. She smiled at the brief, brave streak of independence that had captured her little boy almost overnight. "Sorry, bud. But we need to go home and let everyone eat their supper." To her amazement, he said his goodbyes without a fuss and fell in beside her. "I like your manners, Noah. No fussing means you can go again soon."

"I wanted to eat with Silas."

"Yes, but not tonight. Would you like him to come to your house for supper one of these nights?" He nodded. They made a plan as they walked home. "You can help me make monkey-fried potatoes with ketchup.

And radish roses and celery crunchies? And maybe a cheese biscuit?"

"Silas doesn't eat cheese biscuits. He eats apple muffins."

"Well, maybe he'll like cheese biscuits." She was grateful Noah's cousin wouldn't request hot dogs or pizza like every other child she knew. Managing expectations was easier when the two shared the same restrictions. The buddy system.

Two days later, Samuel stopped by on his way to town to take Noah with him in the buggy. Silas was already perched in the front, and Noah eagerly jumped in beside him. Amanda realized she was clutching the handle of her broom with a white-knuckle grip as Samuel snapped the reins on Prince. *How old is that boy—thirteen? He's too young to be driving anything, let alone a horse and buggy. What have I agreed to?* Her hands felt clammy, and she struggled to breathe. But she sucked in a lungful of air and willed herself to remain calm.

"Have a good time," she called unnecessarily. The boys were already making too much noise to hear.

She prepared dinner with an ear trained for the clomp of horse hooves on the pavement. When she heard a horse pull up and two little boys jabbering in excitement, she slipped through the door and stood on the stoop to greet them. She realized she was holding her breath, an involuntary reaction that recalled the day her father had died after falling out of this same buggy. Noah had been sitting next to him, lucky to have escaped with only a broken leg. But what was done was done; she couldn't carry the past as an excuse to coddle her son. That wouldn't be fair. Her father would have been the first to agree.

She exhaled and her tension headache disappeared. "You guys have fun?"

Noah nodded. "We took provisions to a lady who has no family." He looked to his uncle. "We do a good turn."

Silas stood with his eyes wide, staring at the unfamiliar house and more importantly, the swing that hung empty and inviting. She smiled and bent to welcome him. "Hello, Silas. Are you staying for supper?" He nodded warily and looked at Noah for reassurance. A thought occurred to her for the first time. She had assumed Silas was simply shy around her, but his wide-eyed trepidation suggested another possibility. "Do you speak English, Silas?"

"Nei. Some little." He looked frightened like he was considering jumping back into the buggy with his uncle.

She glanced up at Samuel, whose nod verified her suspicion as he flicked his reins and started home. What an idiot she was. Amish children didn't start learning until they started school. He and Noah didn't need to share a language; they spoke the universal dialect of children. "Noah, maybe you can show Silas your toys. He might like to play a game on your Leapfrog. He doesn't have a computer."

The boys ran upstairs, and she continued supper preparations with a tinge of guilt. What was it she'd read about managing expectations in children? What would Lorie think if her son came home asking for a computer?

She pulled a basket of potatoes from its shelf and

peeled without finding an honest answer to the question. When the boys slid into their seats for supper, she watched the way they communicated. Silas was shy at first, nodding or shaking his head to her questions. When he spoke, she could understand most of his meaning, and what she couldn't, she guessed at. "Silas, *ich saag dank am disch,* I offer thanks at the table." Her best effort at the blessing she'd heard Lorie say. The boy looked up, grinned, and reached for his fork. *Close enough.*

Under Noah's tutelage, the boys made mustaches of their celery sticks and walked their potato crisps around their plates like ponies drinking from a ketchup pool. She tried to imagine John Ruth allowing such antics at his dinner table, but Silas seemed to be enjoying himself, his initial shyness gone. They didn't have much to offer in the way of entertainment, but clearly, playfulness at the table was a trade-off for the allure that the farm held for Noah. Not that she could compete with cow herding, generators and milking machines, hen houses and warm eggs. *It's not like we have a menagerie to attract four-year-olds.*

She smiled. "Silas? Do you visit the zoo?" At his look of puzzlement, she spread her arms. "Elephant?"

He laughed and nodded. "Zoo *wunderbaar gute.*"

She clapped her hands in enthusiasm. "We ask your mamm. Okay?"

She shifted her attention to Jules, who had her mouth open like a little bird, waiting for another spoonful of pureed peas. Noah finished his supplement and resumed his meal without prodding. She had a fleeting thought. *The boy needs a brother.*

She considered driving Silas home in her car, but in

a spirit of fairness, she decided to walk. *Better to check with Lorie before I expose her son to an SUV with leather seats, a six-speed transmission, and surround sound.* The trek up the road felt like trying to shoo kittens into a basket. The boys exploded with energy, tagging each other, laughing, play hitting and ducking all the way to the farmhouse door.

Lorie answered her knock with a concerned expression that hinted that she and her husband had misgivings about their son's new friendship. But she greeted them with a smile, her eyes clear and welcoming. "You will come in for coffee and pie?"

Amanda glanced over Lorie's shoulder to where John sat reading his newspaper under the yellow beam of a single lantern. His face was set in sternness that reminded her of his father Levi, the first time she saw the elder Ruth shoveling manure in the barn; firmly polite but fighting back the obvious urge to dismiss her and send her packing. At the doorway, she bit off a smile when she realized how much he probably regretted not doing so when he had the chance, five years earlier. But now it was too late. His son had fallen in love with her and changed his life.

"No, thank you. We need to get home while it is still light." She hesitated. "It's Noah's birthday next week. We plan to go to the zoo. Would it be possible for Silas to go with us? Jacob will be here to drive." When she saw Lorie's face waver in uncertainty, she added, "Maybe you would like to go also?"

Lorie glanced over to where her husband's newspaper had stilled, his face hidden in the shadow. "We discuss this, John and me. We will let you know our decision. But thank you for feeding Silas tonight. I pray he behaved himself."

After a minute of small talk, Amanda started home. The decision was up to John—and maybe his bishop. She'd done everything she could.

Lorie stopped by on her next trip to town. "John has decided. Silas will be allowed to see the zoo. But he is *naerfich*, nervous this first time, so many new things for an impressionable young boy. Perhaps if you were to invite Grossmummi he would be less nervous? Emma would enjoy the outing."

"And Levi? Should I—"

"Nei. Our father-in-law will not go. He is too bull-headed for such pleasure." Lorie smiled and glanced across the fence at her husband and his father, working in the field.

They laughed together until Lorie saw her husband watching from the field where he was working with a seeder and a team of horses. "Much work to be done. I must be off. *Mache gute*."

"Good day to you, too." Amanda closed the door with a glad feeling. *I'm building a family. Small steps.*

She explained the plan to Jacob when he called that night to tell her his flight number. "We'll pack a lunch, so Silas doesn't get exposed to too many bad habits. I'll make all of Noah's favorite foods. He wants a donut instead of a cake. I'll ask your mother if she wants to come with us. But I thought it might be better if you asked her when you get here next week."

"You are the matchmaker, this is for certain," he teased.

"Well, someone needs to be. And who can resist our cute kids?"

"I think it is better that you do the inviting. Give them time to think on the matter. Especially Daed. Maybe he takes it to the bishop for deciding. Who knows?"

"Seriously? The zoo?"

"More to it than that. He would be encouraging fellowship with outsiders. This is not to be taken lightly."

Another *faux pas* on her part? "I'll never understand your family."

Jacob's laughter made her smile. "If you want a place in the sun, you will have to expect some blisters. If you had married your cowboy, you'd be saying the same thing."

"What brought that up?"

"I saw your old boyfriend, Charlie Rivers, today. He asked about you. I told him you are fat and homely, and he said he's glad he got away." His teasing shifted into an enthusiastic recant of his day. She could hear the happiness in his voice from three thousand miles away. "Charlie talked me into trying my hand at roping. I practiced tossing the rope over a set of horns on a fence until I wore my arm out."

"So...spending time with all my old boyfriends? Did he try to show you up?"

"Ja. He shows me up plenty. But I like him."

Surprise caught Amanda before she could contain herself. "You and Charlie—who would have thought!"

"I could say the same about you spending time with my family."

"So what is this—revenge friendship?"

Jacob's laughter sounded relaxed, as though he'd had a warm shower and a couple of beers. "What you

English call 'payback'? *Nei*. He is a friend. He sees what you and I have together, and he hopes to discover our secret. He makes jokes as if he is looking only for the good times, but inside, he is searching."

This is a strange turn of events. What do they say? The best revenge is just to happily move on and let karma do the rest. "I'm glad you're enjoying yourself, sweetie. You'll have a lot of fun."

"So far, so good. We're not *rutsching*, messing around, out there. He's serious about his horses and everything else. I have to earn his trust before I can work one of his roping horses. They cost a good bit."

"Hey, if you're too busy to get away, I'd be happy to drive us back home again." *If your bromance is that hot and heavy.* She bit off the last thought; it was too hard to explain pop culture.

"*Nei*. I be there, don't make a fuss. I will be a good boy and return home like I promised. I have my flight ticket in my pocket. We celebrate the boy's birthday, a day he can remember when he is older."

"I invited guests," she began, relieved when he didn't pursue the subject. His tone didn't suggest that he was open to another surprise. He sounded irritated at her as if all his talk of old boyfriends had opened an old wound.

Chapter Ten

❧

After a fretful night with Jules, Amanda pulled the refrigerator door open, looking for quick energy. She picked up a jar of strawberry jam and set it back in favor of an English muffin with peanut butter, dropped it into the toaster, and picked up the coffee maker. A moment later she set it down and turned on the teapot, instead.

She aimlessly scrubbed a spot on the counter while she recalled something Carol had told her five years earlier when she'd confessed her growing attraction to Jacob. She'd called Carol to ask whether she should wear stilettos with her form-fitting red dress or tone it down a bit and go with sandals and a more modest look. Carol had been furious with her. The words of her lecture replayed themselves while Amanda waited for the water to heat. *You go putting an idea in that Amish head, he's going to fight temptation his whole life.*

Her conversation with Jacob replayed itself as well. In the crispness of hindsight, it sounded like he regretted rushing into marriage. Was he hinting that he wanted to be a bachelor like Charlie? Enjoying Friday nights at the bar and Sunday mornings roping while she stayed home and tended a brood of kids? *Hey, I'm the barrel racer. I deserve to be out there if anyone does.*

She wished she could pick up the phone and whine to her mother. If life were fair, today was the perfect day for advice. On days like today, her death sliced like a knife. She could almost hear her mother's sage advice, could see her labored response as her spoiled daughter rambled on about her self-absorbed life. For a moment she closed her eyes and conjured up their conversations.

Mom, do you think I made a mistake in marrying Jacob before he got the piss and vinegar out of his system, like Dad used to say?

JACOBFOLLOWEDHISHEART

I know. But what if he made a mistake?

TRUSTHIM.LETGOOFFEAR

I'm not afraid for myself. I'm afraid for him. What if I talked him into something he regrets? What if he wants to make up for lost time?

WHATIFTHESKYFALLS,HENN
YPENNY?

Amanda giggled in spite of herself.

Okay, you're saying I need to call Jacob back. And stop living in fear that he'll leave me and the kids and be a cowboy.

She made herself a promise to follow her mother's advice, but first she needed to brew a pot of tea, her mother's remedy for everything.

A hesitant knock on the door interrupted her futile search for a lemon. She snapped off the tea kettle and opened the door to a young woman in her early twenties, one hand clutching a darling little blonde girl about Noah's age, the other cradling a baby in an arm that trembled under the weight of the newborn.

Behind her, the car they'd arrived in backed out of the driveway. Amanda caught a quick look at the driver, a young, good-looking guy. Probably the children's father. She had the feeling she'd met the girl somewhere, but she couldn't place her. Not Amish, the woman was dressed in a conservative skirt and blouse that hung loosely on her thin frame. Her hair was darker than her daughter's, sandy brown, and she wore it long and straight while the little girl's braids resembled a little Amish girl's, but the sadness in the young mother's eyes defeated her smile.

"May I help you?" Amanda asked.

"I'm here to see Lydia Miller." The young mother stood with her chin jutted forward, a gesture of defiance that contradicted her trembling hands.

Amanda reminded herself to speak instead of simply gawking, but the words sounded as confused as her thoughts. "She's not here. I'm her niece, Amanda. May I help you?"

The visitor tightened her hold on the child's hand and slumped against the door. Amanda scarcely had time to grab the baby before the woman's eyes fluttered, and she collapsed. As she wilted to the floor, the little girl released her mother's hand and stood wide-eyed, tears glistening.

Amanda tried to keep her diverted with a stream of questions. "What's your name? Mine's Amanda. Is your mama sick?" She led the child into the living room and laid the baby on a blanket. By the time she returned, the mother had roused herself. Amanda helped her to her feet and held the door open. "Are you ill?"

"Only a bit." The young woman brushed her hand across her face, her exhaustion more noticeable because of the dark circles under her eyes. Her voice was barely audible. "Lydia is no longer here?"

"My aunt passed away five years ago."

"I'm sorry to hear that." The young woman glanced back at the rapidly disappearing car then at the door. "I am sorry to trouble you."

In the living room, the little girl edged closer to her mother and placed a protective hand on the baby's blanket. Already the young mother seemed restored by the warmth of the house. Her color had improved.

"I'll make us some tea." Amanda brewed a pot while the woman changed her newborn, a boy with a cowlick on his high forehead that reminded her of Jacob. The thought made her return to the living room to glance more closely at the young woman. "Are you here to see the Ruths?"

"I...yes. I'm sorry to be such...I would not wish to trouble you. My name is Beth. Beth Wilbur. I used to be Beth Ruth."

"Jacob's sister?"

The girl nodded.

The fourth Ruth scholar! Mystery solved! Mrs. Zooks at the one-room Amish school down the road had mentioned teaching four of the Ruth children, but Amanda had only counted three: John, Jacob, and their sister Sarah. *The plot thickens.* "Jacob never mentioned you," Amanda admitted. Nor had Emma, or either of the Sarahs. Could a sister just disappear?

"I am no longer one of them. It is our...their way that they not mention me. I accepted it when I married."

"That was your husband in the car."

"Yes...Jeff. He comes for me in one hour." Beth settled her baby to her breast. As he suckled, she smoothed his tuft of blonde hair, almost identical to the little girl's, who sat quietly nibbling a cookie in another chair.

"I have a little boy just about your age. He's spending the night with his cousin, Silas." She glanced at Beth. "John's son. I am married to Jacob. He left the community, and we live in Oregon now. He runs our family business, a commercial nursery." For want of something better, she blurted, "Both boys have the Maple Syrup Urinary Disease. John's wife Lorie has been helpful in advising me. My Noah goes there to visit, and I am not fearful that he will eat something that..." She trailed off when she saw that neither mother nor child was listening.

The mother's eyes filled with resolve. She waited until her daughter was distracted before she spoke quietly. "I have a favor to ask. Would you bring my mother to me?"

Shame at her narcissistic rambling shocked Amanda to her feet. "Of course. I will run upstairs and get my baby. And then I'll fetch Emma. She is probably in her garden at this hour." *But of course Beth would know her mother's schedule.* She fled upstairs before she could humiliate herself further. She strapped Jules in her infant seat without pausing to change her diaper.

Time enough for that, later. In the car, she managed to strap the baby into the car seat before she jumped into the driver's seat. Her foot laid on the accelerator as if every second was precious. At the Ruths', the dog came to the gate to follow her to the door.

"Why, Amanda! What a surprise." Emma opened the door and beckoned for her to enter.

Amanda's heart lurched when she saw Levi at the table with a cup of coffee in his hand. She took a breath and tried to sound normal. "Emma, you have a phone call."

"A phone call for me?" Emma seemed bewildered. "It wonders me. It's not John, I pray. Nothing has happened to him?" She was prattling. "He was only just in the field."

"No, it's not John. A woman. She says it's important. I brought the car so we can hurry." Amanda prayed Levi would not accompany them.

"Better go." Levi gestured to the partially open door. Emma grabbed her shawl and followed Amanda to the gate.

They rode in silence. At the house, Amanda led the way to the door.

Once she entered, Emma started across the room to where the phone rested on its cradle. "Am I to telephone back? Did the woman leave a number where she might be reached?" She glanced back at Amanda, her confusion growing until a baby's cooing from the living room caught her attention. A moment later she dropped the receiver back in its cradle and started cautiously around the corner. At the sofa, a young woman waited with trembling lips.

"Mama?" Beth struggled to rise with the baby in her

arms. She took a couple of steps and halted, still several steps short. "Mama?" The tears she had been holding began to fall. "Mama, I wanted you to meet my children. It's almost summertime. I thought you—this is Adam. Adam Jacob." She gestured toward the little girl. "This is Emily Ruth. She is waiting also to meet her grandmother. She's four now." The little girl advanced shyly, her fingers in her mouth. "Emily, come say 'hello' to your grossmommi. Your grandmother."

Emma's hand slipped to cover her mouth. She stood motionless, studying her grandchildren with eyes grown soft and moist. She smiled and the little girl's hesitation melted away when she seemed to understand that the strange lady in the big white apron was her grandmother.

Slowly, Emma bent to take Emily's hands. "What a big girl you are. Are you a help to your mama? A good big sister with your brother?"

"Uh-huh." The little girl nodded, her eyes wide and curious as she stared at the white kapp on her grandmother's head. She shrank back against her mother.

"Don't be shy, little one," Emma murmured. "I won't hurt you." Her eyes softened, releasing their faded blue color, and she turned to Beth again. "She looks like her grossdawdy." She placed her hand on her granddaughter's downy hair and smoothed the flyaway strands. "*Gott segen eich, kind.*" Without thinking, she had lapsed into dialect. The child gave a startled glance at her mother.

"She does not speak our language?"

"What use would she have?" Beth seemed to catch herself. "My children speak only English."

Amanda decided the two needed privacy. "Beth

isn't feeling well, Emma. Perhaps you'd like to hold the baby while I refill her tea? Would you like a cup?"

"That would be wonderful."

By the time Amanda carried in the full pot and another cup, Emma was burping Adam. Neither woman was speaking, but each seemed comfortable with the silence.

"Shall I serve the tea at the table?"

"No," Emma said.

"No," Beth echoed.

They spoke in unison, urgency in their voices. Amanda brought a TV tray and set it alongside Beth.

The tea restored Beth's energy. "It's good to see you, Mama," she said. "I've thought about this so many times. I could wait no longer."

Emma blinked and glanced down at the baby's blanket. When she lifted her face, her eyes were damp. She tried to wipe them discreetly on a corner of the blanket while the baby played with her kapp strings. "The *kind* has Yacob's forehead."

Beth nodded, her cheeks wet with tears. Emily climbed onto her mother's lap and stroked her cheeks, crooning softly, "Don't cry, Mama. Grandma's here now. You don't have to be sad anymore." Beth nodded again and wrapped her daughter in her arms.

Amanda escaped into the kitchen to feed Jules. The little girl followed, and she tried to think of things to keep her entertained while the conversation in the living room continued.

"Mama, I have an illness in my breast. The doctor said I needed to have an operation. But before we could begin the treatment, I made another baby. The doctor said I would need to choose." She took a deep breath. "I chose to doctor myself with herbs while I carried Adam. Then I needed time to wean him. Now the doctor says it's too late. I tried to think, Mama, what you would do. Mama..." She looked up with welling eyes. "I needed to see you."

"*Ach, dochder.*" Emma reached for her daughter.

In the dining room, Amanda held the baby—Jacob's namesake—and tried to keep him quiet. She set Jules in her highchair and led Emily to the window to watch the horses hauling a load to the field. Emily followed the horses work, clearly fascinated. *If Jacob were here, I'd carry her across the field to meet her uncle.* But it was John handling the reins. Instead, she told her niece about the family.

"This is your grandpa's farm. You have lots of aunts and uncles and cousins who live there now. They look just like you. And they have chickens and cows and horses. And a great big garden with all sorts of yummy foods. Do you have a garden?" When the little girl shook her head, Amanda added, "Wouldn't it be fun to walk outside and pick an apple? Or a carrot? Just like Peter Rabbit. Do you know Peter Rabbit?"

Snatches of conversation came from the living room. She wished she could offer them more privacy, but the women didn't seem to notice.

"...Jeff and I have planned everything. When the time comes, his sister will help him raise the kids. She's...she doesn't have any. It will be best." Beth was twisting the fringe from an old throw pillow, the same fringe that Jacob favored when he was upset. "I just wanted you to meet them," she finished.

"Your daed—"

Beth shook her head emphatically. "He wouldn't

break the Ordnung. That's what's most important. It always has been."

Emma's tone was sharp. "Beth, we do not choose what is easy for us. Your being on the *Bann* was not easy for us, either. Our neighbors took us to task, and we suffered for your decision, them thinking we failed in our duty as parents. But we are true to our ways."

"The only thing I did wrong was to love a man outside of our faith. He is a good man."

"I do not make the Commandments, Beth." Emma's tone hardened, and her words carried into the kitchen. "But I am a woman of Gott. What choice do I have? You rejected Gott. It says in the Bible that we must avoid forbidden marriages."

"I know, Mama. I don't blame you. I just miss you." Beth tried to muster a smile when little Emily broke loose from Amanda and pressed against her with a question.

Amanda heard a car pull up. Outside, Beth's husband waited with the radio playing loudly.

Beth heard as well. She collected the baby's blanket and toy and reached to take her daughter's hand. "We must go. Papa is here. Em, say goodbye to your grandmother." She swung her gaze to Amanda. "He waits for us in town."

Emma sounded weary. "That is where our Sarah works today. She was a *kind* when you left. Today she makes paper ornaments at a shop in town with the other girls."

"Just like I did when I was her age. Is she—?" It seemed as though Beth was afraid to ask too much. Instead, she busied herself with her children and let the question die. "Amanda?" She drew a shallow breath and tried to summon her strength. "I am sorry I didn't meet you earlier. We could have written, exchanged Christmas greetings. I would love to see Jacob happy and settled like me. Tell him for me..." She glanced over at her mother. "That he should have no regrets for leaving. Make him happy, Sister. Be his family. His rock. Be strong for him when he misses his family." She shifted the baby in her arms, her face pale and exhausted. "I must go now. I am sorry to leave like this. But I have given my life over to God's will, even though it hurts so much to think of what I will be missing in this life. Does this make sense?"

Amanda nodded, too overwhelmed to respond as Beth took her daughter's hand and led her to the car. She strapped both children into their car seats and stood, favoring her back as though pain racked her body. When it eased, she settled into the passenger seat. The husband reached over and stroked his wife's cheek. He glanced back at Emma before backing his car onto the road. Seconds later, he headed in the direction of Albany.

"Do you want me to drive you home, Emma?" Amanda asked.

Emma faced the empty road, but her face seemed to have aged in the past hour. Amanda knew her answer before she gave it. "Nei. I will walk."

Chapter Eleven

Jacob's plane glided through a dense blanket of clouds and taxied to a stop on the wet tarmac, while Noah jumped up and down, screaming with excitement. When his dad appeared on the ramp, he broke loose from Amanda's grip and ran forward. "Daddy! Daddy!"

Jacob scooped him in his arms and burrowed his face against Noah's puffy jacket with a fierce growl. "Who is this great big kid? And what did you do with my little boy?"

Noah laughed. "Here I am, Daddy. It's me. I growed bigger than Silas."

Jacob lifted him above his head and pretended to compare their heights. "I think, yet you grew taller than me. I need to get me some of that *wunderbaar gute* drink you use. Or soon you be so tall you must duck to use the door."

Jacob glanced to Amanda, her cue to join their play. Life was too short to waste a moment. Even Jules squirmed to have her father's attention. Amanda pressed a kiss against her daughter's head and handed her to her father. "She hears her brother so excited, and she wants her daddy. Don't you, Jules?"

Hers and Jacob's kiss was unhurried, a promise for later, when the kids were settled for the night. "I missed you, liebchen," Jacob murmured as he pulled aside her hoodie to stroke her neck. "No more late-night phone calls for this fella. I want to see your beautiful face on my pillow, yet."

"Agreed. I will love having a man around again."

On their way to the car, Noah clambered onto his father's rolling suitcase and watched for pedestrians. Amanda followed more slowly. She wanted to give Jacob time alone with his son. Watching the Ruth family with their children and grandchildren had created a yearning inside her that she hadn't recognized until she saw Noah reacting to his father. *Boys need their fathers.* And their grandfathers, her heart reminded her. A moment later she caught up to the two and slipped her hand into Jacob's.

"I promised the nursery workers we will come back next week. I guess we better get *kracken,* heh, little wife?"

Amanda nodded as she shifted Jules in her arms. "Your daughter is getting too heavy to carry. She wants to walk."

"Here, let me take her."

On the drive home, Jacob slowed for a traffic jam where a slow-moving team of horses plodded toward them, guided by men with long poles. Behind, a flatbed wagon held a house that extended over both lanes. He pulled to the side and cut the motor. "Watch this, Noah. This is something to see."

Amanda pulled her phone from her pocket and held it up where she could take a few shots without being too noticeable, out of respect for the Amish men walking alongside.

The strange load lumbered down the road. When it was opposite them, Noah hung out the window, silent and serious as the horses passed just feet away. A short, squat white house set atop the wagon, its doors and windows closed, and the front steps missing. A family followed in another buggy. Judging from the worry on the driver's face, he was the owner. But the men helping to move it seemed to know what they were doing. The horses as well. The house rolled slowly past, and Jacob pulled back onto the roadway. "Fellas around here move from time to time. It's no big deal for local folks," he explained. "But I'm glad Noah had a chance to see a bit of our culture."

"I guess, with no septic system, no electric lines, no water lines, or garage, they just pull up stakes and move? Pretty simple." Amanda shifted to include her son in the conversation. "What do you think, Noah?"

He grinned. "Can we move our house next to Silas, Daddy?"

Jacob met her glance with a rueful smile. "What about your friends back home? Won't they miss you?"

"No. I want to stay here. With Silas and Uncle Samuel. They are my best friends."

"Now see what you have stirred up? A hornet's nest, most likely," Jacob whispered with a frowning glance at Amanda. "You will need to be the one to tell him we're going home. He has found a family here. Even if I have not." His Adam's apple bobbed when he swallowed, as it did when he was upset. His silence spoke for him, the only sign of his frustration.

With nothing to say in her defense, Amanda rode the rest of the way home in silence. In bed that night, she shared with Jacob about his sister Beth's visit. "You should have seen her, Jacob. She was so thin. And she misses your mother so. It broke my heart to watch them. It was like they were each standing on separate sides of an abyss, and neither could get across to the other. They just stood there and yearned to be together."

"Mamm will suffer in her heart, but she will not tell Daed of the visit. Probably not even her sisters or her mother. She will carry this weight inside her until she dies."

"Will she hear of it when Beth...passes?"

Jacob pressed his hand on her back, making slow circles across her skin in his need to be connected to her. "Probably not. It won't matter. Beth is already dead to her. That's what her religion tells her. But I wonder, is such a thing even possible?"

Amanda lay with her head on his shoulder and felt his vein throbbing, as it did when he was upset. She shifted to cradle his head. "Jacob, I got her address. We can write to her. Her husband's name is Jeff. Jeff Wilbur. We can write him. He has our address. And we can send her some money. You should have seen her, Jacob. They're so poor. I'll bet it took everything they had to make the trip from Albany. Gas, motel. Surely they won't drive all the way home in one day."

"Shhh." Jacob pressed his fingers across her lips. "We mail them a check tomorrow. And I write her a letter telling her that she lives in my heart. We can't fix this, but we can make it better. Now let's get some rest and put our heads together on this tomorrow." He smiled against her ear, and she heard the humor in his voice. "My sister does not know her good fortune to meet my wife. But she will soon learn that her bruder marries a firecat."

The next morning, Amanda watched as Jacob composed a letter, his eyes dark and intense, his thoughts somewhere far off. His penmanship was precise, the careful script of a schoolboy as he put down sentences born of hard consideration. When he finished, he handed it to her to read.

Amanda shook her head and turned away to hide her tears. When she finished, she dropped the sheet onto the table. "This is perfect. She needs to know she won't be forgotten. That she is loved."

"Ach, she is loved, all right. Mamm may try to toe the line with the bishop, but her heart does not dry up for her oldest daughter. Even if she tries to make it seem so. I have seen her when she comes across something of Beth's. It is resolve I see in her eyes, not a hardening. No matter that she tries to conform." Jacob slipped the letter inside an envelope and pulled out his checkbook. "I send one thousand dollars. We can afford it. I will send more, afterward. For the service."

Amanda nodded. "Let's include a family photo. She needs to know she's not alone."

Later, she watched the mailman pick up the letter and toss it into a box on his car seat before driving off in the same direction that Beth had driven. After lunch, she walked to the farm with the children so Noah could hand his grandmother an invitation to his birthday party. Emma opened the tiny envelope, and her face flooded with color.

"Ach, what is this? A celebration for my grandson?"

Noah nodded. "And Silas has been *imbited*, too. Uncle John says he can come if you do."

Emma regarded the paper with a frown. She looked up and her eyes were troubled. "I will need to discuss this with Levi. And possibly the bishop." Her frown softened as she gave Noah's head a tussle. "But we see what we can do." She produced a plate of snickerdoodles and offered him one. "When you finish, let us go see what the garden provides us this fine day. Weeds, this is for certain. Maybe you like ta help Grossmummi to separate the useless weeds from the ones we use for healing? Not all plants are unwelcome in the garden. Some are Gott's gifts, if we know how ta use them properly."

She eased Noah out of the kitchen and into the sunshine with little fanfare. Soon he was bent over, nodding gravely as she explained about the bunch of pigweed she placed into a basket. Soon he was pulling dandelions by the root and adding them to the rapidly expanding collection of "good weeds."

Emma smiled approvingly. "We will have a fine mess of greens for supper. A good tonic for Grossdawdi's arthritis. I will tell him that my grandson helps me." She tucked a bundle into his jacket and flattened it with her hand. "Your mother should cook these with a scant amount of bacon grease. It will make your bones healthy and strong." She took Amanda aside and whispered, "I will have an answer for you in two days."

Amanda saw the bishop's buggy on its way from the Ruth farm the following day. The bishop was sitting upright, his face so wreathed in thought that he didn't respond to Noah's wave as he rolled by. Soon, Emma's plump figure appeared in the distance. She arrived at the gate with a pan of roasted potatoes and pot roast covered in a white dishcloth.

"*Denki*, but no, I don't come in. I must rush home." Emma flicked a glance toward the house, and her eyes darkened.

She's thinking of her daughter, and the sadness of letting Beth go. Jacob was right. A mother's heart doesn't let go of her children. Amanda accepted the roast. She returned from the kitchen to find her mother-in-law pushing Noah on his swing. When Noah was soaring, she straightened. "I bring the question to my husband and the bishop. I am allowed to visit the animals. As long as we take a lunch." She smiled. "No loitering in the gift shop or at English shopping malls, is how the bishop phrased it. I tell them my son is not ignorant of our rules. He will honor his mamm as the Bible commands. So yes, I go with you." She gave Noah another push before she offered her farewells.

Amanda closed the gate behind Emma as she returned home, walking nimbly with the ease of a much younger woman.

"We'll pick you and Silas up at ten o'clock on Friday morning," she called.

Emma waved over her shoulder. "I will be ready. A rare treat, to be sure."

❦

On Friday, Noah was nearly wild by the time they settled his cousin and grandmother into the car. Amanda insisted Emma sit up front, beside Jacob. "It will be quieter. And give you a chance to talk." Silas

balked at the child seat she'd borrowed, until Noah
explained it was a spaceship and they were flying over
the world.

The elaborate entrance to the zoo was an adventure
in itself. Inside, Noah hesitated over which path to take,
until the sound of hoots and high-pitched screams lured
him to the monkey exhibit. Jules had graduated to a
stroller, and Emma volunteered to push it. "This makes
my first."

When the boys tired of the monkeys they dashed
off to the African Savanna, gawking at the giraffes and
the elephants. Jacob took turns setting both boys on his
shoulders for a better view, while Amanda taught Jules
the names of animals she was learning in her picture
books. By the time they arrived at the waterfowl lake,
Emma was satisfied to sit and rest while the boys raced
along the walkway, and Jacob returned to the car for the
lunch basket.

"I'm afraid my cooking isn't up to yours, Emma,"
Amanda admitted as she pulled the top off a store-
bought relish tray and watched the little boys snatch the
olives.

"Food is a comfort," Emma said. "I give thanks for
this day with my family."

"Glad you came?" Jacob's expression reminded
Amanda of a little boy's, soft and vulnerable. She
wondered if maybe it was the first time he'd ever had his
mother to himself. Something about his eagerness told
her it was.

"I have a *zeugris*," Emma confessed. "I tell your
daed that I will spend the day with my son, no matter
his opinion. If it is a sin, then I will stand before the
community, later." Her eyes sparkled with mischief.

"This is the first time I stand up for myself." She hesitated and her face sobered. "Seeing my daughter...like that..."

Amanda reached to cup her shoulder. "Beth knows you still love her. She just needed to be reminded. Now she knows for sure."

"We do not speak of her since her shunning...since she turned away from her baptism. But sometimes..." Emma straightened and glanced at a plastic tub. "I will enjoy another piece of your fine chicken. Is there a drumstick? A mother rarely gets the treat of the drumstick—what with all the *kinder* clamoring for it."

After the lunch crumbs were cleaned up, Noah led the way from the primate enclosure to where the cats paced behind a wire enclosure. "We should have brought Timberly. She would make a new friend," he said.

"More likely some animal's dinner," Jacob teased.

"Jacob!" Amanda warned. She turned to soothe over the looks of shock on her son's face. "I read the rules. We can't bring Timberly to the zoo because she might bring a disease. And she'd get scared by the loud roars and screeches."

As if on cue, one of the lions nearby roared.

Silas stood rooted in place, nodding uncertainly, clearly longing for his mother. His grandmother noticed and leaned to whisper conspiratorially, "*Ach du lieva, kinder, such schmunzla!*" Emma's stage whisper made Silas laugh. A moment later he was chattering with Noah and pointing to a panther lolling in a tree.

Crisis averted. "Thank you, Grossmummi," Amanda mouthed to Emma. In the moment she felt a shift in their relationship. She reached to place her hand over Emma's on the stroller handle and felt pressure returned. Emma looked up, her warm blue eyes soft and understanding. *She noticed it, too.*

"Let's go to the Australian Outback. Safari time, Birthday Boy!" Jacob swung Noah up, oblivious, and Amanda smiled as he galloped down the sidewalk with the boys. *Each to their own. He's making his own connection.*

She followed more slowly, with Emma favoring her hip. "This is the last exhibit," she explained after checking the map. "Will your bishop allow you to stop for ice cream? It's Noah's birthday treat."

Emma smiled and nodded. *"Die gute gubbotta dawg.* I have the good birthday party today. I remember this always."

The ride home was made in silence, with three small children and one grandmother nodding off in the back seat. Jacob drove slowly, humming a soft tune with the radio while Amanda rode beside him in silence.

At the farm, Lorie came to the door wiping her floury hands on a towel. "So how was it? Did you see big tigers and zebras like in your picture books?" Silas nodded, his face a mix of melted ice cream, dirt, and little boy adventure. She laughed. "Did you bring home the *buwe,* the boys? Or the monkeys? I can't tell for all the dirt."

Noah's face screwed comically. "Silas is a boy, Aunt Lorie. He's not a monkey."

"Gute gubbotta dawg, Noah. Happy birthday. We have a gift for you." She handed him a package wrapped in an old copy of the *Budget.*

Noah solemnly unwrapped the paper and drew out a small hammer and handsaw. He stared a moment before looking up with a grin. Amanda reached to intercept the tools before he could cut his finger, but caught herself and pulled her hand away. "Daddy will need to show you how to use them. You can make your own blocks."

Noah's eyes shone with pride. "Thank you, Aunt Lorie, Uncle John."

From inside the living room, a newspaper rustled.

"We best get you in for a bath before bed, *sohn.*" Lorie's smile included all of them. "Thank you for including him. He had a *wunderbarr gute* time. Clearly."

Silas nodded. "*Denki, Uncle.* Aunt. *Gute gubbotta dawg, Noah.*"

Emma gripped Amanda's hand. When she turned to do the same to Jacob, her eyes shone with unspent tears. "*A wunderbarr gute dawg, sohn. Denki.*" Her eyes seemed to want to say more, but the newspaper inside John's house rustled again, and she broke away.

Noah insisted on holding his new tools on the way home. At bedtime, he agreed to set them on a shelf until his father could make him a toolbox. "So Jules doesn't get hurt," he explained.

"Well, that was a success," Amanda murmured to Jacob after getting both children to bed. "I'm glad it only happens once a year."

"More likely once in a lifetime. That was something I never thought to see. My mother taking a day to herself!"

Amanda reached to rub the soreness from his shoulders. "Miracles never cease. I think you're getting too old to ride four-year-olds on your shoulders." She lowered her hands to his back.

His body quickened and he groaned. "I'm not too old for this," he teased.

She laughed. "That's good to know. You got anything in mind?"

Jacob flopped to his side with a grin. "Count on it."

Afterward, he caressed a strand of her hair between his fingers. "Wife, it's time we go home. You said the birthday party was the last thing on your so-called bucket list. We start home day after tomorrow. Right after breakfast."

She reached to couple his fingers in hers. "Noah's going to be heartbroken."

He reached to give her a final kiss. "Maybe so. But his daddy's not."

Chapter Twelve

The roosters woke Amanda in the middle of a dream where she was burying her father's ashes next to her mother's. Fully awake, she lay with her eyes still closed, contemplating the meaning of the dream that seemed to be telling her it was time to go home. She slipped out of the covers, restless with regret. In the depression of the mattress where Jacob had slept, an empty pillow still held the indentation of his head. She tiptoed down the hallway and tapped on the bathroom door. It swung open to an empty room. Downstairs, his boots no longer sat on the linoleum next to the back door. His hat was missing, as well. She smiled when she heard the moos of cows being pushed into the barn for milking. *He's going to miss this. Even if he pretends he won't.* She saw him standing outside the barn, waiting to hit the switch on the generator that would power the milking machines.

Unseen by either him or his brother John, their father was on the other side of the barn, climbing the tower to the windmill, a grease canister hanging from his waist. Amanda looked around, but his sons were oblivious to the danger. Either one of them would gladly do the task that consumed their father this morning. She'd heard them chastise their father before about attempting something that was meant for a younger man.

No! You're too old for that, Levi, you'll hurt yourself. Leave it for one of the younger guys. She watched, mesmerized as her father-in-law continued to climb until he reached the tiny platform next to the blades. In the cool of the morning, the wind hadn't started up yet, a tiny mercy, and maybe the reason for the early-morning climb. But the metal steps were probably still damp with dew.

Upstairs, Noah called for her, diverting her attention from the windmill. When she turned back, she heard a shout. In the distance, three figures were running to the tower, climbing. She recognized the stout form of John at the bottom. He was shouting to a nimble climber that could only be Samuel. Jacob was just behind him, both climbing to the top where Levi clung to the tower.

"What's wrong, Mommy?" Beside her, Noah clutched his Teddy bear in one hand.

"I'm not sure, bud. Maybe something happened to grandpa."

"Should we call Daddy?"

"He's there now, helping. Maybe we should call 9-1-1." She looked around for her phone and remembered she'd left it upstairs, next to her bed.

"Grandpa says the Pennsylvania Dutch take care of their own." Noah stood with his chest puffed out, as though he were a little Amish boy, himself.

"Good point. Let's wait and see. Your daddy's got this." She eased him away from the door while she kept an eye on the drama down the road. "Let's get you some breakfast."

"I'm going to be a fireman when I grow up. Then I can save grandpas when they get hurt."

"Sweet thing, you've seen too much in your short life. Like me." She tried to find her smile. "Maybe we should both be firemen. We like to save grandpas." When her son began making his supplement, she returned to the door to watch Samuel helping his father climb down, while Jacob waited in case he was needed. They descended slowly, one step at a time while Levi protected an obviously injured hand.

In the background, Noah's blender whirred, blocking out the sound of Jacob and his brother. A noise from upstairs confirmed that Jules had woken. "Time to get your sister."

She was carrying Jules down the stairs when Jacob rushed in, panting. "Where's the car keys? *Schnell,* quick! An accident at the farm. I need to go."

Amanda dropped Jules into her highchair and grabbed her purse. "Here...take mine. We saw what happened. Is he okay?"

"My father caught his fingers in the windmill. They are mangled. I need to take him to the hospital." He grabbed the keys and rushed out.

A moment later she heard the tires spinning on the gravel before the car sped off toward the farm. In what seemed like seconds, Jacob raced past in the opposite direction, on the way to the hospital. A few minutes later a white van pulled up to the farmhouse. When it passed her door again, Emma was inside, her mouth pressed in worry.

Amanda quickly fed and changed Jules before she hurried to the farm.

Lorie answered the door, her lips furrowed with concern. She met Amanda's eyes and included the children in her greeting. "Noah, such small ears have no need to hear adult conversation today. Perhaps you would like to see what your cousin is doing? He and Samuel are in the barn, feeding the cows."

She waited until the door closed before she offered Amanda a cup of coffee. "A setback for Levi, this is certain. He was determined to complete the task he set for himself, even if his sons felt it was too difficult for a stout, older man to do. He set himself above their wisdom and look what happens! He is distracted. The brake comes off the windmill and the blades begin whirring when a stiff breeze suddenly blows from the northeast. With his fingers mangled, he can only hold on. No time for shifting weight from his injured fingers."

She lowered her voice and leaned closer. "We wrap the fingers in a clean scrap and place them in a bowl of raw milk for the trip to the hospital. With Gott's grace, the good doctors will be able to reattach them."

Levi crippled? He is so careful. A hundred thoughts ran through Amanda's mind. She had seen John riding in the car beside Jacob, both of their faces set in worry. How could the farm function without a second set of hands? Who would pay for the medical care? What if infection set in? How was Emma taking it? She managed to utter the least worrisome thought she could muster. "So, John went with them."

Lorie tucked a stray hair to her kapp and returned the coffee pot to the stove. "My husband and yours drove their father to Medina in the automobile. Jacob phoned ahead to arrange the surgeon. It happened so quick we are still a bit shaken." Her hand shook as she sipped her coffee, but her voice remained calm and reassuring.

"I saw Emma leave. You didn't go with her."

"Nei. It makes no need for us all to be there. Levi is in Gott's hands. I stay behind and prepare the meal. They will be hungry when they return. Samuel is trying to keep up with the feeding and field work, but it is only him alone with the horses. Young Levi is no help. He has hired out on a neighboring farm each day, for after school and this summer. John felt he had no need of him."

Amanda hesitated, unsure to what degree she was allowed to know the family secrets. "I haven't seen Samuel around much."

"Ja. The boy clashes with his daed and even his brothers. He used to be such a sweet boy, but now since he turns into a teenage boy, he thinks he knows all the answers." Lorie laughed. "But we have faith. Wait and see! He will end up the most upstanding of the lot. It happens this way in our community. We write no one off. Everyone is redeemable if they put their faith in the Lord. And if they want this life bad enough."

Even Jacob? Maybe he left too soon. "Samuel is a hard-working boy. Perhaps he will take after John."

"Ja, we see." Lorie glanced toward the kitchen where a huge pot of beans was simmering on a gas stove that had been added since Emma lived in the house. "A wedding present," Lorie explained. "Our ordnung agrees that such a stove will cause no harm. I suspect a number of wives had a hand in convincing their husbands of their decision. I do not miss adding wood to the firebox every time I bake my cakes."

"Agreed! I have enough trouble with my microwave." Amanda bit her lip to stop herself. "I should be going. We were supposed to start packing for home today. But now, with this—"

Lorie nodded. "It is only John alone on the farm until Samuel completes the school term. The authorities are firm on regular attendance. They will not make an exception, even with this."

"When does he get out of school?"

"Three weeks more. His daed's accident kept him home today. but he must resume his studies tomorrow or the authorities will knock on the door." Lorie sighed and looked again at the boiling pot. "Gott will provide for us. We do not fret."

Amanda walked home slowly, taking time to watch Samuel struggle with the huge Belgians on the corners. She recalled the way Jacob handled the team on his trip into town, as though he had last driven them only days before, not five years. At her gate, she waited for Noah to push the stroller through and latched the gate behind him.

She had supper on the table when Jacob rushed in. He brushed past her to scrub his hands in the kitchen sink and dropped into his seat at the table before emitting a long sigh. "A long day. Daed is home now. But the fingers will not be reattached. He will need to make do with his left hand."

"Is he in pain?"

"The doctor gave him medication." He chuckled

and fanned his hand in a wiggle-waggle gesture. "It is some kind of powerful pain killer. I never knew Daed to be so jovial. When I left, he was chattering like a tree squirrel."

Amanda smiled at the image. "And your mother?"

"She and John are at the house." Jacob scooped into his mashed potatoes like he hadn't eaten since early morning. A pork chop disappeared, and with it, a good portion of the cabbage and apple casserole she'd prepared for Noah.

She finished the dishes while Jacob went upstairs to take a hot shower. She was wiping out the sink when the bedroom door snapped shut, a clear invitation to follow him upstairs.

A few minutes later, she waited for his breathing to slow before she brought up the subject that had been worrying her all day. "This is John's busy season."

Jacob scowled and pulled his arm away. "Each is a busy season for a Pennsylvania Dutchman who farms with horses. Even the winters. Chopping forage for the cows, milking in darkness, morning and night. Even the ride to town on frost-bit days are a struggle for us. Having to harness the horses to the sled every time we wanted to go into town—" He paused and leaned in so that his breath fanned her cheeks. "Wife, what goes on in that mind of yours? Should I be worried?"

She attempted to appear surprised, as though she hadn't just been concocting a plan that would alter their travel plans. "I was just thinking. Young Levi is working for the neighbor this year." She sighed. "I suppose the authorities will allow Samuel to skip school to help John." She feigned a look of innocence and continued.

"...after all, school is nearly out for the summer. Only another month or so—"

Jacob raised on his elbow, his voice loud in the small room. "Enough, wife! You've been talking to Lorie." In the other room, the baby stirred, and he lowered his voice. "You have some plan in that pretty head of yours. Spill."

"*Ach*, no need to go all *techy*," she teased. "I'm just wondering how John will manage for the next three weeks, that's all. Till Samuel gets out for the summer, I mean."

Jacob shifted elbows, his face nearly touching hers. "I know what you're scheming, little wife. But we're in the same spot with the business, what with your father gone."

"But you have our foreman."

"He's a good man, but he can't do it all. What would you have me do?"

"Jacob, think about staying another two weeks. Help out? Work side-by-side with your brother. Would it be so hard?"

"Hard? You betcha."

She shifted so that her hip touched his, causing his body to react. "Your poor mom. All that worry at her age. If only she had someone to help out."

He chuckled and moved closer. "You're trying to make me *narrish*. But I don't get nervous. Five farmers will be at the farm tomorrow morning before sunrise. They'll trade off, send their sons over along with food for the family. The community will step in like always."

She stretched her arms wide and yawned. "Maybe you should get there before they do." She kissed him lightly and reached for the light. "We better get some sleep. Morning comes early."

He hesitated until he saw that she was serious. "Sleep? This is what you want? Wife, you are a hard woman, even for an Englisher."

"Good night, Jacob."

"Harumph!"

It seemed that she had only just fallen asleep when she was awakened by Jule's sleepy cry. She checked the clock and waited, but the cry intensified. Her hand slid across the sheets to Jacob's side of the bed and found it empty. In the corner, his work pants were gone, as was his jacket.

On her way into the baby's room, she peeked out the window and saw a lantern pushing cows into the barn. Outside, a buggy clipped past, with two men inside. By the time she finished feeding and changing Jules, the buggy was on its way back in the direction it had come.

An hour later, she was dishing bacon and eggs onto a plate when she heard Jacob's boots clomp on the mat. He entered and slung his hat on the rack, slipped out of his coat and headed to the sink to wash up. "You got breakfast timed to the minute, wife. You make a fine Amish farmer's wife."

"And you look to be working side-by-side with your brother. At least he didn't throw you off his place."

"Yet." Jacob reached for his coffee and drained most of it before he set the mug back on the table. "I forgot how much food it takes to be working with horses." He forked an egg in half and slipped it in his mouth. "I figure to help with the seeding. Last week's storm washed out the seedlings, and we're going to need to replant. Crop will be late this year, but Gott willing, we can manage."

Amanda leaned to press a kiss on the soft part of his neck where his shirt gapped. She stifled a gasp when he twisted to intercept her mouth with a proper kiss. "One day at a time, liebchen. We see how it goes."

He wolfed his breakfast and was back in the field before the sun rose over the top of the barn. She watched him throughout the morning, driving the horses, refilling the seeder, and spelling John and Lorie as they raked the seeds into the earth, neither man smiling. She was too far away to hear whether he and John were speaking, but it didn't matter. Small steps.

In the afternoon, she loaded her kids into the car and drove into town for groceries. "If Daddy's going to be a farmer, we better make sure he has a lot to eat, Noah, don't you think?"

"I want to play with Silas."

"I know, sweetie, but we can't go over there every day. They have work to do. And so do we."

"That's not fair."

"Noah, where do you learn to talk like that? TV? Silas's mommy won't want a boy around who talks smart to his mommy. Do you think Silas talks to his mommy like that?"

Noah rode in silence, considering. When she thought he'd forgotten the lesson, he surprised her. "I won't talk smart, Mommy. Silas says it's a sin."

"And he's right. You know your Commandments. 'Honor your mommy and your daddy? Well, that means no more smarty-pants."

Noah nodded enthusiastically. His good intentions lasted through two aisles of sugar-coated cereal, carbonated drinks and snack bars with enough sugar to fuel an engine. With little objection, he settled on apple snacks, pretzels, and Goldfish for treats. She followed the grocery bagger out to the car, fished in her purse for a couple of dollars to tip him, and thanked him a third time when he found a safe spot to nestle her wine bottles between the frozen vegetables and the loin chops.

The theater in Medina featured a movie with evil-looking cartoon characters running around causing trouble. "Maybe Silas's mommy will let us take him to the movies. What do you think? Shall we ask her?"

"I want to see *Minions*, Mommy. That's my favoritest."

At home again, she set Jules on the living room rug with a stack of toys and got Noah settled with a book before she started toting in bags of groceries and stacking them into bare shelves and cabinets. *We were out of everything. The shelves are bare. What was I thinking? Oh, yeah, today was supposed to be Packing Day. We were going home. That's what I was thinking.* Not a muddy farmer tromping in at night, expecting meat and potatoes and a fresh dessert to sate his ravenous appetite. No matter what she cooked, it wouldn't smell or taste as good as his mamm's. Double whammy. *This plan better work. John and Jacob better not have a dust-up or we'll have to pack all this food home with us.*

Chapter Thirteen

✦

A t suppertime, Jacob described how he'd plowed straw into the soil in the far pasture, and how the Belgians remembered his voice. His fingernails were edged with dirt that not even a nail brush would completely clean. After supper, he sat in the living room, in his stocking feet, stacking blocks on the floor with exaggerated caution while Jules giggled and clapped. At his daughter's urging, he puffed his cheeks and pretended to blow the towers down while he nudged with his finger. Each time the tower tumbled, Jules's giggles filled the room.

Amanda watched as she folded freshly laundered cloth diapers. "I've gotten rather used to using these for Jules. I hang them on the line and the sun purifies them."

"What happened to the disposable ones? You were set on them with Noah."

She shot a look at him to be sure he wasn't mocking her. "Yeah. About that. I caught Lorie looking at the super-sized box I brought home in the back of my car.

She didn't say anything, but I could tell what she was thinking. I took them back and got these."

Jacob looked up and grinned. "I tell you, liebchen, you're 'going Amish.'"

She poked him with her bare toes and twisted away when he tried to catch them.

In the corner, Noah was playing with a wooden toy Silas had given him, quietly running the toy horse and wagon on the floor with "click-clock" sounds while Jules demanded that her father make another stack. The room still held the scent of broccoli casserole and slow-cooked beef stew they'd had for supper. An apple pie was cooling on the counter for later, when the children were in bed, and they had a minute to themselves.

She finished nursing Jules and laid her in the crib. They stood together at the open door and watched their children settle into their beds. Jacob followed her into the kitchen and took a seat at the table for his pie and coffee. "Is it my imagination, or is our life easier?"

Amanda laughed as she handed him his cup and slipped into her chair. "You might be right. I feel like I can breathe and take time to play with the kids. Tomorrow, Noah wants to pick wildflowers along the creek. We'll fill a basket. He wants to take some to his grandmother."

His eyes seemed wary. "She won't set them inside the house. They believe flowers are best appreciated in nature where God intended them. I don't want him to be disappointed."

"He'll be crushed."

"Crushed? Not likely. Our son takes the differences between his family in stride." Jacob laughed. "Maybe better than we do. He and his cousin don't let much get in their way of friendship. Unless they argue over who will start the generator."

"Our son's learning to milk cows. Who would have dreamed!" She recalled a memory of her father watching Noah try to coax a drop of milk from his first cow. "I'm so glad Dad came with us. He got to live his youth again."

Jacob gave her hand a gentle squeeze before picking up his coffee. "Your camera captured it. Noah will remember this time."

"I hope so." She remained in her thoughts while the sounds of the house settled around her.

The rest of the week passed slowly enough for her to accomplish everything she needed, and nothing she did not. Jules learned to say "ma-ma" in her highchair while she beat the tray with her spoon. She learned "da-da" when Jacob stepped into the kitchen with his boots covered in thick black mud and manure. He kicked the boots off at the door and swooped his daughter up from where she had crawled across the floor. "You call for your papa to swing you over his head...like this!" Her giggles filled the kitchen until he deposited her in her highchair and turned to wash his hands. He reached to give Noah a playful swipe over his unruly hair. "How is my helper tonight? Tomorrow, you want to ride with me and help drive the horses?"

Noah's vigorous nod caused his blonde locks to fan out, covering his eyes. When he finally stilled, he turned to his mother. "I need gloves like Daddy. He wears them for blisters."

Somewhere in the cellar, she'd seen a pair of small leather gardening gloves. She caught Jacob's amused glance and mouthed a silent "thank you." To his credit, he blushed. *He's a better father since we arrived. John's example must be rubbing off.*

The next day, Amanda captured photos of Noah sitting on his father's lap as he handled the reins in his cut-down gloves, his hair riffling in the spring breeze. She filmed a video of them riding to the end of the row and circling back, Noah's eyes straight ahead as his father pointed out something that made them both laugh. The scene was one for her memory.

She finished filming and set her camera down when her daughter clamored for attention. "Shall we walk up and see what Aunt Lorie is doing today, Jules? Maybe Grandma has some *wunderbarr gute* cookie for you today."

Jules reached to be picked up. Amanda settled her on her hip with a shock of realization. Jules had already outgrown most of her clothing. Her hair would soon be long enough to braid like an Amish girl. "Come on, sweetie. Let's get you all dressed up for Grandma."

She walked the quarter mile, pushing Jules in her stroller. Emma was sure to pile her up with produce and baked goods; she'd need the wheels to carry the treasure home.

Emma was mending a pair of Levi's suspenders. Her sewing basket sat on the table, filled with scissors, thimbles, threads, and darning needles. Dozens of well-worn tools filled the basket, most of which she didn't recognize, but Emma seemed to use every one of them.

"I wish I knew how to sew." Amanda deposited Jules on her grandmother's immaculate floor. "Lorie helped me to make Jacob's suspenders, but that's the extent of my ability."

Emma peered over the top of her mending. "A

handy skill for a woman ta master. Even if you purchase your clothing ready-made, think of the rips, tears, and altering that a small child creates. It makes better ta be frugal. Waste not, want not. Sit. I show you a few simple tips for mending." She pointed to the torn pocket on Amanda's jacket that had been unsuccessfully repaired with a safety pin. "Here. Take this needle and run the thread through it."

Amand spent the afternoon basting stitches along the edges of a handkerchief until she was proficient enough to lay a row of close stitches on her torn pocket. When she tied off the knot with her teeth, as Emma showed her, she lifted the coat to inspect her handiwork.

"See? Nice, straight stitches." Emma smiled. "Maybe when you return home, you will sit in a sunny window and pass the time in mending. Find another young woman and do your sewing together. It is a chance ta visit, and the work goes faster. A good way ta build friendship among older generations. They are sometimes unable ta thread the needle on account of their failing eyesight, and they will welcome someone ta do that tiresome chore for them. Sewing gives us old ladies purpose."

An image of Jacob's friends, Rosie and Tibbs Bell occurred to Amanda. The image of sitting in Rosie's Wyoming kitchen, darning old wool socks brought a blaze of loneliness for the old couple. She'd remember to ask Jacob if they had time to swing by the Bells' Sheridan ranch on their drive home.

"You find yourself a pair of good, sharp scissors and don't let Jacob use them for any but their intended purpose. A man and woman live as one, but a woman's scissors aren't part of the Lord's plan." Emma paused to snip a thread with her teeth.

"I will. I promise." Amanda laughed. "I have my aunt Lydia's old *Brother* sewing machine. Maybe I should take a lesson."

Emma nodded. "An electric sewing machine is a wonder. I have a treadle machine that I make good use of. You are welcome to use it to hem another handkerchief. If I know Jacob, my son is always losing his."

After Amanda mastered the art of threading the ancient machine with white cotton thread, she concentrated on maintaining a straight line as she worked her foot on the peddle. For the first few minutes she felt like a kid learning to ride a bicycle, pumping and steering at the same time. "There's a lot to learn," she said. "But I think I'm getting it."

"Slow and straight, in the beginning. Speed will come with practice. Some of our ladies can sew as quickly with the treadle machine as the Englischers do with their electric machines." Emma's eyes held a glint of teasing. "But this way we can afford to eat a nice piece of schnitz pie for supper. For us, every task requires motion. No idle sitting unless we are stringing beans for supper." She glanced at the grandfather clock and set her mending down. "Which reminds me, I must start supper for Levi."

"How's his hand?"

"He gives thanks to Gott that it is only the two fingers that he loses, not the whole hand. That is a blessing, for sure. He is in pain, this is for certain. It will be some time before the skin heals. Until then, he does what he is able."

"Is there anything he needs?"

Emma shook her head. "Only his Bible and a good cup of coffee, he says." She glanced out the window to see him teaching a lesson to the small boys. "He is anxious ta see how he makes out in his shop. It will be a challenge for him now, but he welcomes the difficulty." She smiled. "I hear him now, saying, 'if you aim at nothing, you're sure ta hit it.' Already he is thinking on how ta sand the toys he makes. No longer will he be able ta craft the small boxes that the tourists like. But he can still make a pie table and a simple chair. He will sand and stain the pieces his sons make."

She smiled again and her blue eyes shone with joy. "It makes no difference. He will find a new way to serve Gott and his community." She tied her apron and prepared to pump water into the wash basin for her hands. "Who knows, maybe Gott calls him ta preach, after all these years."

Amanda tried to accommodate the stern man who had set aside his daughter—and quite nearly his son. "Is that likely to happen?"

Emma shrugged as she picked up a basket and motioned for Amanda to follow her out the back door to the root cellar. Inside, she leaned over a bin to pull three baking potatoes out. The potatoes were at the bottom, covered in straw, but their size was impressive. She picked out the last of the carrots and retraced her steps. "Our new crop will come in soon. And just in time, praise Gott. We spared what we could for families in need. We always grow more than enough for our household. It's our community's way."

Amanda glanced around at the meager supply of rutabagas, squash, gourds, and pumpkins neatly stored and covered in straw or sand. Nearly empty racks of dried herbs lined one side of the dugout. On another side, a few packages of smoked meats and ham hung from the rafter.

"Almost bare, this time of year. Most things last until spring. We rely on the garden in the cold months. Levi and John will butcher hogs when the weather makes cold. Until then, we will use such as we have— chickens and cold storage meats." Emma winked. "I buy my liverwurst at the meat market. I can't get the texture to suit me when I try it myself. Easier to exchange eggs to the butcher."

"You store milk and eggs here, too."

"And butter, whipping cream. Lorie has the good gas fridge in her house now, but I do things the old way. It works well enough." She indicated a small jar on a shelf. "Fetch me down the heavy cream. I will whip some to serve with that delicious pineapple you brought me. A real treat for Levi." Amanda watched as she locked the cellar door against raccoons.

Inside again, Emma added a few sticks to the fire already burning in the cook oven before she added the potatoes. She layered three pork chops in a cast-iron pan between slabs of cabbage and raw apple slices, seasoned everything, and placed it in the oven beside the potatoes. With scarcely a break in her pace, she dusted her hands on her towel and returned to her sewing machine to watch Amanda finish her stitching.

"You make everything seem so easy, Emma. Will I ever be as skilled?"

Emma peered over her reading glasses as though the question puzzled her. "Our skill comes from necessity. You buy much of your needs at the market. What need will you have to crock sauerkraut or brine pickles and watermelon rind? We choose to provide for our needs. To live independent. But there is a price we pay for this. We work long hours. Those who don't will find themselves short of provisions when the cold weather comes —and likely lacking in grace at the Final Judgment."

"But you won't let them starve?"

"Nei. The Lord is clear about this. We provide for the poor among us."

"I've heard of the Christian Aid Ministries."

Emma nodded as she snipped a thread and folded the shirt she had just finished mending. "My sisters and I will spend our next Sister's Day canning chicken for the poor overseas. Good, nutritious meat. In this way we glorify Gott and help enlarge His kingdom."

Amanda nodded. "...whatsoever ye do, do all for the glory of God. 1 Corinthians 10:31."

Emma looked up approvingly. "You know the verse. It is a credit that you do so."

Amanda hesitated before she admitted, "I Googled it. On the internet. I was curious."

"As long as you live by the verse." Emma rose to add another piece of wood to her cookstove. "I sometimes think it would be nice to have a stove like Lorie's. But we make do. We often eat with John's family. I don't cook as much as I used to. Samuel eats at their table more often than not. He sleeps in their house—in the room that John shared with Jacob."

Amanda went to the window and lifted the plain cloth shade, keeping a tight grip as the powerful spring rolled the shade to the top of the window. "Aunt Lydia had these in her windows." In the forties and fifties. As soon as venetian blinds came out, she replaced them. "I have some stored in the basement if you want them."

Emma glanced over her spectacles with a smile. "Waste not, want not. We make gentle use of our shades. They should last for a good while yet. But you could donate them to the Mennonite Relief Fund. For others who are not so fortunate."

Amanda scanned the yard for Noah and found him perched on the wagon seat, watching the seeder spill its load into the dirt. "My son and his father are going to be hungry tonight. It's time for me to start home, as well."

"Already? Maybe the baby has a bit of applesauce before she goes. I have ignored my little Jules in my haste to finish my sewing today. You will bring her back so I might have a proper visit? She is growing with every day. She is already pulling herself up. Soon she will be trying to walk. She takes after her father in this."

Amanda stood beside her mother-in-law as Jules balanced against a table leg. "I suspect you're right. She's curious. And I hate to say it, but she's got a bit of a temper."

"Jacob was the same at this age. I fear we considered him rebellious when he was only curious. His daed and he often clashed about the principles of our faith. So many questions my son asked. Always challenging our ways. Our other son, John was accepting from the start. I wonder now..."

"Jacob tried to remain, but he felt like an outsider."

Emma gazed out the window at the men working in the field. "I remember the day he left. It was a shock to me. I wanted to follow him outside, but Levi shook his head, and the bishop as well. I could do nothing as they helped the poor girl out of the service. When we get home, I knew without needing to be told, that my son had taken his things and left us." She seemed to be reciting a story from heart. "I heated supper for my family, but I held my sorrow inside. I sat at the table in silence while the bishop discussed his leaving as though he had committed a grave sin. But I knew the truth. It was required of me to forgive John, and I did gladly, for he was truly repentant. But my son Jacob was robbed of his moment. Surely he would have made his testimony and announced his marriage that day." She stroked her granddaughter's curls without seeing the child, her face wreathed in momentary pain. Then it was gone, replaced by her clear-eyed intelligence and hope.

"You are wise to bring Jacob home for reconciliation with his brother. I know this was your plan. A brother against his brother is warned of in the Bible. But one of my sons has committed a sin against the other, and my Levi does not believe the fault was John's."

"Because your husband is complacent in the sin," Amanda said.

Emma looked up without speaking and then dropped her head. Outside, a shout to the horses meant that the men were finished for the day.

Emma's actions clearly indicated she didn't want to speak of this day again. Like her daughter Beth, the secret of Jacob would remain between them. Amanda gathered Jules from her grandmother's lap. "I must hurry home and start supper. Noah will get a rare treat of hamburger tonight. He's earned it."

She started down the steps as Jacob was showing Noah how to pull the harness off the team. When she looked out of her kitchen window later, she saw Jacob walking home with a sleeping Noah on his shoulders.

Chapter Fourteen

❧

"Jacob, I had a note from your sister, Beth. She is worsening. The cancer is taking its toll. She frets that nothing is going as she had prayed it would. She doesn't say what the problem is, but she seems concerned. Should I write back? Is it too much to expect an answer?"

"Nei. Write her. Our women love pen pals, and a shunned one is no different. Something to take her mind off her troubles." Regret crossed his face, leaving his eyes coached in sorrow. "She will harken to news of her family, even if she doesn't ask. She has a good heart. She will welcome to know you, even if only for a short time. And who knows, maybe Gott spares her." He pulled on his hat and coat before lacing up his work boots. "I am off to finish seeding today. Give Beth my love. She was my favorite. We shared some fine adventure when we were *kinder*."

In the silence that followed, Amanda took out her box of fancy stationery.

Dear Beth,

We didn't have a chance to visit, but my heart wants to know you, if only to bring me closer to Jacob's childhood. Like ships passing in the night, your light has touched me. I begin by telling you how adorable your children are. Sarah resembles Jacob so much. She stole my heart the moment I saw her, and I feel as though we have a deep connection. And baby Jacob—named after the man we both love so dearly. My prayer is that he will grow into half so good a man as the one I married.

Your mother grieves your absence—and your illness—even if she doesn't speak of it. I sat with her only yesterday as she taught me to sew on her treadle machine and you were there with us in spirit, as I know you will always be for her. You will not be forgotten, no matter the rules that govern their faith practices.

Jacob sends his love. I have enclosed a photo of our little family for you to share with yours. If you want, I will write as often as possible, so your children will know they have a family that loves them. I would appreciate a photo of you and yours

for the same purpose. Family is precious
and rare. Let us keep each other in our
hearts as we are able.

Jacob finds himself lending a hand on
the farm for a few weeks, until Samuel
finishes his school term. Your father lost
two fingers in an accident, but Levi is of
good cheer, if such can be said of him.
Emma bears up with her consistency and
good cheer. I truly love her and sometimes
wish I could share her life in its entirety
and that of our sister-in-law, Lorie, whom
you would love if you knew her. She is as
bright a light as John is gloomy, if I
may speak plainly. Jacob and John are
moving closer to settling their rift, a betrayal
that I will not burden you with, only to
say it weighs on them both like an anchor.

My children are, as you well know, the
center of my life. Noah is often with his
father and the horses, trying to be a four-
year-old farmer. As does his cousin Silas,
who is the same age. They share the
MSUD, and Lorie has offered good, prac-
tical advice for me in his struggle. We were
able to have an appointment with the
specialty clinic here in Ohio, but so much
information is available online that I felt

already "Ahead of the curve," if I may use my teacher language.

Jacob and I are divided on whether I will eventually resume my teaching career. I may home-school my children for a few years. That is his hope. We shall see. I have so much energy, and hopefully a degree of talent for teaching. But he wants me to channel it into parenting our own children for the time being. As much as I hate to admit it, he may be right.

I will close now and save further news for another time. Our prayers are with you. We love you and feel such sadness at the missed opportunity of knowing you better. Take care and love to your family.

Amanda Miller Ruth

"There, that'll do for now." She placed the letter in an envelope along with a photo of her family and another of Emma and Silas, taken at the zoo. "I hope she writes back." Upstairs, Jules was calling to be picked up. *And so the day begins.*

Jules had soaked her crib and was badly in need of a bath and a change of clothing. Amanda was running the tub when Noah appeared, still rubbing his eyes. "Mommy, this house is cold."

"Hop in here with your sister and warm up," she suggested. "Here, I'll help you with your PJ's."

The enormity of Beth's tragedy grew as she watched her own children splashing and giggling. When the water began to cool, she wrapped her wiggling daughter in a towel as Jules insisted on drying herself. Beside her, Noah stood complacently, waiting his turn. What different personalities her children had. Noah was a lover, while Jules would take on the world.

Noah waited for her to open the door before he followed her to the bedroom. She picked out a set of warm-weather clothes and handed them to him while Jules fought Amanda's attempt with sleeves and leggings. She was winded by the time the last button was fastened and two kicking feet laced into soft shoes for warmth. "Jules, you are a feisty little thing. You remind me of your daddy."

"Am I like Daddy?" Noah stood waiting to go downstairs for his breakfast.

"You, my little man, are a lot like me." She hugged him and felt him against her, satisfied at her answer. *Don't break my heart one day by leaving me.* She formed a mental image of Emma in her little house, grieving the loss of an adult son and daughter who left their community and never returned. *At least you have Jacob for a few more weeks. And then he, too will be gone.* "Do you love your grossmummi, Noah?" He nodded and pressed against her for another hug. "She's the bestest baker, isn't she? And you have her pretty blue eyes."

After breakfast, they took a late morning walk to watch Jacob unharness the Belgian draft horses from the wagon. He led one of them forward and tied it to a post outside the barn. Trailing a hand on its side, he walked around to examine a loose shoe on its hind leg.

In the yard, a pair of Amish men stood talking to

Levi and John. Every so often, they glanced over at Jacob and their conversation fell. She made her way to the barn and found Jacob wearing a leather farrier's apron and searching for something in the tool storage area before he returned to the tied-off horse with a heavy hoof jack and pair of nippers in his hands. Without looking up, he set the horse's huge hoof on the jack. Using the nippers, he pinched off the first nail-head, continuing until the last one was free. The worn-out horseshoe fell to the ground with a thud.

He worked with one ear cocked to the conversation in Pennsylvania Dutch dialogue being spoken outside.

"The legislature's set on their law. John will need to see to the carbide spikes he puts on his buggy. Ice or no, he's going to need to fix the problem."

When Noah left Amanda's side to steal closer, Jacob motioned for him to stand a safe distance away. "Don't startle the horse, Noah. Quiet steps." He handed Noah the discarded horseshoe and straightened with a hand on his back before he plucked a hoof pick from his apron pocket.

Amanda took advantage of the moment to ask, "Is your brother in trouble with his community?"

Jacob grinned and bent to pick at the dirt compacted in the horse's frog. When he finished, he began paring the overgrown sole with a pair of nippers. "The English claim the carbide spikes we use on the buggy wheels are tearing up the fresh-laid asphalt. John's stubborn and sees only the safety of his family. He's been fined once, after a warning. The deacon is here to warn him that the community has agreed to mend their ways with the legislature. A compromise."

"What will he do?"

Jacob released the hoof and gave a covert glance at the men talking excitedly outside. "John won't like it, but he'll buckle down to the rule. Sometimes they are allowed to cut the spikes to a better length that does less damage. A compromise will be made. The state has rules, but we are large in number around these parts." He looked up and grinned. "I mean to say the Amish are."

She heard the slip of tongue. "How are you getting along with your brother? Any change?"

"Change? Nothing I can see. He is stiff-necked, that one. He's glad of my help but unwilling to admit he needs it. But I do my duty, and my conscience will be clear." He bent to inspect the hoof in the sunlight of the open door. "These horses are bred 'base-narrow.' This means close-footed so they don't trample the furrows. But in time the hooves require adjustment, or they will become crippled before their time. Good only for the glue factory." He indicated the hoof he had just picked up. "The fit on this has been off for a while."

"Nothing wrong with the horse. Let it be and get about your business." John strode into the barn, his anger causing the horse to shift off the hoof jack. Jacob jumped back to avoid being stomped.

"This one's in need of leather pads or he'll be crippled." Jacob stood glaring at his brother, neither of them willing to cede their position.

Fresh from the humiliation of his church representatives, John raised his voice. "My brother, always the expert. He comes back after running away. Five years gone, and he comes to tell me how to manage my horses!"

Jacob shrugged and picked up the opposite hoof.

He clinched off the nails without waiting for permission. "Just stating the facts, bruder. The proof is here. Horse is wearing hard on the outside. You need to compensate in the shoe."

John stood with his arms folded across his chest, his lungs wheezing with fury as Jacob finished cleaning the second hoof and filed the outside. Samuel arrived from school and stood uncertainly, watching.

Jacob released the horse and gave it an encouraging stroke. Inside the cinder-strewn workroom he had a layer of hot coals burning on the farrier's brazier. He took no notice of his brothers as he walked back and forth from the horse to the fire, pounding the shoe to red-hot and lifting it to eyeball the fit. When he was satisfied, he hung the shoe from a hook to cool.

"Dunk it in the water and be done. At this rate you'll lose the sunlight." John shifted in impatience.

Jacob kept his head down as he shook his disagreement. "Hoof size is a factor here. Water cooling is fine for the buggy horses, but there's too much metal on these. Slow cooling is better." He selected a thick piece of leather from a package the Fed-Ex driver had delivered earlier.

John scowled. "What's that? Another expense? At this rate I would be better off sending you packing and doing it myself."

Jacob traced the pattern of the shoe onto the leather and began to rough-trim it. "Leather pads ease the horse's legs," he explained. "I paid for these. No need to fuss. But you will be a fool not to order more when these are gone."

"No charity needed. I pay my debts," John grumbled. "But that horse was well enough before you took him out to the field."

"Maybe. Maybe not." Jacob directed his advice to his younger brother. "Samuel, you show this horse some common sense, you'll get another few years of work out of him." He tacked the shoe and pad together and started to fine trim the fit. When he was satisfied, he picked up a can of packing salve and smeared it over the hoof, taking care to get into the crevices. The horse shifted, showing signs of restlessness. "Easy, boy. Almost finished." He tacked the shoe and pad to the hoof and straightened. When the horse stood on all fours again, Jacob squinted until he was satisfied. He bent and began nailing the shoe on with a handful of square nails clenched between his lips.

John stood watching, scowling. When Jacob tacked the last nail, he found his tongue. "You learn that after you ran off?"

"Nei," Jacob said. "A Pennsylvania Dutch fella out of Akron taught me."

"Hurrumph."

Amanda watched from the sidelines with the small boys. When they began to get restless, she whispered, "You need to be very quiet."

Jacob straightened to relieve his spine before he started on the next hoof. Sweat ran down his temples from the heat bathing the barn from the brazier. Two hours later, he untied the horse and slapped its rump to gauge the fit of the shoes as it ran through the gate. "I do only the back hooves today. Less stress on the horse if I break up the work."

John watched his draft horses nuzzling each other in the pasture. "Whole process will need to be done again in a couple of months," he grumbled. "Take good part of a week to do it your way."

Jacob began putting his tools away. He smothered the coals and picked up his coat. "I finish the front hooves tomorrow, when Samuel gets home from school to learn. Best you work the horses during the morning. They stand easier with their vinegar out."

John walked toward his back door without acknowledging his brother.

Chapter Fifteen

Lorie walked out of the house in time to fill in the gaps of her husband's rudeness. "Thank you, Bruder Jacob, for the kindness. That old horse was foot sore. John was telling me we would be forced to replace him before the next season." She offered a smile. "One less problem to vex him. Gott gives him enough these days."

Jacob acknowledged her without returning her smile, his eyes dark with a blaze of anger at his brother's curt dismissal.

Amanda approached Lorie, who stood with a stiff, embarrassed smile. "Have you talked to John about allowing Silas to attend the movie show with us? It would mean a lot to Noah."

From the top of the stairs, John waited. "No Englischer movie for our son. We know about minions. They are mindless creatures who become the instruments of the devil. You wish to teach your kinder that sin is cute, that is your concern. But our son does not be knowing such values. And neither should yours."

Amanda stood, wishing she could disappear.

Lorie headed back into the house, apparently in agreement with her husband. From the open door, she offered a slight wave. "Thank you again, bruder, for tending the horses. It is hard for one man to keep up with all the chores required on a farm. Your labor is welcome."

Amanda waited until they were clear of the gate before she spoke. "You did a kind thing today, Jacob. You taught your brother a new skill, whether he wants to admit it or not."

Jacob scowled. "At service he will be the one telling others how it should be done—like he was the one who invented the process."

"But he'll know who taught him. And he won't forget. Ever. Neither will Samuel. He has high regard for you. He wants to learn."

Jacob slipped his arm around her and brought her body close. With his son perched on his shoulders, they followed the edge of the farm where the smell of sorghum in the adjacent field offered a bit of relief from the tension in his muscles. "True, little wife. Let's forget this day and go home. I pray you have something ready in that slow cooker of yours. Or my stomach will make a meal of my ribs."

She heard herself chuckling, a welcome feeling after the tense afternoon. "Barbecue ribs and coleslaw."

After his last day of school, Samuel stopped by. At her bidding, he ducked his head and entered the kitchen to take a seat at the table while she scanned the report card he pulled from his waistband. She wasn't surprised to see that he'd gotten C's in most of his subjects.

He accepted a cup of coffee and eyed the loaf of banana bread she brought from the oven. "I'm free to take over the farm work now. Give me a chance to earn my keep this summer. I watched the way Jacob shod the horses, and we won't be repeating the same mistake, Gott willing." He looked down at his heel resting on the rung of his chair. "Wish it was Jacob, was running the farm," he muttered. He glanced up with pinked cheeks, obviously embarrassed that he'd spoken aloud.

"If wishes were horses, beggars would ride." Amanda handed him a carton of cream for his coffee and two slices of banana bread.

Samuel looked up. "You learn that in school?"

"It's an old Scottish proverb. My father used to say it when I complained."

Samuel grinned. "I liked your daed. He was easygoing. Not like—"

"Levi?" Amanda smiled at his look of chagrin. "My father thought your father was a good man. He brought you kids up well. You have a remarkable family. Don't take that for granted. I have no one."

"No one? Surely you are my sister now, part of our family. And we are yours. Silas talks every other word, the name of his cousin, Noah. Even he boasts of his *Oncle* Jacob. This makes our brother John narrish, crazy. He is thinking, what does his younger bruder do that even his own son likes the oncle better?" Samuel's laughter caught in a snort.

Amanda paused in her laughter to give him a peck

on his cheek. "I will remember this moment. One of my favorite memories." She smiled at his embarrassment. "But *shuss*, little brother. It will be our secret that Jacob is our hero. He must never suspect, or he will be hard to live with."

Samuel's face blazed pink. "Ja, our secret." He leaned in to whisper conspiratorially, "Even Mamm, she likes Jacob best. Even more than me and Young Levi. He is her favorite. But she can tell no one, especially Daed. He is only for keeping the Ordnung."

"That's not so bad. Everyone lives by rules, even the English. Don't think the grass is greener outside your community, Samuel. It's just different."

"Ja. Crabgrass. Weeds that take root where it chooses."

She laughed. "Exactly."

Noah woke from his nap and ran downstairs to hug his uncle. "Can I walk home with you and push cows, Samuel? Daddy says we have to go home in two days."

Samuel looked up. "You leave in two days? We will miss you."

Amanda smiled at the panic in his voice. "The road we take goes both ways, brother. Remember that. Maybe you want to come visit us next year? After you start your rumspringa? Jacob would be glad to have you. A chance to see the world before you join your community."

"Ja. That sounds like a plan." Samuel rose and picked up his hat. "Noah, I make tracks to get the milking done. You better get your shoes tied if you want to be a farmer."

Amanda closed the door behind them and picked up an empty packing box. She climbed the stairs and carried Jules to the window to watch Noah trudge beside his uncle, looking for all the world like a little Amish boy with his hands clasped behind him and his little straw hat shading his blonde curls.

The next morning, Jacob pulled the self-enclosed trailer up to the front door and started loading the heaviest furniture in the front. Amanda carried out a box containing most of her kitchen supplies. "We've been invited to Lorie and John's for supper. She says she owes us a meal."

Jacob hefted a box and glanced down, obviously irritated that she had left such unwelcome news to the last minute. He swallowed hard. No point in ruining the day. "You forgot to tell me this?" he inquired softly.

She glanced around at the amount of stuff they'd collected in only two months. "Well, with all the packing..."

"Wife?"

She straightened from the loading ramp and tried to ignore the storm that was building both in the sky over his shoulder and in the lines of his face. She walked over to wrap him in a hug. "Let it go, sweetie. It's our last day. Surely you can eat a simple meal with your brother and keep the peace. We'll be gone tomorrow. Give your mother the satisfaction of seeing us all under one roof. She deserves that."

He eased around her to drop his box and turned toward the kitchen. "I would like to taste my mamm's schnitz pie one more time," he admitted.

Amanda waited for him to hold the door open. "She gave me her recipe. I'm going to get it right this time."

"I will be a happy man if this is true."

"Speaking of happy, do you remember what day it

is?" When he shook his head in puzzlement, she slid a wrapped box from her apron pocket. "Happy Birthday. This is why your mother wants you to come tonight. She plans a special meal for you."

He unwrapped the gift, careful to fold the paper so it could be reused. He lifted the lid and stared with a look of confusion until he lifted the suspenders out. "A pair just like my mother used to make me." He looked up with dawning recognition and grinned. "You made these? From my mother's instructions?"

She nodded, her heart pounding as he inspected her slow, careful stitches. "If you look closely, you'll see the crooked ones. My stitches weren't as tiny as your mother's, so I used her treadle machine. I pumped until I was blue. It was quite a project."

He slipped them over his shoulders and ran his hands along the margins to test them. "Now truly I can get old and fat. Nothing stands in my way."

"I found metal clasps. They really are better than the buttons. Trust me on this. I asked Wiser Good at the Mercantile, and he gave me the honest truth."

He snapped the suspenders onto the front of his Wranglers and pivoted to do the same on the back. "So, not a true Amishman, after all. Some old ways, some new."

"Fair enough." She stood back and admired her handiwork. "Very handsome." She pressed close. "Happy birthday, Jacob."

He lingered over the kiss, and she felt his warmth against her. "It means a lot, your stitching them for me. I will take care to save them for special occasions." He gave her a look that brought heat to them both.

"Knowing my little wife, I won't expect a second pair if I wear these out," he whispered into her ear.

She laughed. "Good plan. Quit while I'm ahead."

For a moment the air seemed alive with the energy of their teasing. She looked around at the old walls and considered the lives that had known this kitchen, this old house. "I think I'm ready to let it go now, Jacob. Time to go home. Whatever I was searching for, I've found. Dad got to see this place one last time. If Noah wants to visit when he's older, he can stay with Silas. I have a feeling they'll stay close, no matter what. They'll be pen pals when they learn to write. And after that, they can build a friendship."

"You're ready to let this go?" Jacob smiled. "No more living with one foot in the old family house that belonged to your aunt Lydia?" He lifted her chin to better gauge her mood. "You're no longer leaving your heritage behind?"

She shook her head. "I can't have it all. I have to choose. Lydia's gone now. I don't have to feel guilty about not loving her enough, or in the right way. I don't have to feel bad for my father, either. I'm ready to sell this place and go home."

He hesitated. "Liebchen, you are sure about this? I thought you were set on a plan to rent the house out to tourists."

"I can't do that. Your parents don't want strangers staying down the road. New neighbors every week." She paused to give Jules a teething biscuit and a sippy cup. "Everything is changing. Let's use the money to buy a motorhome. We can come back and visit when we want to."

Jacob's look of astonishment was comical. "Wife?

It's hard to keep up with you. What makes the sudden change of heart?"

Wonder rode the moment. She sensed the shift inside her, freeing her from the past. "I was thinking about Beth and her children. The life she'll never have with them. I want to see things. Do things with our kids. Not just sit in one house, looking out at the same fields forever. We can work hard, but we can play hard, too. See new places." She hesitated. "Maybe even go see your sister one last time."

His eyes darkened with emotion. "This is about your daed, isn't it?"

She nodded, her lashes suddenly damp with tears she was trying to hold in. "He had so many plans to travel. To see Florida. He realized this dream—coming back to his old home again—but he had so many other plans. I want to realize his dreams for him. For us."

"So we get a motorhome?" Jacob straightened as the idea took hold. "I would like that. We could set aside a few weeks and just travel. Spend holidays at the coast. Visit the National Parks that I read so much about."

"Jacob, let's sell this house and do it."

He stooped to lift Jules out of the highchair. "You'll need a brother or a sister to play with, won't you, little one?"

Amanda felt the easing of her father's death. His memory, never, just the awful details of his passing. She felt as though he was up there, watching her, approving of her plan. "We'll drive back to visit Carol and Rennie when the baby arrives. We'll make the trip every year. Reach out and touch, as the saying goes."

"What's to stop us driving into Canada? Or Alaska?" he asked.

"I want to see Sarasota Springs, your old stomping grounds. Go swimming in a bikini and scandalize the rumspringa boys."

Jacob gave her an exaggerated look of disapproval that would have done his father proud. "For sure they would notice you," he teased. "But I don't share you with anyone."

"Back atcha. You're mine. Don't let those suspenders swell your head." She glanced at the clock. It was nearly time to start for the farm. "We're hooked up to the trailer. Do we drive down to your folks' or walk?"

Jacob gave a long look out the window at the field he'd just cleared of its first hay crop. "We walk. I want to appreciate my labor of the past weeks. I work hard. Even if John thinks I don't do the work of a ten-year-old."

A memory flashed through her, and she smiled, remembering. "Do you recall the day I came to the farm for the first time? Your father telling you the same thing?" She lowered her pitch in a near-perfect imitation of Levi Ruth's voice. "'Jacob? You plan to go into business for yourself, best I hire young John Yoder to do your work. It won't be much work I'll be missing by hiring a ten-year-old in your place.'" She wrapped her arms around his neck and pressed against him. "I think that's when I started falling in love with you. You looked so sweet, standing there all embarrassed and blushing, defying your father for my sake. You were my hero." She welcomed his kiss. "You still are."

"Careful, little wife, or you make us late for supper."

She took his hand and led him upstairs where Noah

was playing with his toy trucks with Jules, both of them oblivious to anything but their play. Amanda tiptoed out of the room and shut the door. "We have twenty minutes."

"Wunderbaar gute, liebchen," he whispered. "I make good use of the time."

Chapter Sixteen

✥

At the Ruth farmhouse, John sat in his chair reading the newspaper when Lorie opened the door. Behind her, the table was set for twelve. Their daughter Sarah worked in the kitchen, ladling stewed cinnamon apples into a bowl. A pork roast steamed on the sideboard, its skin crisped to a golden brown. Stewed cabbage, small baked potatoes, and glazed carrots filled a platter, along with the season's first green beans.

The back door opened, and Emma walked in, carrying a birthday cake decorated with chocolate pinwheels and peppermint drops. Levi followed, his fingers still bandaged.

"*Wie ghets?*" Levi glanced over at Amanda and repeated his greeting in English for her sake. "How's it going?"

Jacob nodded without meeting his father's gaze until Amanda shot him a look of warning. "Same as ever," he admitted. "I have worked up an appetite with the horses. I will welcome this fine meal."

"My wife uses the foods Gott provides to nourish our bodies." John looked up from his paper and folded it on its creases before carefully setting it on his chair. A subtle reminder that his reading had been interrupted.

Jacob's jaw clenched at his brother's actions, but he made a vain attempt at humor. "My wife places her trust in both Gott and the Aldi Market." He winced when the joke fell flat. "She says Aldi's is for sure an Amish store because there are spaces for buggies in the parking lot."

His jest brought a frown from his father, but he apparently felt reckless tonight, baiting his father with an outsider's joke to show that he was no longer one of them.

Amanda jumped in. "Jacob means I'm not a scratch cook like the women in this family. But I know my way around a box of macaroni and cheese."

"I might try doing the same." Emma offered her a kindly smile. "It would give me joy to try a product that is recommended by my family."

Bless your heart, Emma. Amanda set Jules on the floor and watched her crawl to her grandmother, who picked her up to play with her kapp strings. "We leave first thing tomorrow morning. I will miss you, Emma. And I know Jules will. She has warmed to her grandma in the past two months."

Emma's fingers traced the outline of Jules's plump cheeks. "So like her father, my Jacob. He was a happy little boy—a curious little thing." She waved a hand toward the heavy pie table in the kitchen. "He would often climb up to help himself to the molasses cookies I kept in a red tin. He would pound on the top, thinking perhaps ta pry the lid open." She looked over and smiled. "Instead, the rattling would alert me ta come and set him on the floor with a swat to his behind. Soon he would try again." She included Jules in her smile. "You would like a cookie?"

Jacob helped himself to one of the cookies as well. "Mamm grows soft after all these years. For all my life, she tells me 'to spare the rod is to spoon the child.' And now she does just that." He included his mother in his teasing. Even Levi smiled.

Lorie appeared from the kitchen, wiping her arms on a hand towel. "Perhaps this is time we share our news." She glanced at her husband and waited for him to speak.

"It seems that Gott plans another Ruth baby soon joins the family."

"In December." Lorie smiled at her husband. "John wants to wait to share the news, but I am eager to tell."

"Congratulations." Amanda leaned in to give Lorie a hug and caught herself as Levi shook John's hand. *No hugging*.

"Gott blesses us," Levi said. He patted Lorie on the shoulder. "We should give special thanks this day."

John stood beaming beside his wife. Jacob apparently couldn't ignore the chance to rib his brother. "So, what is this I see on my bruder's solid Amish face—*hochmut*? Such pride is a sin."

John's face fell, the moment spoiled. "First, remove the plank out of your own eye, bruder," he growled.

"Enough! No scrapping, or you two will eat in the barn," Lorie scolded. "Sarah, put the little one in the highchair. Others, take the seats for supper."

John took his usual spot, and Jacob took a chair at the other end, next to Amanda. She smiled and whispered, "Your mother doesn't give you the birthday chair?"

"Nah, a slice of her birthday cake is enough." He leaned back with his hands tucked into his suspenders. "Ask her for the recipe—that is all the gift I need."

Emma took her seat in time to hear the last. "I will copy it, for sure. She scooped a ladleful of soup into her bowl. "Lorie serves us 'Rich Man's Rivvel Soup' tonight. Made with last year's corn. And chicken broth from a stewing hen we don't carry through the summer."

"It's delicious," Amanda offered.

"Whets the appetite for the meatloaf," Jacob teased.

Lorie shook her head. "Nei, tonight we have ham that's been holding for the right occasion."

"The big ham? I intended that for the fundraiser auction coming up." John glared at the platter Lorie was carrying in.

"We have other hams. Husband, you would deny your bruder the fine ham?"

"Harrumph!"

Levi frowned, and the tension seemed to grow heavier. "John's right. The meat would have served our fellow Christians in need."

Jacob speared a piece of ham, hesitated, and took a second while his brother waited his turn. Down the table, Samuel and Young Levi watched with wide eyes as John grabbed the platter and slid three pieces onto his own plate. He passed the platter down the table without looking up.

Amanda speared a small slice and set it on a plate along with sweet potatoes and peas for Noah. For the next few minutes, the click of forks and knives, requests for food, loud chewing and the occasional belch created a strange cacophony of sounds that didn't include the human voice. When she finished with her son's plate, she set some peas and ham in front of Jules to occupy her. By the time she started on her own plate, she slipped a fresh slice of ham from the platter when it made its second pass around the table. The men finished before the women, but it was Lorie and Sarah who jumped up to clear the table and refill coffee cups. She popped a last bite into her mouth and half-rose, embarrassed at their efficiency.

"Stay sitting, Amanda. Mind the baby. We got this." Emma reached to take the empty bowl of mashed potatoes and another of cucumber salad.

"Just like at home," Amanda joked. "Two hours of food preparation eaten in ten minutes."

"I thought you folks ate store-bought chicken already cooked. Seen that in a store once. Englischers was snatching them up while they was still smoking," John said. "Made me think they were throwing good money after bad."

Levi nodded at Jacob. "You eat that way, you'll be fretting where your next dollar's coming from. Wondering where it went."

Jacob straightened in his chair and glared at his brother. "My wife's a pretty decent cook. Not so much butter and cream in her meals. Keeps my heart healthy, I'm told." His tone sounded like he was settling in for an argument. Amanda flashed him a warning and shook her head just enough to send a message. *Don't you dare!*

Too late.

John glared over his coffee cup. "Fresh cream don't be causing anyone harm in our neck of the woods. From what we read, the preservatives in your store-bought food are the problem." He scowled. "Our women got solid flesh. Not the unhealthy flab we're seeing on you outsiders."

"Wouldn't know. Haven't seen too much store-bought food on my table." Jacob's face blossomed with color. "Fact is, my wife's damn health conscious."

"*Ach du lieber!*" Emma's hand flew to cover her mouth.

Levi pounded his fist on the table. "There'll be no taking of the Lord's name in this house!"

Jacob looked over at his mother, chagrined. "Sorry, Mamm. I forgot myself, for sure and certain."

Levi eased back into his chair, still frowning. "Where is this cake? *Ich saag dank am disch.* I offer thanks that we enjoy the meal in peace."

Lorie carried the cake in and set it on the table in front of Jacob. "*Gute gubbotta dawg,* Bruder Jacob."

"Happy birthday, Jacob." Samuel and Young Levi joined their sister Sarah in a boisterous greeting.

Jacob beamed as he took a bite while Lorie cut thick slices with a dozen quick flicks of her wrist. When the last plate was passed down the table, she took her seat.

Amanda's first bite melted in her mouth. "This is delicious!"

Lorie nodded. "An old recipe of my grossmommi. I make it for special events. John favors it."

"I'm surprised he didn't save it for the Mennonite Relief Fund," Jacob mumbled. Amanda aimed a toe at his calf and felt a stir of satisfaction when he winced.

"We donate our fair share each year. You remember all the things we load into our wagon when it is time ta hold the sale?" Emma's eyes were lost in thought. "Such a *wunderbarr gute* time we have each year. It is a shame you don't be staying for another month. We will have a chicken barbecue and a singing. A pie bake sale and even games for the kinder." She glanced at Noah. "You would enjoy to see this, ja?"

Noah nodded, his face smudged with chocolate frosting so that his eyes seemed like blue saucers. "Can I can go with Cousin Silas?"

Amanda's smile wavered. "We talked about this, Noah. We are going home tomorrow, to see your other friends. Silas needs to stay here and help his daddy. Just like you do." When Noah's eyes filled with tears, she added, "We'll write to him."

"Don't be filling the boy with ideas," John warned. "We obey the Ordnung in this house. No exceptions for any fella chooses the low road. I won't have it!"

Jacob glared across the table. "I'm good enough to get you through a tight spot. Is that it? Fix your mistakes with horses half-crippled from your neglect. But when it's time to go, I can count on your righteous lecture about what a sinful fellow your bruder is." He picked up his empty cup and lowered it again in disgust.

"You wouldn't know the low road if you stumbled on it. You're on no road at all! Leaving the community is sin enough, but having no church?"

"I keep Gott in my heart. That's more than you can say." Jacob's Adam's apple bulged with anger. "I came back here to set things right between us." His mother watched, pressing her lips as though in pain, her blue eyes shaded with tears. "I wanted to make amends with my bruder. Throw off the weight. Amanda asked it of me. And I agreed." He scraped back his chair and stood, legs apart as if braced for a stiff storm. "I don't wish to upset my mamm like this. But my bruder's stubbornness leaves me no choice."

"I'm not the sinner here, Englischer! Proof that you have lost your way." John's face raged scarlet as he leaped to his feet, his beefy arms planted on either side of his dinner plate like the thick legs of the table beneath him.

The two little girls began crying. Noah looked from one person to another, his face crusted in fear. Lorie reached to comfort her daughter while Amanda uncoupled Jules from the chair and rocked her, oblivious to anything but Jacob's anger.

"Enough!" Levi's fist pounded onto the table, causing the cups to shake in their saucers. "Take this outside. We don't have the bishop stopping by to tell us to mend our ways. Outside!"

Jacob glanced at Amanda. He swung his hand up and pointed a trembling index finger. "Say your good-byes, liebchen. It's time to go."

She collected her children, with Noah protesting that he didn't want to go. After thanking Lorie for the delicious meal, she stood fighting tears as her sister-in-law promised to mail the recipe for the chocolate cake. She shook hands with Samuel and saw his eyes troubled and doubt filled. "It will work out. Don't fret."

One by one, she shook hands with the women. Sarah hesitated before leaning in to give her a hug. "I wish we'd had more time ta visit," she whispered. "I dunna want to make Daed mad, but I hope we meet again, even with you living across the country."

Amanda managed a hug with Jules between them. "One day we'll come back. When the men have made their amends." She leaned in. "Send us an invitation to your wedding when you find the right boy. We would like that."

Jacob bent to collect the diaper bag and her purse.

Emma pressed a kiss on Jules's forehead and tried to extricate her finger the toddler held in a death grip. A moment later she bent to take Noah's hand in hers. "You be a helper to your daed, grandson. And stay strong in the Lord. *Gott segen eich.* God bless you."

The sun was low in the sky as they started past the gate where Amanda's father had died. She toed the dirt one final time, looking for some sign of his passing—a coin from his pocket, a broken eyeglass, even a spot of darkened earth to make the tragedy seem real, but the site had been swept clean of any reminder. Not even a wreath of plastic flowers. Nothing to mark her father's passing.

She walked silently, feeling invisible. With Jacob lost in the weight of his anger, there seemed no point in trying to keep up. She slowed until she was walking ten feet behind, with Noah's hand in hers and the baby cradled against her breast. In the comfortable cadence of their footsteps, she heard the lowing of cattle in the field, the croak of frogs and the song of nightbirds; familiar sounds that underscored the finality of parting. The smell of fresh-mowed hay infused the air around them; she looked up and saw the field where Jacob had been working with his father and mother on the fateful day when lightning had claimed their barn.

At home again, she squinted as she adjusted to the brightness of the electric lights after an evening spent under kerosene lanterns and candles. Without speaking to Jacob, she climbed the stairs and started the children's bath. When the water was ready, she went through the motions of washing ears, faces, and hair. Later, she nursed Jules while she read Noah his favorite book. Finally, she snapped the light off and left the door cracked.

Downstairs, she folded the last load of laundry and slipped everything into a suitcase except for the things they would need in the morning. When she was satisfied that nothing remained to be done, she climbed the stairs and filled the tub for herself.

Jacob was still outside when she made her way into bed. So many farewells, but his was not the way to say goodbye. She stood at the window, allowing herself one final inspection of the farm and the farmhouse with a faint glow of lantern light downstairs where they had just eaten. Without waiting for Jacob, she doused the light and climbed into bed. She woke when he slipped into bed alongside her, but she feigned sleep. Time enough to sort this out tomorrow.

Chapter Seventeen

❧

Amanda woke to the sound of the SUV door slamming as Jacob packed a few last-minute items. She reluctantly rose and dressed in the first thing she found in the suitcase, a long skirt and top she'd brought along to appease her in-laws. She stripped her bed of its sheets and blankets and managed the load in her arms. With a last look at the empty room, she closed the door and slipped downstairs.

Breakfast was a chaotic clamor of whining and whimpering. Jacob ate the last of the eggs before she could have a bite. Noah pouted because his favorite swiftie cup was already packed and he had to use a mug. Jules spilled her sippy cup on her clean outfit and needed a change. Amanda tried to muster an upbeat tone, but everything she said sounded worse than the silence. Finally, she set Jules on the floor and tossed her a Tupperware container and lid to occupy her while she carried the highchair to the cargo trailer. Inside, she saw her father's ashes tucked in a safe crevice. *We're taking you home, Daddy.* She slumped against the loading ramp to steady herself, and let her tears spill out. *Mama, I need you today. We're a mess. Nothing's going right.*

Her mother's advice seemed to beg a listen.

YOUASKINGTHEIMPOSSIB
LE?

For two grown men to settle their differences? That's impossible?

NOTYOURSTOSAY

You mean I need to mind my own business?

WHONEEDSTHIS,YOUORJAC
OB?

Hmm, I'll need to think on that.

She returned inside to do a final search for missing socks and the pink pacifier that would be the mother of all disasters if it got left behind. *Check and check.* She climbed the stairs and searched closets and crannies. *Last moments in the house. My nostalgic trip of memories.* Too bad it was ending on a sour note.

On the spur of the moment, she fished her phone out of her pocket and rang Carol. "Hi, it's me. Life's slamming me hard this morning. You sure you want us to stop by? I'm warning you, I have issues."

Carol's laughter was balm to her soul. "Sweetie, it won't be my first rodeo with your emotional baggage. Bring it on, baby! See you in half an hour. I made cinnamon rolls and mimosas."

She responded to Carol's over-the-top mood with laughter that felt foreign, a clue that she should probably laugh more often. "I love it. We'll be drunk by nine in the morning. I can always count on you!"

Outside, she heard Jacob talking with someone. When she peeked through the kitchen curtains, John stood beside his buggy, wearing his familiar straw hat. She tried not to eavesdrop, but snatches of their conversation filtered inside the open door while she occupied herself with essentials, like wiping down the empty refrigerator for the third time.

"Maybe I find truth to what you tell me last night." John sounded hesitant. "My wife tells me my heart is no longer the one she married. Maybe she is right."

Jacob's resentment shifted into begrudging concession, but he insisted on speaking in English. "Best listen to the wife. Amanda can tell when I'm being a horse's ass."

"Ha ha. I will remember that one. Ja, it is the same with mine. When I let her, the wife keeps me steady."

The men spoke in a louder tone than they needed, but their hands and wary movements told the story. Healing was happening. Amanda moved away from the window.

"The horses look good," John admitted. "They like their new shoes."

"Good to hear."

John shifted with a look of chagrin. "I send for a pack of twelve pads so I have them handy. In the past, I think to save money, only pad them for the hard surface road. But they walk heavy. Seem to like the comfort."

"Seems so."

John shifted and directed his gaze to the ground while Jacob fiddled with the luggage rack on his SUV. When silence stretched, John looked up. "I was shamed to face you, bruder. I made it in my heart to blame you. Easier that way." He shifted and uncrossed his arms, his sternness softening to something akin to regret. "Everybody thought the same, I guess. That you were the black sheep, couldn't be counted on."

Jacob's hands stilled, but he kept his face hidden. The sun cleared the row of ash trees and spread the morning with light that laid itself across his face, fading the storm clouds of resentment as his brother's words penetrated his mind.

"The lie of your unworthiness became the truth for all of us. Blowing at the smoke don't help if the chimney is plugged, the bishop told me. The chimney ain't good for the community, anyway." John darted a quick glance at his brother. "That day at the service marked itself in my thinking. When the girl I sinned with moved away, I thought that was the last of it. But I find myself reading the *Budget,* looking for your name. The births of your children. I don't hear from you, and I know the reason why." He straightened, pulled his hat off, and twisted it around his fingers, something Amanda had rarely seen him do—and the hat off out of doors? Never. "You come back, and I think maybe you've forgotten all about it. Live and let live, I think. And then, first thing, it comes up. And I back off like the stubborn horse's ass that I am."

Jacob looked up with a trace of a smile.

"Bruder, I sinned against you. And Gott." John's eyes looked tortured. "And I ask forgiveness."

Jacob released the luggage cord he was gripping like a lifeline, and took three slow steps toward the buggy. He met John's proffered handshake while his other hand snaked out to clasp his brother's forearm. A moment later he slipped his hand away to embrace his brother. When they broke away, John nodded. He replaced his hat and reached to collect his reins. "Best go about my way. I guess this is goodbye, then. *Gott segen eich.*"

"Gott bless you, too, bruder."

Amanda watched the buggy until it disappeared around the curve. When the road was empty again, Jacob roused himself, and she caught a glimpse of his eyes bright with joy. On the way back inside, he bent to scoop up his daughter from the porch and tickle her belly with a loud raspberry. She giggled and mouthed a jumble of words. But the last one caught Amanda by surprise. "Daddy."

He glanced toward the house, his voice excited. "Look at that! This is turning out to be a *wunderbarr gute* day." He carried his daughter inside and gave Amanda a kiss. "We got any of that good coffee left, liebchen?"

"I saved you a cup. It'll last until we get to Carol's."

"Carol's? We are stopping there? I planned to get on the road by nine."

She barely hesitated as she gathered her purse and started toward the door. "Change of plans. Make it eleven."

❦

"Amanda! You're deserting me in my hour of need. Look at me! I feel like a stuffed cabbage." Carol's pitiful complaint didn't quite mask her excitement as she tried to postpone Amanda's departure.

Amanda laughed. "You *are* a stuffed cabbage. Bun in the oven."

"Stop. Don't make me laugh with this hot coffee pot. I'm losing my best friend, and I'm consumed with angst. We didn't spend enough time together while you were here. We should have taken a weekend trip to Branson. Ran over to Nashville. Made a loop."

"Yeah, right. Dollywood. Hit Graceland on our way home." Spoken aloud, the idea sounded perfect, except for Carol's incessant morning sickness, a toddler, and her father's untimely accident. *Dad would have loved it.* "Next time."

"Promise?" Carol's eyes glistened with tears.

"We'll go to Disney World. Take our new RV." Amanda shot a look at Jacob when his exaggerated brow suggested another version of the plan. "Don't look at me like that, Jacob. We agreed to pull the plug on the Ohio house and put our assets into a travel rig."

Jacob emptied his coffee cup and set it where Carol could refill it when she came by. "We think not to get tied to the land like our families," he explained. "We take another track and see how it suits us."

Carol nodded, transfixed by Jules, who was exploring the living room with her ungainly forward crawl. "Julebug's morphed into a stinkbug." She dragged her gaze away and gave a quick, surprised chortle. "No more Miller House. You guys are cutting the ties to your family home?"

"Ja. It makes time."

Carol bit her lip. "We were hoping you'd move back. Let our kids grow up together. Do the parent-teacher thing together. You the teaching and me the helicopter-parent thing."

Their laughter rang through the kitchen. "I'd like that," Amanda said. "We could grow old together. Sit with our slippers propped on the coffee table while we complain about our daughters-in-law."

Carol giggled. "Is that what your mother-in-law does?"

Amanda considered the question. "I've never heard an unkind word from Emma's mouth. But I wonder if she even considers me a daughter-in-law. She's never said."

Carol's gaze was shiny with tears. "You did great, kid."

Amanda sent Jacob out to the SUV to get the sack of baby clothes that Jules had outgrown. When he returned with a bulging container of onesies and terry sleepers, Carol pawed through them with excitement that was infectious. "What happens if you need them again? I mean, hey, it's not out of the realm of possibilities." She held up a shirt that proclaimed, *Grandpa's little darling*. "Maybe you should keep this one. For the memory book." She folded it and handed it back without looking up.

Amanda clutched it against her. "I miss Dad so much. I miss his corny jokes and the way he looked after me. Us." She glanced at Jacob and bit her lip. "I mean...you know. You're still a kid while your dad's alive. No matter the age."

"Our parents give us everything we need. Hang on to that."

"Yeah."

Carol glanced at the clock. "Enough, already. You guys gotta get on the road." She scooped Jules up and nuzzled her. "You're just too cute." She relinquished her to her mother. "I put in an order for one just like her." She patted her baby bump and followed them out of the house. At the car, she gave Amanda a hug and backed away.

Amanda's gaze lingered on her friend, standing at the edge of the road until distance obliterated her. In the back seat, Noah was flying his plastic airplane around Jules's car seat. When his sister giggled and grabbed for it, his high-pitched protest shattered the mood. "I just realized, Jacob. I'm sitting where Dad sat on the trip here. I—"

Jacob reached to squeeze her leg. "Your father was a good teacher. I have new appreciation for the land we travel." He gave her a long, appraising look. "He told me about your ancestors' trip over the Oregon Trail, the troubles and the hardship. We don't learn that in school. It makes me understand how a family forms itself in new land."

He drove through commuter traffic until lunchtime when the afternoon crowd thinned and the freeway opened toward the midwestern plains. At some invisible point, it seemed that the memories of Ohio and its regrets morphed into excitement for what lay ahead.

Two days later, Jacob crossed the Oregon state line and headed toward Portland with his air conditioner on. The Columbia River lay to their right, crowded with windsurfers and sailboats playing on the whitecaps. After spending the night at The Dalles, they made a stop at the Multnomah Falls for a picnic and a hike before piling back in the car for the last stretch of the drive.

Jacob pulled into the driveway and parked while Noah fumbled with his seat belt. Once free, he took off toward the field to greet his horse, Yankee, who whinnied in recognition.

Amanda released Jules from her car seat, keeping an eye on her son as he crossed the driveway after checking in both directions for vehicles. "Look, Jacob. He's not the same little boy who left three months ago. He's a brand-new guy."

Jacob reached to encircle her while late afternoon light illuminated the row of firs on the distant hillside. He drew a deep, audible breath and she copied him, taking in the scent of loamy soil, evergreens, and summer cropland. "We are each of us changed by our journey, liebchen."

"For the better, I think."

Chapter Eighteen

✦

"Jacob, we got a letter from Beth. Your sister says she's been accepted into an experimental program at the Mount Sinai Hospital. She's being admitted this week. The chances are slim, but she's praying the doctors will find a cure, for her children's sake."

"This is good news. Write her and tell her we add our prayers."

"She says her husband Jeff lost his job. The company was downsizing. He used up all his sick leave, and he was one of the first to be let go. They don't have any savings left."

Jacob glanced at the door, his work jacket in his hand. "I know you, wife. You have already a plan in mind. How much do we send this time? Five thousand?" He grinned when he saw her guilty nod. "Your heart is in the right place. Beth needs our help. It is money well spent."

Amanda set aside the letter and leaned into his

arms. "You're a good brother and husband. We...none of us...deserve you."

He smiled against her hair, and she felt herself responding. "No thanks to me. I know better than to refuse you this request. Even though you are a modern woman with your own money, take it from the joint account so that we do this together." He teased her neck with his lips while his jacket slipped forgotten to the chair. "We are a team, liebchen. In everything."

Amanda reached in her purse and handed him the checkbook and a pen. "She'll be comforted to see your signature on the check. And better yet, a personal note."

After complying to her request, Jacob snuck a glance at his watch. "I have a delivery to ship. I call my sister tonight and explain that she owes me nothing. She will feel the obligation, I know this. Better that she concentrates on her health and leave the worrying to others. Anyway, I do a Zelle transfer. You need to keep up with the times, wife."

Amanda's first stop after dropping Noah off at preschool the next morning was to the grocery store. On the way home, she stopped at the city park to swing Jules on the toddler swing where each pass brought memories of the "Grandpa Swing" and her father. At home again, she booted up her computer to create an e-vite for her father's Celebration of Life. It was time.

Lucy Knowles was the first to respond, but the numbers kept growing. She recognized names from church, from the neighborhood, from the other growers in the area. On her next trip into town, she dropped by the newspaper office to hand the clerk a hand-written obituary notice, along with her credit card.

"You know, you can do this over the internet." The

clerk gave a sympathetic nod at the baby backpack where Jules was struggling to escape and run around.

"Yep." She pulled a sheet of paper from her purse that represented three hours of writing and rewriting that expressed her father's life in his own terms. "This is a life moment. It needs to be honored." She glanced up to see the clerk nod.

"That will be three hundred and twenty-six dollars."

She spent the next two weeks collecting balloons, a guest book, plastic wine glasses, tablecloths and an array of paper plates and napkins. She considered getting a floral arrangement, but at the last minute she visited the greenhouse and created arrangements of holly and evergreens that had been her father's life work. She twined strands of fairy twinkle lights through the branches and added red and white poppies to honor his proud military service. When she finished, she stood back and admired her work. *Serviceable and to the point. Just like him.* She wrapped the tubs in red crepe paper and set them in the shaded porch before she started on a memorial speech.

When she finished, she read her notes through a sheen of tears, made a correction, and set the paper aside, overwhelmed by feelings so raw and fierce that she was trembling. She'd written a letter to herself, almost too personal to share, but she was determined that others would understand her loss. Outside the ranch house, the summer was in full bloom over the pasture where Yankee grazed. Jacob was on the forklift, his hat tilted to the side in the same way her father had worn his. She gathered her notes and walked out to the porch with her heart pounding.

At closer inspection, she realized Jacob was wearing her father's favorite cap, the one he hung in the mudroom every time he walked into the house. Jacob had grabbed it this morning instead of his straw hat. She squinted into the brightness of the morning sun as he spun the forklift in a half-circle, just as she'd watched her father do a thousand times. *Dad would be proud of us. Of Jacob. Of the family we are forming.* With a last glance, she returned to the house where Jules was waking from her morning nap.

"Let's go see the horsey, sweet thing. We'll take him a carrot. Would you like to carry it?" With Jules firmly attached to the treat, they started slowly out to the corral, with her holding her daughter's hand while Jules took her first, hesitant baby steps.

The mailbox held a letter from Tibbs and Rosie. She tucked it in her pocket and continued down the lane, with Jules now protesting in her backpack. A rare morning for exploring the blackberry bushes just forming buds, and the hazelnut farm next door, its newly planted trees in neat rows that stretched into the distance. Ash, white oak, and bigleaf maples shadowed the roadway in a showy display of foliage. Here and there a dogwood thrust its bloomy superiority into the mix, clearly bent on outdoing its plain-Jane neighbors. She inhaled the scent of red cedar, warmed by its familiarity. "This is where my mama grew up, Jules. I hope one day you love it as much as I do. I hope you get to live here when you're all grown up. Would you like that, sweet thing?" Jules's mishmash of words and gargled sounds indicated her enthusiasm, if not her ability. "You can't wait to talk, can you, Jules? One day you'll open your little mouth and the whole dictionary will spill out. Just like mine did. You're going to be a talker."

"Ma-ma. Da-da."

"Yep, you got those down. Can you say 'grandpa'?" She caught herself with the realization that Jules would have no understanding of her grandfathers. "You came along too late, sweet thing. Grandpas teach you to dance and show you the names of every flower and why butterflies cluster on the bushes. They teach you how to spell your last name and how to tie your shoes." She added this last with tears. *You left us too soon, Dad.*

She walked along the road, immersed in memories of her dad and Noah playing with their Legos on the floor. When they reached the crossroads, Jules was squirming to be put down so she could walk. "Time to head back. We need to pick up your brother from preschool."

Noah bubbled with excitement as he ran toward her at the sign-out table. In his hand he held a miniature dinosaur made from a lump of blue clay, with enormous, misshapen feet and a horn that was nearly as large as its body. Amanda squatted to cup it in her hands as she made her careful inspection. "Look at you, Noah! A wonderful dinosaur. I'm scared it might eat me."

He shook his head seriously. "It's a Ceratops. A horn top. It eats plants with its teeth."

"In that case, would it like to ride home in the car with us?"

When Jacob came in for lunch, Noah explained his Ceratops to his father. Clearly Jacob had never had a miniature dinosaur before. He examined it from every angle and pronounced it fierce. Amanda watched the two of them examining the horn with their fingers. When Noah left to wash his hands, she remembered the letter in her pocket and handed it to Jacob.

"For me?" He sounded surprised. In retrospect, he didn't get much mail. Only bills and official notices from the government. He used his thumb to tear a slit across the top and slid the note out before he started reading. When he finished, he folded it carefully and slipped the sheets back. "Rosie wrote. Tibbs has taken a turn. She thinks he's holding on through the summer, waiting for fall. Says he likes to watch the storm clouds over the Bighorns. 'Snow peaks, turning leaves, crisp promise of something that ain't come yet,' is how she put it. He likes the anticipation."

Amanda laughed and picked up the letter. "'He likes to dream, but he likes his feet planted solid.' That's how she describes him."

She set Jacob's sandwich in front of him and opened the refrigerator for iced tea, letting silence envelop the room. Noah was quietly feeding a slice of tomato to his dinosaur between his own bites, a rare balance between their usual chaos and letting silence have its moment. *This is perfect, each of us knowing when enough is good.*

Jacob picked up his cold beef and tomato sandwich and took a bite. "These ours?"

She nodded, pleased that he recognized the effort everyone had put into growing them. "Beefsteak tomatoes out of Dad's seeds. Noah helped me pick them yesterday."

"Seems your garden is thriving, yet."

She laughed. "Not sure I can call it mine. Your workers did most of the work. Mr. Gomez is a whiz

with the garden. I think he may be as good as my dad."
She set a handful of peas in front of her daughter and
chuckled when Jules slapped her hand away. "Looks
like we're ready for finger foods. She wants to feed
herself."

"Stubborn like her mama," Jacob teased. "Hope
she's as pretty."

Amanda glanced at the unfinished note on the
counter. "I was working on my eulogy today. Do you
think I'm as stubborn as Dad?"

He looked up and grinned over the top of his sandwich. "Define 'stubborn.'"

She tossed one of Jules's peas at him and laughed.
"Only ehen I disagree with you. The rest of the time
I'm clever and adorable."

"And your point?" He picked up the pea and sent it
sailing back onto her plate. Jules squealed and fanned
her hand across the highchair tray, scattering her peas
across Amanda's lap. Jacob started to laugh, caught
Amanda's warning scowl, and slipped his hand over his
mouth. "Wait till she can handle a spoon."

"I wonder if I'm trying too hard to hold on to memories. Dad's? Jules's babyhood? Do you think I'm just
afraid of change?" She reached to hand Jules another
spoonful of peas. "Tibbs is failing. Who's next? I feel
like I'm losing everyone. I don't want to be alone,
Jacob." She reached to confiscate Noah's dinosaur until
he finished eating and lowered her voice. "I don't want
there to be just us, a little nuclear family."

Jacob glanced around the table at the four of them,
his eyes reflecting the same uncertainty as she felt. "We
give thanks for what we do have, liebchen. We don't
complain and demand more. Gott knows our needs."

She rose from the table and stacked the lunch dishes in an effort to curb her agitation. "You're right. We're not alone—we still have Rosie and Tibbs." She carried a stack to the sink and turned. "Jacob, we need to go say goodbye. Tibbs wants to see us."

Jacob's eyes darkened in thought. "We have only returned home." He shifted and his eyes held a look of resignation. "Set it up with Rosie. We leave in a few days?"

Amanda sighed. "We have the celebration of life for my father on Sunday. Let's have no commercial trucks driving in that day, okay?"

He tipped his fingers in a mock salute. "Ja. Right as rain."

On Sunday, with Jacob standing at her side, she greeted old friends and neighbors, church members, and a few customers and suppliers. Some brought their families, and Noah led two small boys off toward his fort while the adults gathered in front of a row of ice chests. She introduced Jacob to those who hadn't attended the wedding and kept a careful watch on the ladies she'd hired to put on the luncheon. When it was time to make her speech, she handed Jules to one of her teacher friends and took a deep breath.

"Thank you all for coming. I look around at the decorations, the picture board, the memory books—all the trappings for a celebration of his life, and I wonder if anything can truly reflect the bigness of the man whom I called my father. I can just hear him chuckle in appreciation. 'Close enough for government work' was his favorite saying. Gosh, he hated mushy sentiment. And stubborn! He'd rather lose a toe than read the sign." She paused for laughter. "Dad was a doer, not a dreamer. A worker, not a slacker, and he didn't abide people who weren't. I learned early the lessons he may not have known he was imparting. I think everyone who knew him did, or they didn't stay friends for long.

"Bob Miller was a hard man to know. He kept his thoughts inside, where they belonged. His words, not mine. He loved his wife and his daughter with the ferocity of a lion. He held us close. He kept us safe. He let us know that we mattered. And he died the way he lived, in a burst of fierceness. Our hearts are broken but we should never, for a minute, question the way he left us. He despised the slow cloud that was claiming his brain. Better for him, the brief, glorious blaze of glory.

"*Vaya con dios*, Dad. Go with God. Be with Mom again, as in the early days, when life was a promise. We will miss you, Dad. Thank you for your service."

Someone raised a glass in salute, and everyone took up the chorus, adding their cheers and salutes to the photo of her father she'd placed between the festive tubs of his evergreens. *Dad, you did good. So many good friends and people who loved you. You ran the good race, Daddy.*

After waving the last guest off, she returned to the kitchen to slip the kitchen helpers each an envelope that included a generous tip. Outside, the tables were already broken down, ready to be returned to the rental company. The dumpster overflowed with paper. Chairs had been neatly stacked. She waved the women helpers to the leftover food and insisted they take it for their families. When the last car disappeared down the driveway, she collapsed on her sofa and allowed Jacob to rub her feet.

"You did good, liebchen."

She smiled. "Funny, I was just thinking the same about my father. He had a lot of friends."

"The mark of a good man. He made a difference. Lived a good life. Left behind a good daughter."

"I'm not so sure about that. I can be *techy* sometimes. You've pointed that out more than once."

Jacob squeezed her foot and ran his hand along her calf. "*Techy,* A good Amish word. You've been listening to my mamm." He tickled her kneecap and continued upward with agonizingly light touches. "You plan on going Plain?"

She glanced over to where Noah was playing on the carpet, building a tower of blocks. Jules played nearby, trying to swat the tower down. "Jacob...stop!" she whispered, trying not to giggle as she pressed her hand against his and felt their fingers intertwine.

The enormity of the day pressed down with crushing effect, so much that she struggled to breathe. Her father's ashes now interred with her mother's in the mausoleum plot they had purchased a year after her mother's accident. It had sat empty for thirty years. Now it held two wooden boxes with their names engraved along with their dates. Her father had spent most of his adult life caring for his wife. He had survived her by only five years, filled with plans for the future. "It wasn't fair," she complained. "He got a raw deal."

"He would not agree. He was lost without purpose. Your mother gave him that. I never knew her, but a life without purpose...without someone...can be empty."

"He had purpose. He had us."

"Ja. This is true. But we had each other. He felt the burden. He wanted to be free." Jacob lifted her chin to meet his gaze. "I know the feeling. Racing out of my father's barn on a perfect spring morning. Fresh breeze washing over me. My horse wild for freedom and me wanting the same. I see your daed. And I know what he was thinking at the end. He was alive. And then he wasn't." He pressed a light kiss, and his breath caressed her. "Think hard before you regret the way he passed. Noah was thrown out and suffered his grandpa's rashness, but he healed and has a story to tell."

"But I feel bad for my dad," she insisted.

"Feel bad? I don't feel the same."

She sat quietly, hearing his words resonate in the silence. He was right. There was no upside to her father's future. No happy ending. At the end he had struggled. He'd talked of climbing the tree to fix the ropes on the Grandpa Swing, and the possibility of him falling from the huge tree was real. This way was better. The coroner claimed he'd died quickly, his neck broken. Ironically, the same thing that had crippled her mother.

Jacob rose from the sofa and gave a one-shouldered shrug to relieve his tension. "Best put this behind you, liebchen. He's in Heaven now, safe and happy. Don't dwell on the small, mean thoughts that come into your head. Others will require your kindness now. Tibbs and Rosie want us to visit."

Amanda felt the storm departing with the reminder of more pressing issues. "Can we fly up this time? I've had my fill of driving for a while." She understood his reluctance because she added, "Otherwise I'll drive while you sit in the back and keep the kids occupied."

Jacob grinned when he realized she was joking. "You win. We fly up."

Chapter Nineteen

❦

Rosie's tiny frame barely showed through the windshield of the Chevy pickup where she sat waiting at the loading zone of the Sheridan County Airport. She slipped from the seat in time to open the back door for Noah, who ran to greet her.

"Howdy, neighbors! Come give old Rosie a bearhug, youngster. If you ain't the handsomest young thing I ever saw. You gonna give your dad a run fer his money one a these days. I declare, you've grown six inches since last time I seen you, Noah. What you been eating? I need to get me some or you're gonna shoot past me like I was drought-stunted."

Noah giggled and ran to throw his arms around Rosie's neck.

Jacob loaded suitcases into the bed while Amanda strapped the baby seat in. Noah's toddler seat fit in the middle, leaving her room to squeeze into the other side. Rosie resumed her place at the wheel and pulled out into the traffic without looking back. "Don't do much good. Mirrors are still set for Tibbs. But he ain't been driving lately."

"Maybe I can fix the mirrors while we stop at the market," Jacob offered, with a quick glance at Amanda.

"Great idea. We can buy fixings for a few meals. Cook ahead and freeze them while we're here." Amanda gripped the handle and prayed until Rosie pulled into the Walmart and slipped into a space between two other pickups.

"Nothing to it," she said when Jacob complimented her on her parking. "Used to trailering the horses. Now that's a challenge, if you ask me." She handed Jacob the keys and claimed a shopping cart from the rack before leading Amanda toward the doors. "Oughta be ashamed of myself, shopping in a chain store. But it's all about convenience these days. 'Get 'er done.' That's my mantra."

They piled the cart with fruits and vegetables, corn-bread mixes and ice cream. Amanda kept an eye out for the gluten-free section and added some low-protein cereal for Noah. She pulled out her charge card and inserted it as soon as the last item was rung up, grateful that Rosie was too busy chatting to notice.

Jacob loaded the bags into the back with an eye out to the weather. "Rains, we'll be in trouble."

Rosie squinted at the sky as she headed to the passenger side. "Won't rain before 3:00. We'll be home afore that."

Jacob pulled into the ranch with fifteen minutes to spare. He had time to carry in the last bag of groceries and set it alongside the luggage before the first raindrop fell. He looked up to see Rosie grinning.

"I'll take that sack of spuds, you don't mind,

cowboy. Figure we'll have fried chicken tonight. Save a nice drumstick for Tibbs."

Amanda eased into the living room and pulled up a chair alongside Tibbs's worn leather recliner. His dog lay on a ratty rug near the hearth, panting with exertion after slipping out of the house to chase a rabbit across the pasture.

"Tibbs. How you feeling?" She reached to enfold his veiny hand in hers, surprised at how cool his skin felt. She caught the gleam of humor in his face and leaned closer. "You look like you ate a plate of roadkill."

He winked and his grin crackled across his grizzled face like thin ice on a skate pond. "I'd a taken you for a liar if you fudged yer opinion, missy. Truth is, I feel worse than I look. But you're even purtier than last time I saw you. That man a' yours must be doing something right."

She laughed and reached to wipe his chin with a towel Rosie had left nearby. "That man of mine's almost perfect."

"That's good, honey. You just keep thinking that way and everything will be fine."

She leaned to smooth his hair back into place. "Does he have a character defect I don't know about?"

Tibbs snorted. "He's good enough..."

"...for government work." She laughed. "My dad used to say that."

"Did he now? He must have been in the service. We all used that a lot."

"He was. Where did you serve?"

Tibbs leaned back in his recliner with a shrug of his shoulders, a cue that he was planning on telling a long story. In the kitchen, Jules was crying for something to eat, and Noah was reaching for a second helping from Rosie's cookie tin. Amanda looked around for Jacob.

Rosie stuck her head out of the kitchen. "Tibbs, let the gal tend to her little ones. That story will save until after supper. We'll carve out time for it. I know they both want to hear." She bent to offer him a kiss on his whiskery chin. "Youth before beauty. You're a fine hunk of manhood, but the little ones need to come first."

Tibbs nodded and reached for Noah. "Can you bring me one of those cookies? Rosie hides them like they're diamond gemstones."

After a supper of fried chicken, mashed potatoes and pan gravy, pineapple coleslaw and carrot curls dipped in ranch dressing, Amanda managed to get Jules to sleep with a half-dozen picture books and a stern warning. In the living room, Noah read his dinosaur picture book to Rosie while Tibbs dozed. His story would have to wait for another time.

She finished wiping the counter and hung the dish towel to dry in time to hear him trying to coerce another story. "Uh-uh, Noah. You know the rule. Time to get ready for bed."

Jacob waited in the hall to draw her into a dance as the radio played a Texas shuffle. When the music ended, he led her to the sofa and sank into the cushions. "Been a long day. Maybe we should get some rest."

Rosie winked. "Rest? Is that what young folks call it these days? Always thought Sunday was the day for that."

"Rosie, you got a wicked mind!" Jacob laughed and slipped his arm around Amanda. "A man ought to get as much rest as he can. Seven days a week."

Rosie looked over at Tibbs, still asleep. "That man was a great one for resting."

Amanda smiled. "My dad used to call it 'having pie.' Mom told me that before the accident, he used to leave the tractor idling and come into the kitchen yelling, 'Time for pie!' Funny thing was, he never had much of a sweet tooth. But they used to laugh about it afterward."

"Before the accident?" Rosie's eyes dimmed to the flat cast of a desert sage. "Such a young thing to lose your mother like that."

"She wasn't lost." The words came out before Amanda had a chance to reconsider. "She just lived a different kind of life." She glanced over at Jacob. "I didn't know how much she taught me until I had my own children. Then the lessons came back. The memories." She looked up to see Rosie studying her and she admitted something she'd never shared with anyone. "I feel her presence sometimes. I think she's watching us."

"She is, sweet girl. You can bet yer bottom dollar she is. What mother would give up the chance to be a grandmother!" Rosie's face flushed with emotion and her lip trembled as she leaned to rouse Tibbs from his nap. "Come on, you old cowboy. Time to hit the hay. We need to let these kids get their rest." She winked at Jacob and started down the hallway with Tibbs on her arm. "Night, all. Don't let the bedbugs bite."

Noah came to the bathroom door with his toothbrush halfway to his mouth. "Mama, does Rosie's house have bugs?"

"Shhh. No bugs, kiddo. Let's get your teeth brushed."

❧

Amanda woke during the night with the feeling that something wasn't right. She listened to the coyotes in the pasture. A moose cow she'd seen earlier that day bawled at her calf in the darkness. A nightbird rustled in the hickory tree outside the kitchen. Down the hall, Rosie's bare feet padded across the wood floor. Her bedroom door squeaked and her hands brushed the walls when she made her way down the darkened hallway, as though she were blind and needed to feel her way.

Amanda slipped from bed and followed Rosie as she groped for the light switch and lit up the kitchen. When she looked up, her eyes were pools of pain. The tight lines of skin across her cheekbones had aged ten years in the three hours since she'd gone to bed. She gripped the cord of the landline phone as though she wasn't sure she wanted to make a call, after all. Amanda followed the direction of her stare, back down the hallway.

"What is it, Rosie? Is it...oh, no! Not Tibbs."

Rosie nodded, silence caught in the grief written on her face. "He's gone. My sweet cowboy. Gone to meet his maker."

Amanda helped her to a chair and ran a glass of water that felt shockingly cold in her hands from the well outside. "I'll start coffee. It'll likely be a long night."

Jacob appeared in the doorway, scratching his head. "What time is it?" He glanced from one to the other with a look of confusion.

"Jacob...it's Tibbs."

"Tibbs?" Comprehension spread across his face as

he saw Rosie, grief-shattered and slouched at the table. He backtracked down the hallway and pushed open the door to Tibb's room. A click of the light switch was the only sound until he gently closed the door behind him and returned to the kitchen. "You'll want to sit with him, Rosie. Say your goodbyes. We won't leave him alone tonight." He reached for Rosie's hand and guided her back into the room. Afterward, he carried two chairs to the bedroom and set them in a semi-circle at the end of the bed. "Amanda, heat some water. When you're ready, we will wash him proper. No need to call the coroner yet. We'll say our goodbyes like he'd expect us to."

Amanda nodded, grateful for her husband's presence. He was their friend. Rosie's rock.

Rosie sat stroking her husband's hand while her lips trembled in silent prayer, seemingly unaware that they were there. Except for the ticking of the grandfather clock in the hallway, the settling of the house and an occasional sound of a sleeper, the house might well have been empty of life.

Amanda sat absorbing the moment. *I've seen more deaths in my life than births. How strange.* "He lived a splendid life. His stories were of another era."

Rosie looked up long enough to nod her agreement. "He sure didn't fit this one anymore. A pure dinosaur, this man. As outdated as those plastic T-Rex figures Noah carries in his pocket."

Jacob stood at the doorway. "He told me right off he was raring to go. I thought he wanted me to take him for a ride in the pickup, but he waved me off. Said he wanted to pass through the veil." Jacob's voice trailed off from where he stood to make room for them to sit.

"He waited for you folks to come. That's what he told me on Monday. And you made it." Rosie chuckled, a short, raspy sound that passed for laughter. "He always said he didn't want a bunch of vultures standing around, waiting for his death wheeze. That's what he liked to call it. But he didn't want me to be alone, that was a fact."

"I was surprised that you wrote a letter," Amanda said.

A smile flitted across Rosie's face. "Figured posting a letter would give us a few more days together. Told him he needed to hang on till you got here."

Jacob glanced down to study the wedding ring on his left hand while time occupied the silence, broken only by the chime of the clock. When it toned the four o'clock hour, Rosie slipped to her feet and rolled her sleeves. "I suppose there's no putting off what God and Heaven declare." She unbuttoned her husband's pajama top. "Never wore one of these things in his life —just the bottoms—until he started feeling the night chill. It was either bundle up or add another quilt. Expect he liked the feel of air on his body parts."

Jacob found a rubber sheet in the linen closet and slid it underneath before he slipped out and left the room at Rosie's request. Amanda picked up a sponge and soaped his arms while Rosie lathered his chin for a shave. Left alone, the two women worked in silence, performing a sacred, timeless ritual.

The sunlight rose as Amanda finished trimming Tibbs's hair. She slipped Rosie's worn scissors back into their case and set it on the tray alongside the safety razor. They had dressed Tibbs in his best suit, a western-cut suit of gray worsted wool, with a couple of snags from helping out a neighbor on the way home from church one Sunday.

"He never attended again after our son passed. Mad at God, I suppose. Said he'd already suffered his earthly trial and he'd skip the rest." Rosie stood like a statue, slowly wrapping a scrap of toweling around her fingers as if the act of busyness might postpone whatever came next. "He wanted to be buried in his boots. Suppose we should slip them on before the rigor sets in." She walked to the closet and selected a pair of size nine boots that nearly dwarfed her tiny figure. "We may need a man's help with these."

"Jacob?" Amanda stole into the hallway, keeping her voice low. *Just give me another half an hour before the kids wake.* How many times had she had that same thought? Surely a universal mother's prayer. "Jacob? We need your help in here."

Jacob slipped in and took the boots from Rosie. When he finished, they stood silently as sunrise lit a path across the room, softening the grizzled lines of Tibb's face. "He'd thank you for this, Rosie. He looks wonderful *gute*."

Rosie straightened with a show of resoluteness that defined her intentions. She was having no pity. "I had my time alone with him. Word spreads fast around here. Time we call the mortuary. Folks will show up with food and good wishes. Flowers if they've anything still left in the fall gardens." She picked up the cup of coffee cooling on the dresser, her eyes fading to exhaustion.

At breakfast, Amanda waited until Rosie sat down before she handed her a plate containing a scrambled egg and fried sausage. "You need to eat something, Rosie."

Rosie shrugged. "You gonna stand there till I clean my plate, I suppose?" At Jacob's nod, she started eating.

By noon of the following day, the viewing room at the mortuary was filled with ranchers and their wives. Occasionally someone lapsed into a story about Tibbs that brought laughter from the others. Amanda sat in the last row, holding Jules while people came and went.

The funeral was held on the third day. Rosie donned a dark tweed skirt and long-sleeved brown shirt that topped a pair of western boots and her own western hat, a twin to the one that graced Tibb's casket. Her voice was strong and sure as she joined in singing "The Old Rugged Cross."

The reception was a loud, raucous affair. A dozen young ranchers were among the old timers and their wives who had driven in from two counties over, according to Rosie. She recognized them by the color and shape of their western hats. Judging from the stories the younger men shared, they had been classmates of Tibbs's son, Steve. Their parents, and in a few cases, their grandparents, arrived in western-cut suits and cream felt cowboy hats, denims, and long-sleeve western shirts with straw Resistols. "Country proud," Tibbs had called the tendency for true westerners to show up sporting their best threads. Every man and woman seemed to have a story of Tibbs wrecking a pickup, learning to drive a Model AA, and breaking either horses or bones. They shared stories of bringing home the glory at local rodeos followed by as many girl-chasing and nice-guy stories.

Ranchers' wives filled the tables with green bean

casseroles and hams alongside potato and macaroni salads. Amanda made a plate of veggies and ranch dressing for Noah. A friend carried a plate to Rosie, but she set it aside without drawing attention to herself.

Amanda shared a table with a couple who ranched east of Sheridan. She introduced herself and was surprised when the woman leaned in, whispering over her husband who was sharing a story with another neighbor. "You were there with Rosie when he passed, I hear. Helped her with the laying out?"

Amanda nodded, surprised to see respect reflected in their faces. "Ole Tibbs got his share, but no more," the woman's husband was saying. "He figured, no point in being greedy."

She listened as these longtime friends honored a man they respected. Nobody mentioned how many acres he'd accumulated, or how new his pickup was. Apparently in Wyoming, the test of a man was his character, not his bank balance.

"He was never one to take a second helping if there was an empty plate down-table," someone said.

"Amen to that. Tibbs was a square shooter, that's for sure."

Across the room, Rosie was nodding to someone who was sharing a similar story. As another hour passed, weariness pasted itself on her features until Amanda suggested Jacob ask if she was ready to go home. When he did, Rosie's quick look of panic seemed at odds with the serenity she had maintained all afternoon. He helped her to her feet and steadied her when she wavered, until she rallied. Amanda followed them as Rosie gave everyone a thank-you wave on her way out.

Chapter Twenty

A manda glanced from the kitchen where she was putting together a vegetable soup of leftovers. When she glanced into the living room, Noah had climbed into Tibbs's empty chair to read a picture book the two of them had shared. Under the glow of the reading lamp, it seemed as though Tibbs was still there, wearing a halo.

Rosie fidgeted with the lace cover of her reading table; her worn Bible opened to the twenty-third Psalm. She looked up when Jacob stomped his boots on the outdoor mat and entered with a whoosh of cold. She stared intently in the dim light, squinting as if her eyes were playing a trick on her before she slumped back in disappointment. "Thank you for seeing to the horses. I'm not sure what to do with them. Tibbs was good about feeding, but with the snow coming on, I don't envy the trek to the barn ever morn." She glanced out the window at the snow-peaked mountain range in the distance. "We're expecting white by mid-November. Don't expect we'll see drift for another month."

Jacob disappeared into the bathroom and Amanda set the cooking ladle on the counter. "Come home with us. This place will be here in the spring."

Rosie's momentary hesitation was quickly replaced with a look of steely determination. Backed up by a hitch of her shoulders, her voice gained strength until she sounded, as Tibbs had once claimed, "like the pretty young thing who used to wear Rosie's dancing boots."

"Sweet thing, I got to sit out winter right here, grieving and tearing my hair. I got to don my widow's weeds and see the season through. There ain't no getting around that part. No running from the pain, you understand?"

Amanda thought back to each loss in her own life. Here in Wyoming, the sun would set early and rise late, the snows would pile, and the winds would howl. Rosie would doubt her decision a thousand times before the late spring sun cleared a path to Oregon.

She realized Rosie was still speaking. "Pain's the only scrap Tibbs left behind, and I'm fighting to hold on to it. By spring, good memories will flow back along with the longer days. Time then to visit the ocean, and make homemade ice cream in the back yard, and laugh at the children's antics." She was staring into the fire, mesmerized by her own thoughts. "Till then, tears'll be my companion. I'm holding them off till I see that plane of yours disappear down the runway. You know."

"I *do* know, Rosie," Amanda murmured.

"Yes, sweet thing, I expect you do."

"When's supper ready?" Jacob stuck his head through the doorway in time to catch the last bit of conversation. "Anything I can help out with? Rosie, I fed the horses the last flake of hay. We'll need to bring in some more before we head home."

"When you expecting that'll be?" To her credit, Rosie's smile didn't waiver. She'd buried her husband, but her ember wasn't extinguished. Amanda imagined she'd just seen it spark.

"Wednesday. That'll give us a few days to see what needs to be done around here. Winterize you. I remember the order of things. Tibbs had me doing them in reverse, digging out for spring, he called it."

"The pump house needs the heat light set. The insulation checked that the rodents haven't made a mess in there. Faucets shut off..." Her voice trailed off. "Gosh, my memory must be fading. I can't recall what else he did every winter, Jacob. Seems I should remember."

"It wonders me you recall as well as you do, Rosie. You had a shock. Your memory will serve in good time."

"Supper's served." Amanda cooled a bowl of vegetable soup for Jules and set a bowl in front of Noah.

"My, but she's growing. Feeding herself now." Rosie smiled as the toddler gripped her spoon and lifted it to her face. When she managed to get a diced potato into her mouth, she dropped her spoon and clapped. "Well good for you, missy. You got the knack, that's for sure." Rosie's eyes lost their bleakness while she urged Jules to take another bite.

Amanda remembered clapping when her mother learned to operate her computer for the first time. *Life goes not backward. Not tarries with yesterday.* Someone had famously written that. Kahlil Gibran. She had a book of his poetry on her bookshelf back home.

"Soup hits the spot." Rosie finished her bowl, even

if she declined seconds. "Maybe I'll just sit in my chair and take a cup of tea like we do every ni—" Her head popped up with a surprised look. "Well," she managed, "I'll need to start a new tradition."

Jacob kept his gaze on the floor, unable to think of anything to bridge the awkwardness.

Amanda piled empty bowls on the counter in silence. *Life doesn't hand us a rulebook for grieving. No apologies needed. No explanations required. No platitudes.* "I'll set the tea kettle and join you as soon as I finish these dishes." She ran the sink full of soapy water and plunged the bowls in. Alone in the kitchen, she noticed the path worn across a strip of ancient linoleum that contrasted with the sunny yellow walls they'd painted the last time they visited.

Her aunt Lydia had taught her about *doing for,* her way of leaving someone's life a little better than when she arrived. In her own small way, she'd kept them from collapsing under the weight of despair. After each visit, she left a new lawn planted, a room painted or papered, or a shabby chair recovered, cheerfully minimizing her efforts by saying she enjoyed "doing for others." Over the years, her projects had meant the difference between living in a dilapidated house and an updated fresh one. She instilled pride and industriousness in a ten-year-old motherless girl's brain and made it seem like a game.

Amanda glanced around at the old farmhouse's furnishings that looked like they hadn't been touched since the house was built at the end of WWII. When Jacob wandered into the kitchen to help dry, she voiced her idea. "Jacob, Rosie agreed to let me sew up new curtains for her den. We saw some fabric in town that would be perfect." She washed a stack of bowls while she considered. "The problem is, new drapes will make the paint look dowdy and old."

He looked up from his dishcloth and shrugged. "I don't see the need, but if it's okay with her, I'll pick up a gallon of paint while I'm in town."

"Desert-Glo. Satin finish. Ace Hardware has it." She ducked when he tried to swipe a fingertip of soap-suds across her cheek. "How's Rosie set for firewood?"

"Good. Tibbs saw to that. Had three cords deliv-ered and stacked. His apology for leaving her out here alone, he told me. Bought it cut and split this year because he knew he wouldn't be here to do it."

From the living room, Rosie's voice crackled over the sound of Noah reading his picture book aloud. "Hey, I heard that. Never a mention about the wife who toted and stacked right alongside him for sixty-five years. Worked toe-to-toe with that man, and he still insisted he did all the work himself!" Her snort filtered back into the kitchen as the tea kettle began to whistle.

Suddenly the day seemed long, filled with false bravado and postponed grief as they proposed chores to occupy themselves from the hard job of grieving. Left to itself, silence clamored louder than the tears it sought to mask. Rosie must have felt it as well when she stood and made her way down the hall without saying good night.

Jacob lay awake in their bed when she came in and clicked off the lamp. He reached to draw her into the heat pocket he'd created in the cold sheets. "We buried a good man today, liebchen. Everyone had something to say about his character. Good things. Generous things. I feel honored to be his friend."

"You're a good man, as well. A good friend, Jacob. You care for his widow and stack her firewood, and when the time comes, you'll see to his monument in the town cemetery. You carry his legacy. I saw it in people's faces today."

Jacob hesitated. "We are not the ones to take over this ranch. He knew I'm not suited to this life. Rosie, too. They know my heart is not here. Not like their son's." Outside, the wind rattled the leaves of the maple trees along the driveway. "He and Rosie were fixed to this life, like my daed and mamm. But I am not my brother John, willing to take over. They were two old people struggling." He shifted. "Now, only one."

"She loves it here." Amanda shivered at the sound of the wind. "She wants to stay through the winter and grieve. She told me so. And emerge in the spring like a crocus."

Jacob laughed quietly. "She *would* say that."

"She has the right."

He lay in silence, his breath the only sound. "She thinks we are her next of kin. But the law gives us no right to interfere. What do we do?"

"Give her time to figure it out for herself?"

He shifted in the bed and considered the question. "Yeah, I guess."

Amanda lay quietly until she heard his first soft snores. For her, sleep came in broken dreams and strange sounds. The night passed at a frustrating pace; it seemed like an eternity before the first rays of sunlight colored the window shades.

She woke, groggy and pale, to find Jacob sitting on

the edge of the bed, rubbing his hands through his hair as though deciding whether to face the day or to drop back into bed. Jules settled his decision when she padded into the room dragging her favorite stuffed toy, a blue whale that Tibbs had bought her at the lighthouse. She climbed up and settled in between them, with a hug for her daddy.

Rosie was outside, feeding the horses before Jacob managed to find his work clothes. She reappeared from the barn wearing an oversized ranch coat and mud boots that came nearly to her knees. Her thin white hair was covered with a floppy western hat that had seen better days, but her face held satisfaction.

Jacob escaped into the crisp morning to collect two days' worth of mail and newspapers. By the time he returned, Rosie was already in the kitchen, whipping up pancakes. Amanda hurried to help her.

"I figure I can do my grieving after you kids go home. No reason to waste what precious days we have together. Let's take a hike after breakfast, out to the far coulee, and see what it looks like this time of year." She wielded her spatula like a saber, flipping several strips of bacon before she placed a pancake on a plate.

"You sure?" Jacob reached for a knife and began cutting the pancake into bite-sized pieces for their toddler.

"I'll have my share of solitary hikes. Do me good to have company."

"You think you should be walking around here by yourself? After we leave, I mean?"

Rosie laughed. "Bite your tongue, boy! You want me to get one of those 'help, I've fallen, and I can't get up' thing-a-ma-bobs? Like the little white-haired ladies, live in cities?"

Jacob snatched a piece of pancake off Jules's tray, and she giggled. "That's not a bad idea."

She planted a fist on her hip and leveled a scowl at him. "I just buried the bossiest man on the planet. I don't need another one. I can fend for myself or suffer the consequence. I ain't nobody's fool." At the stove, she hesitated before turning to point her spatula at him again. "And don't be bringing up that fluke thing happened with the boxes falling on me when you were living here. That has nothing to do with this."

Jacob's face flooded at the reminder of the day she almost froze, unconscious and trapped in the snow. He glanced over to catch Amanda's eye and grinned. The story had acquired the rank of a legend in the family annals.

"I knew it," she sputtered. "At my age, all a woman's got is her grit. Leave me my dignity. If I need help, I'll give a holler."

"On a phone thingie that's hanging around your neck?" he teased.

"Maybe! Maybe I'll get a cell phone for my pocket. That make you happy?" She picked up the plate of bacon and set it on the blue checkered oilcloth table-cloth next to his plate. "Now let's eat before this maple syrup gets cold."

Noah staggered in, rubbing sleep from his eyes. "Maple syrup's already cold, Rosie."

"Not mine. I heated it in a pan. Keeps the hotcakes warm. Now hop up here and try it."

After breakfast, they followed the creek toward a rock outcropping standing sentry on the rolling, golden grassland where a creek fed the aspen and willows along the bank. The aspen grew in a clone forest with leaves fall-dried and already falling with the early fall cold nights. As they approached, the leaves shook like bones racked on a skeleton for Halloween, in Amanda's mind. She held the thought to herself; it would take too much explanation.

Noah discovered the crisp fallen leaves of the quaking aspen, and he stomped in circles, his little boots making noise disproportionate to his size so that he kept bobbing his head up to see if everyone noticed. When Jules squawked to be let down, Amanda let her crush leaves with her brother. When they tired of the game, she handed Jules off to Jacob. "I wish she'd hurry and learn to walk by herself."

"So she can go running off when you go to the market?" Jacob joked.

"Folks tend to wish for what they don't have. I'm here to tell you, don't be in a hurry for them to grow up. Savor your time with those little folks. They grow up fast enough." Rosie found a limb to use as a walking stick and stalked ahead.

Amanda wasn't the only one panting by the time they found a spot for their picnic, but she tactfully avoided pointing it out. When they finished eating, she let Noah scatter the scraps for the coyotes while she reclined against an aspen. "If I lived here, I wouldn't move from this spot. I'd bring my paints and capture this image and hang it in every room in my house."

"Why not just build a house on this spot?" Jacob asked.

Rosie looked up, frowning until she realized he was joking. "Folks tend to spoil the best spots by civilizing them. Ought to tuck themselves out of the way and leave the wild places be."

"Agreed. Cluster the houses and leave the vistas alone," Amanda said.

Rosie gave her a sharp, penetrating look. "You had me worried for a minute. Thought you might be mutating into one of them Portland liberals with your green talk. Heck, we been living green since forever. Wouldn't know how to do otherwise. Green!" Her snort of derision seemed to include the view outside her window. "Book-smart idiots thought that one up. Live out here and a person'll come to know, only way to have anything is to stay clear of the stores. Make do or do without."

Jacob laughed. "You sound like my mamm."

"Your Amish folks aren't wrong in their beliefs. But they got a mix of stubborn makes them ornery, some of them. Your old man like that?"

Jacob hesitated. "To my mind, ja. But sons and fathers clash in every culture."

"Mine sure did. Wish I could go back and rewind that particular clock. Sour memories got a hold in me I wish I could shake." Rosie's gaze held on something in the distance until a noise from the children caused her face to soften. "Children are life's chance to do it all over again with the hope you get it right."

"I hope we get it right the first time," Amanda said.

Rosie shook her head. "You won't. Sorry to say that, but your kids'll have a few things to say about that after they're grown."

"Did you?"

"Oh, my. Different world back then. Beans and bacon, morning, noon, and night, sometimes. Rural electrification come late around our parts. Beef was selling for two cents a pound, sheep, even less. We didn't have the money to bring the poles into our place from the main road. After our region formed a coopera- tive and got a loan, my father couldn't afford the appli- ances. Finally got Mama a refrigerator, but when the first bill come, she sat down and cried. We never got an electric range till Tibbs bought me one for a wedding present. We pinched pennies, paying that $3.50 elec- tric bill ever' month."

"What else do you remember?"

"Ain't much I don't. Farm life was one of drudgery. Same chores done over and over till they was seared in your brain. Waking in the dark, working cold and hungry, walking out to see the cash hens huddled together in the henhouse, and all of them a frozen chunk of ice—dead and all your hopes gone with them. We grew up fast and serious in those days. No time for childhood. We had to get onto the business of survival. Rodeos were for sport and a way to unwind." She paused to study the far horizon while her thoughts settled.

"That's why Tibbs had such a set-to with our boy, Steve. We thought it was time he settled into the work, but Steve had his own ideas. Wanted to rodeo profes- sionally and that set hard with us. Especially Tibbs. He'd had to give up his rodeoing days to tend the ranch, and he thought Steve should do the same. They quar- reled and neither side won. Not really. They lived under the same roof, but it weren't good for neither of them. Steve said there was no way he was bringing home a wife to live in the same house as his father." She swiped at her eyes, and her voice lowered to a whisper.

"Fact is, I ain't sure it was a wife he was in the market for."

Amanda sat quietly, waiting for Jacob to think of something to bridge the tension.

"We let him go like we was dusting the dirt off our back. What was we thinking? He was our kin, for God's sake. Our own flesh and blood. We loved that boy. Didn't matter. Nothing mattered. And then we got the call, and it seemed like nothing was ever going to matter again. Ranch went to hell. We stayed home, afraid that folks were pitying us behind our backs. Then Jacob showed up, like an angel in them funny Aimish duds of his. We thanked our lucky stars he needed a place to stay." She raised her head, uncaring that her cheeks were shiny with tears. "And here you folks are, worrying that I might get hurt out here? Heck, you're the most good come of this place in four generations."

Jacob shook his head. "That's not true, Rosie."

She smiled. "I know it. But that's why I need the winter alone out here. To put my facts straight. I got grief and gratitude mixed up and needs straightening. Come springtime, I'll know spuds from taters and I'll be fit for polite company again. You get what I'm saying?"

Jacob nodded. "But you'll get a cell phone?"

"I have my landline. It's trusty. I won't be hiking out here in the snow." She grinned. "Unless I'm looking for a lost horse or one of Santa Claus's reindeer got off-track." She stretched to relieve her back muscles and prepared to rise. "We best be getting back. Cold comes on quick in this country."

Amanda trailed the others on the way home, setting her boots into the tracks already laid in the wet grass. She studied the snow-capped Rockies in the distance, and the smaller ranges that encircled the ranch like a mother's arms, protecting it from the fierce winds of the plains. In the crags, wildflowers still held their own against the coming winter, fierce, defiant little things determined to live. Rosie was like that, a flower out of her time, clinging to the land because it was all she knew. And yet her soul yearned for the ocean, just like Tibbs. That summer day when he'd stood at the lighthouse, breathing in the harsh sea wind, the scent of salt and seaweed and freedom—Rosie had admitted it was the best day of his life. The one he recalled as he lay sinking from life's burdens in the bed they'd shared for sixty-five years. Now he was gone, but the sea remained.

That night in bed, Amanda waited until Jacob rolled to face her before she whispered, "I'm homesick. I'm ready to visit the ocean and say a prayer for Tibbs."

The next morning, she watched the sun climb the distant ridge while Rosie carried in a small buckskin bag and set it in her hand. "This is for you. Tibbs wanted you to take it. It's a cutting of his hair, the day we laid him out, and his nail trimmings. A few gee-gaws he'd collected that meant something to him, and some sacred. A pebble from the butte, sage, a feather, and a shell from your ocean. He wanted you to take them back and let 'em go. He didn't cotton to cremation, but he wanted a part of him to be set free at the ocean he loved." She squinted an appraising look and asked, "You'll do that for him, won't you?"

Amanda nodded.

Rosie looked relieved. "Thought you might think it was some New-Age nonsense. He wanted you to take it to that lighthouse he visited. Yaquina Bay. He liked the wind there. Said it felt familiar." She hefted the leather sack and placed it in Amanda's palm. "I'll come out later and see the ocean. But this was something he wanted done soon as he passed. I don't know. He was some part Native Indian. Full of contradictions he never talked about."

Amanda felt the buttered leather, warm against her skin. She glanced at the tiny, hand-stitched seam, the leather lacing, and a tiny pattern of colored beads that formed a design on the front. "This is a medicine bag."

Rosie nodded. "He kept the claw of a bear he killed when he was a boy. Some other trifles that held meaning to him. He was a Christian, but a part of him never shed the feral. I reckon he wants to release that to the sea, so it'll live on."

Amanda closed her hand over the soft leather. "I'll honor his wish."

Rosie nodded, her eyes bright with unshed emotion. "He watched you with the children. I think he saw the future and it gave him hope. Like he'd had a hand in producing something better than the world he was born into. Strange, you aren't really kin. but I think he forgot that. Especially in the end. He talked of you when he was dying, and he thought you were his own."

Amanda bowed under the weight of emotions flooding her mind. She recalled his strange, soft, shy glances—pride if she was hard-pressed to give it a name. Satisfaction. Peace. He'd watched the children with such love. Rosie's eyes seemed to understand.

Chapter Twenty-One

❧

Amanda inquired about a local Uber driver to take them to the airport, but Rosie insisted. "I need some things at the market, anyway. My neighbors see me driving to the airport, it'll give me something to crow about."

At the loading zone of the crowded terminal, she stood beside her pickup wearing the scarf that Noah had taken from his neck and draped around hers. Because he loved her, he explained.

At the boarding gate, Amanda sat with her cell phone, killing time. She downloaded her emails and read one. "Charlie's dating someone. Good for him." She finished reading. "Sounds like he needs a roping partner next weekend. You interested?"

Jacob nodded. "Ja. maybe. I been practicing on the barrel back at Rosie's. I don't think to shame myself if I try my hand competing." He glanced over, and it seemed that they shared the same thought. Charlie was a good friend; Charlie with a wife would be even better.

By the time they arrived home, Jules was cranky

with lack of sleep, and Noah was begging to eat. Amanda dropped her bags at the door and put together a quick snack before she started their baths. As soon as they were down for the count, she poured herself a glass of zinfandel and headed to her bathroom for a hot bath.

Later, she slipped into her bed and enjoyed the luxury of her own sheets again. When Jacob joined her, she let out a long, satisfied moan. "I'm glad we're home."

"Thought you'd want to check the mail, first thing," he teased.

"Tomorrow. Life can wait. I'm in heaven."

"We see about that," he whispered as he slipped in beside her.

She giggled. "Thank God no one can hear our bed squeaking except us. Those quarters at Rosie's are a little tight."

The next morning, she sat with a cup of coffee and a letter opener to sort out the solicitations from the actual letters and bills.

Jacob reached past her to gather the pile. "The English ask for so many donations. Look here." In his hand, a dozen solicitations clamored for attention, some with gifts inside: tiny pencils, a quarter, one with a real dollar bill evident from the see-through plastic panel. "If they saved their money from sending these things, they could afford to feed the hungry child."

"You get no argument from me. Let's choose one cause to sponsor every month and toss the rest."

"Growing up, I know only the Christian Aid Ministries. Everyone contributed what they could. Which of these makes a good cause?"

She scanned the pile. "I like this one. Dad always gave to them."

"Then we continue the tradition. Out with the others."

"Wait, what about—"

He gave her an exasperated look. "You do what you need. It makes little difference. But not the one that sends us a dollar bill." He waved his hand over the pile of letters. "My sister writes. Maybe she is feeling better with her chemotherapy treatments." He slit open the envelope and read the letter aloud.

"Dear Bruder and Schwester,

How strange it seems to write those words after such a long time. Many changes for me here in Albany, but none worth wasting time or paper on. My family is good. Growing in leaps and bounds. Baby Adam Jacob looks more like his oncle every day. Little Sarah asks about the pretty lady she met at the tall house, the one who showed her kindness and told her about her grandparents. I tell her that Amanda will always have her in her heart, and this makes her happy. No good news on the cancer, it is in God's hands. Jeff's sister has taken a new job in Chicago, but she assures me when the time—and need— arises, she will help my husband with the children. He is struggling with his job. The company threatens cut- backs, and we pray that his new job is secure, and also the medical insurance we so rely on. I felt lonely today and wanted to write. Perhaps you would welcome a phone call. My number is at the bottom of this page. But if you are busy, I will understand.

Love to you and yours,
Beth."

Amanda added Beth's number to her contacts. "You need to call her today. She's worried."

"How does the sister-in-law think to help if she lives

in Chicago? There is something Beth doesn't tell us in her letter."

Amanda was half-listening as she opened a short note from Emma and read it aloud.

"*Fall is here, and Gott offers us wondrous beauty in the countryside. We made a short visit to the bishop's home to tell him of John and Lorie's news. Another baby boy born healthy, thanks be to God. Silas is helping with the milking now. He sets the machines and cleans the barn afterward. Sometimes it makes hard to get him out of bed at the early hour, but he will soon get used to his chores. Although he doesn't have the physical strength due to his protein intake. I have included a few recipes. When Jacob and his brother were growing up, we had many meatless meals, such as spaghetti and vegetable stews, but later, as they grew to teenagers and were able to help with finances, we were able to afford canned meat and hamburger. Of course, lots of milk and cream. Gott saw that we didn't starve.*

He is good, always.

Emma."

She closed the letter and sat considering the news. "Silas is working in the barns now? He's barely five. Noah's age. He's still a child."

Jacob nodded.

A few minutes later, Noah came padding down the hall with his favorite action figure under his arm. He pulled a stool to the sink and filled a glass of water, carried it to the table and reached for a bowl of oatmeal. She handed him his special milk and smiled proudly at his independence as he insisted on pouring it himself. An image of him proudly pushing the cows into the barn contrasted with the sleepy boy sitting in front of her. He loved the chores. But every day? At five in the morning? She tousled his hair and leaned to give him a kiss. "How's my boy this morning?"

"Fine." He shrugged from her touch and dug a spoon into his cereal without further comment.

My baby's growing up. "Would you like to help your dad in the nursery this morning?" When he looked up and nodded, she felt a stirring of abandonment. *I won't be one of those overprotective mothers. Jacob wouldn't let me, even if I wanted to be. But above all, I intend that my children have a happy childhood.* "And tomorrow you can go see your friends at Pre-K. I'll bet they missed you while you were in Wyoming."

"I wish I was at Silas's house. I like pushing the cows. They're nice. And I like watching the milk come out. And washing the barn."

"Would you like to do it every day...like Silas?"

He thought a moment. "I'd rather watch *SpongeBob SquarePants.* Silas's mama doesn't let him watch TV."

Lorie thinks I'm permissive. "No TV today. You're going outside with your dad."

She considered their conversation from the kitchen while she watched Noah help steer the tractor and operate the levers. Together with his father, they picked up the pallets and transferred them onto the trailers, his face shining with pride as he concentrated on his task, not even looking around to see that she was watching.

That night, she waited for Jacob to finish brushing his teeth before she shared the worry that had occupied her thoughts for most of the day. "Do you think television is a bad influence on Noah?"

"No question. It'll make him fat, lazy, selfish, and stupid." He ran tap water to rinse his brush and caught her eye through the mirror. "It doesn't take a genius to know this."

"Do you think we should shut it off?"

"Permanently? Tie up the cord and set it in the closet?" He dried his face on a towel and frowned. "I would say *yes*! But it is not just the television. It is the smart phone. The internet." He slipped in beside her. "But everything is not a sin. It depends on how we use it. Better to teach our children a higher standard, you know?"

She let out a breath she didn't realize she was holding. "I love you, Jacob."

"You better." He captured her against him in a way that made her forget about television and everything else.

The phone woke her the next morning. Carol's voice sounded excited, and a little tired. "Hey, say hello to the newest member of the *Mommy Club*. I'm worn out, sore in places I didn't know existed, and so happy I'm through the roof."

Carol's joy was contagious. "Congratulations. I'd ask, boy or girl, but I was with you when you did the sonogram. What did you name her?"

"Serenity Grace. With two crazy parents, we decided she could use the zen."

Amanda's laughter bubbled out before she could stop it. "Serenity!" You are truly weird, Carol. But I love it."

"Wait till you see her. She's so beautiful. Dark hair and blue eyes. But the nurse says that might change."

"So give me her vitals—the APGAR rating. But of course she's a ten!"

They chatted until Amanda looked at the clock. "Hey, I gotta get Noah to school."

On her way home, she stopped at a florist shop and ordered a huge bouquet to be delivered to Carol at home. "My friend's lucky. Her mother's coming for the first two weeks. What I wouldn't have given for that. I lost mine." The clerk's pitying look caught her short. What was she doing, moping to a complete stranger? Lucy Knowles had stopped by every day to bring food and laughter as she adeptly changed the baby and offered little tips that elevated Amanda's skill set—and her self-esteem. *Family comes in all packages. I should count my blessings.*

She ran into Charlie at the market when they both grabbed the same package of bacon. He was with a cute, wholesome-looking girl in a long-sleeved, plain-colored dress, and long, straight hair pinned up and topped with a plain black cap. *Mennonite.* She noticed the look of adoration he gave the girl. When another shopper grazed their cart, his arm whipped out, guiding his girl out of the way.

Amanda waited for the other shopper to pass before she got his attention. "Charlie, long time!"

His head jutted up in surprise while a grin spread across his face like sunlight on shadow. "Amanda." He placed a protective arm around the girl at his side. "Carrie-Anne, I'd like you to meet one of my high school friends, Amanda Ruth. Amanda's married to the Amish guy I was telling you about." He waited for them to exchange greetings. "How's it going with you two?"

"We're doing really well. It was hard at first, you know, with the compromises. But he makes me a better person." She heard her earnestness and laughed. "And he says the same about me."

"So you're good?"

His nervous look conveyed a message that she understood. *He's serious about this girl.* "We just got back from visiting his parents. He reconciled with his family." She expanded her explanation to include Carrie-Anne. "They weren't thrilled about us at first. But we get along fine now with his family." She was gratified to see the girl nod and relax. "In fact, his mother just sent a letter today. Some recipes she thought we'd like."

"So, they accept your marriage?" Carrie-Anne's voice sounded timorous.

"He hasn't been baptized, so that's not a problem for them. Our son inherited one of their blood issues, so they've been helping us to cope with that." She was revealing more than she intended, but their interest extended beyond simple gossip. "Jacob's nephew and our son both suffer from MSUD. It helps, having family that understands. We hope one day the boys can spend summers together."

Carrie-Anne nodded and smiled adoringly at Charlie. When they made their excuses and headed off toward the butter department, Charlie's shoulders relaxed. From the back, he seemed relieved.

At lunchtime, Amanda could scarcely wait for Jacob to wash up. "You should see him, Jacob. He was so happy. I've never seen him like that. Content. More mature. He was...complete."

Jacob grinned and reached for a sandwich. "Love will do that to a fellow."

"But Charlie? Drinking, partying Charlie? Who'da

thought?"

"He was in his rumspringa. Happens to the best of us. All it takes is a good woman, and we trade our vices for a homebody."

"I guess. But *Charlie?*" Jacob frowned and bit into his sandwich without answering. His irritation caused a stirring of realization in her. *That's what people thought about him. Judgment by people who didn't know him changed his life.* "I hope we get a wedding invitation." He nodded and continued chewing.

A month later, she pulled the invitation from the mailbox. A simple ceremony in the Salem Mennonite Church. "What will we get them?" she asked at supper that night.

Jacob settled into his seat at the table. "How about a barbecue smoker? We saw one at the Grange when we went for horse feed. I saw the way he looked at it."

She considered for a moment. "Great idea. I probably would have gotten them towels." He nodded and speared a piece of steak.

Charlie phoned to ask Jacob to be his best man. "It means planning my bachelor party. But no booze. I mean, nothing radical. I promised Carrie-Anne that I'd be bright-eyed to face her parents at the church the next morning. Maybe some pool and a couple of beers? Run up to Seattle to see the Sonics play? Something like that?" He sounded hesitant and a little timid.

"Marriage is making a mouse out of him," Jacob complained to Amanda. "He's afraid of his mother-in-law." He popped the cap off a Michelob and took a sip. "I'm not pushing him into drinking, but he needs to find his reasons. His own moral line."

"Agreed. Or he won't hold fast to his vows."

Chapter Twenty-Two

❧

Amanda paused at the sink and watched Jacob spin circles in the driveway on his motorcycle while Noah hung onto his back like a burr sharing the magic of the moment. A spear of terror lanced her heart. *Here we go again.*

Spring had warmed the fields, and across the yard, frantic little wrens had stuffed her birdhouses with dried grass. Soon they would be scooping bugs from the air to feed their little hatchlings, but for now, the nests were quiet. She shifted from the birdhouses to the two riders kicking dust in the driveway. A year ago, she would have marched out and demanded that Jacob put his son on the ground. Today, the joy in their eyes matched their determination like warriors training for battle. An image of Silas pushing the cows in the darkness brought conflicted feelings; she didn't want to coddle her own son.

With the warming sun illuminating the porch, she walked to the door and stood twisting her dishtowel in her fingers while the motorcycle dipped and wove in figure eights, so slowly that it seemed impossible for the bike to stay upright without Jacob dabbing his toes. Despite her misgivings, her admiration lingered. *Jacob's a really good rider.*

He looked up, saw her watching and guided the bike closer. From the seat, he cut the engine and sat without moving, waiting for her reaction. She considered a dozen responses and decided against speaking. Smiling seemed safer. Small steps.

"So, what's for lunch?" His look of innocence contrasted with the fact that he was garbed like a medieval warrior.

"Lunch? We just finished breakfast."

"We bikers work up an appetite, don't we, son?"

Noah nodded. His cheeks glowed with happiness and health beneath the helmet he insisted on wearing to bed each night while they read their books. When it was time to sleep, he allowed her to set it on his dresser with the promise that it would be there in the morning. "You've created a monster," she told Jacob the night he brought it home.

Amanda turned away to hide her smile. "Leftovers," she called over her shoulder as she started down the driveway to the mailbox. They could wait for lunch. Or they could fill their own plates. She didn't want them to get the idea that she was only good for cooking and cleaning.

That night, she waited for Jacob to finish in the bathroom before she brought up the fear that had occupied her mind for most of the day. "Are you taking our son riding on the street?"

Jacob paused with his hand on the light switch. He clicked the light off, and his voice in the darkness sounded gravelly. "I don't encourage him. He comes and asks me. Every time."

She sighed. "He wants to be like you. He won't be content until he's your clone."

"I don't know this word, clone. But he doesn't want to be sickly and worried. He learned from Silas that his disease is not an excuse. Now he wants to be like other boys. Like me." In the darkness, his voice became a smile. "Is this so terrible?"

She brushed her fingers across his ribs and heard his sharp intake of air. "Not terrible," she teased. "He'll grow up to be a heartbreaker—like you."

He chuckled. "I don't know about this 'heartbreaker,' but I take your word for it. I mean to help him to manage his disease and still have a safe childhood. What is it I must do to keep his mother from worrying?"

"I keep thinking of your accident, and I wonder what would have happened if he'd been with you." There, she'd said it. Not so hard.

In the darkness, his voice sounded shamed. "I was angry. And maybe I'd had a beer or two, I don't remember. But this I promise you, liebchen. I do not take chances with our son. You are right to be concerned for him."

"Then how do we compromise?"

"I buy him a small dirt bike and safety gear. We will go out on safe trails, and he will learn to respect the machine. If later, he decides to ride on the street, he will have skills."

"So, not until he's older?"

"Yes. Much older."

The alarm clock woke her the next morning. She lay in bed beside Jacob, waiting for the moment when the sunrise caught his face, and he opened his eyes. When the moment came, he blinked and reached for her with sweet promises that this day would be a good one. By the time she headed for the shower, the sun was visible over the far hills. Jules stood in the hallway with her rag doll clutched in her fist.

"How did you get out, sweetie?" Amanda back-tracked into the nursery where she discovered the crib intact and the sides still up. She heard Jacob scoop Jules up and carry her back into the room. "Did you crawl out? Jules, what are we going to do with you?"

"Makes me wonder if she's going to be feisty like her mother."

"Like me? More like you." Amanda bent to drop the side panels of the bed. "No more crib. She's a toddler."

"No more babies in the house? Maybe time we make another." Jacob's eyes held a tinge of sincerity. He wasn't kidding.

"I...I just got her weaned." Amanda lost her train of thought in the chaos churning through her head. Another baby? So soon? "Come on, Jules, let's get you ready for breakfast."

On her way home from taking Noah to Pre-K, she stopped to let Jules play in the park. While she pushed her on the swing, her phone rang. It was Rosie. She clenched the phone to her ear and heard the snap of a woodstove in the distance. "Hey, winter's officially over. You made it through the winter."

"Yes, with Tibbs here in spirit. Burned through most of my cordwood. Learned to create a few new soups, and I baked a slew of bread that I fed to neighbors and the horses. It was good—all told. I trekked out to the barn enough times, the horses are sick of seeing me. I let them run loose a few days ago. Now they've abandoned me for greener pasture."

It was good, hearing Rosie's voice. "Noah's asking for you. He's growing up fast." Amanda caught herself from blurting out her frustration, saying only, "Jacob's going to get him a minibike for his next birthday. A little one, so he can touch the ground."

"You all right with that? I know you have your opinion about bikes." Rosie sounded hesitant to get in the middle of things.

Amanda carried Jules back to the car and snapped her into her car seat. Rosie's voice came in on the Bluetooth as she started the car. "Apparently, I've been outvoted. Jacob says we can't stop them from growing up. Jules, too. She's not a baby anymore. Jacob wants another one."

"Oh my. What do you think?"

"Truthfully? I just gave away all my baby clothes. I'd need to buy it all new again."

Rosie hesitated. "None of my business, but don't spare yourself a big family or you'll be like me. One isn't enough. Even two."

Amanda laughed. "I have a few minutes before I have to decide, don't I?" She pulled into her driveway and heard the landline phone ringing inside the kitchen. "Rosie, can I call you back? That might be Noah's school."

The call was from Beth. "I hope I didn't disturb you. I wanted to wait until it was late enough. I thought..."

"It's fine. This is a good time. What's new?"

Beth's silence added heaviness to whatever she intended to say. On the other end of the line, Amanda heard her gasp in pain as the bedsheets rustled restlessly. *Not a good day, she's too weak to make it to her chair.* Silence grew until Amanda was tempted to hang up and redial, but Beth's weak cough on the other end hinted of desperation. "What is it, sweetie? Are you okay?" Sniffling on the other end was followed by a cough. "Would you rather call back later, when you're stronger?"

"No. I won't be stronger. I need to say this." Beth shifted and took a shallow, pained breath. "Jeff's sister called us. She's getting a divorce. Her husband met someone. There's no chance for them, she says." She took a breath and started again. "She needs to work to support herself. Her apartment is expensive, but she likes it in Chicago." Beth allowed a sob to break her monologue. "She doesn't want to move back to help Jeff with the children."

"Oh, Beth, I'm so sorry."

"Are you really? Because I need to ask something. My doctor says it's only days now. My lab tests, the experimental treatment, nothing is working. Jeff has taken the kids to the park so I could call you. He lost his new job. This company laid him off because he was losing too much work. That's not the excuse they gave, but he was included in the first batch of layoffs. We have food stamps and some of our neighbors are bringing food. If it weren't for your checks, we wouldn't be able to make our rent." She coughed and took a drink of water. When she was able to speak again, her voice was a whisper. "Thank Jacob for his kindness. It means everything."

"He's happy to do it. We both are."

Silence grew on the line until Amanda heard a weak cough. "Amanda, I have a question..."

"Anything." She choked back tears and heard her voice crack. "What is it, Beth?"

"Jeff he has nothing here. Maybe he could work with Jacob? And you could help with the children? They're so little. They will forget me unless Jacob... unless you keep me alive for them." She sobbed uncontrollably. "Amanda, don't let them forget me, please?"

Amanda squeezed her eyes shut and mouthed a silent prayer for the pain she heard in her sister-in-law's voice. When the silence seemed interminable, she realized Beth was waiting. "Bethie, you honor us. I've loved little Adam Jacob from the first time I held him. And sweet Emily Ruth is so precious. I see myself in her. She deserves to remember you."

In the next minutes she described her own mother's auto accident, and how her aunt Lydia had kept the two of them connected, with projects and favorite foods that her mother remembered, and by firmly pushing Amanda into a deeper relationship when she could easily have pushed horse riding and excursions that would have left her mother behind. Lydia encouraged her make special gifts for her mother and included her in every achievement. Even though her mother was paralyzed from the neck down, Lydia had cooked and made jams from the blackberries that grew along the fence line while the three of them shared recipes in the kitchen. She recalled how much her mother had loved the taste.

"My aunt was so loving. I think, without her, I would have been broken by my mother's injury. But when I grew older, I realized I had two mothers, and I loved them both." She heard weeping on the other end as she waited for Beth to speak. "Beth, I need to talk this over with Jacob, but I know he'll agree. He wants to build a family. We will keep your memory alive."

There was silence on the other end, followed by a sob. Finally, a timid voice asked, "Will you ask him soon? I don't have much time."

"I'll go find him in the field. We'll pray, and then we'll call you back. Can you wait for an hour?"

Beth's chuckle sounded lighter. "I have that long. I'm not gone yet."

Chapter Twenty-Three

"Jacob, say something!"

Jacob sat on a log he was cutting for firewood, his chainsaw resting in a pile of sawdust. The oak tree had died prematurely, felled by disease in its prime, but its leaves were emerging, even though the trunk was already dead. His brow knitted in a frown; his shoulders hunched. *This is too important to botch.* She held her breath and waited.

He raised his chin and his eyes pierced hers in intensity. "What is in your heart on this matter, liebchen?"

She wanted to hug him. "I heard your sister's voice. It was like I was a kid again and my mother was in the hospital, unable to move. My aunt came and convinced me that I would be okay. Without her, I would have stayed in my room and just wasted away."

He squinted and leaned in. "What about your teaching job? Your career? Everything that is important to you? Are you saying you will give up the chance to teach in a classroom?" He stared at her as he considered. "You will be willing to raise her children?"

"Are you?"

"I love my sister. We did everything together. Always her and me, not John. I miss her. She left home, and I had so many things I needed to talk to her about. If she left the community, where was the hope for me?"

"She's asking you to keep hope alive in her children. If we don't, who will?"

He nodded and rose to his feet, gathering her to him while sawdust clung to them both. "Liebchen, never have I loved you more." He released her and fished his cell phone from his pocket. "I call her. Give her hope in these last days."

"Maybe you should go to her."

He nodded and returned the phone to his pocket.

❦

The U-Haul truck pulled up just before supper with a sedan following close behind. Jacob eased out of the moving truck and waited for his brother-in-law to find a parking spot in the yard.

Amanda rushed outside in time to Beth's husband extract his children from their car seats. Unbuckled, Emily Rose approached shyly. With her fingers in her mouth, she edged up against her father and hugged his leg while her eyes filled with tears. "I want my mama," she whimpered. Amanda felt her own eyes welling as she searched for something soothing to say.

Noah saved the moment when he slipped past and ran to give his cousin a hug.

Amanda knelt to eye-level and introduced herself. "Do you remember me, Emily? When you came to see your grandma at the farm? We looked at the cows in the field." The little girl nodded. "I met your mama, and she was lovely."

At the mention of her mother, Emily gave Amanda a fierce, tight hug that seemed to cement them together. Amanda's heart melted. *I remember being starved for a mother's touch.* She raised Emily's chin and looked directly into her blue eyes. "I'm Amanda. I'm your uncle Jacob's wife. And your mama was his most favoritest person in the world. Did you know that?" When Emily nodded and removed her fingers from her mouth, Amanda brushed the little girl's tangled braid. "We're going to be good friends, sweetie. Pinkie promise."

Amanda reached to intercept a wiggling Adam from his father. Apparently, trust was easier with a one-year-old. As long as it included a promise of cheese crackers. "Hello, Adam. Would you like a Goldfish? I think we have some in the kitchen." She gave Jeff a quick glance as he lifted a suitcase from the back of his car. "Jeff, hi. We'll meet later when the kids are settled." His look of relief was almost comical. Clearly Beth had known what she was asking when she requested help.

In the den, Emily and Noah were already pulling Legos from the box. Jules toddled over, squawking when she saw her mother holding another baby, a territorial move that ended well when she leaned in to give the baby a smacking kiss on his lips. "Baby."

"His name is Adam Jacob."

"Adam-wheeee!" Her excited shriek bounced off

the walls, piercing the silence. She gave another half-hearted shriek when Amanda deposited Adam in the highchair that had been hers.

I'll be deaf at this rate! By the time Amanda had supper on the table, everyone's hands and faces washed, and plates made up with chicken nuggets, mashed potatoes, peas, and squash, she was exhausted.

Baths next. She ran the tub with four inches of water and set the youngest two in. With a careful balance of firmness and tact, she managed to get half a week's worth of dirt off Adam before she dressed him in a fresh diaper and a clean sleeper. Keeping a firm grip on him, she used her free hand to run clean bath water for the older two.

Later, she laid Adam in the crib and tried to pacify Jules's outraged cries. Finally, when all else failed, she sighed. "You can sleep with me tonight, Jules."

Afterward, she returned to the living room where Jeff was slouched in a recliner, reading an industry magazine of her father's. She poured herself a glass of chardonnay. "Want one?"

Jeff shook his head. "We don't...didn't drink. Beth thought it wasn't healthy."

She sipped in silence while he abandoned any pretense of reading and sat with his head back on the sofa, his eyes closed. When it was time for bed, she dimmed the lights without disturbing his soft snores.

"Don't get too comfortable," she warned Jacob when he came in a few minutes later. "We have a visitor in the bed!"

Jules spent the night sprawled between them until, finally, Jacob grabbed a spare blanket and made his way to the sofa.

Breakfast was a chaotic blend of Cheerios and sliced bananas, while she tried to find a solution for the single highchair. Noah got ready for preschool with Emily crying because she wanted to go with him. Jacob gave her an apologetic glance on his way out the door with Jeff, to introduce him to the staff and to show him the office where he'd be working in his new position as office manager for the Miller Nursery.

Amanda made a quick visit to the elementary school and obtained an application for Emily. *First grade, here we come.* Emily could begin school as soon as she provided proof of vaccination and a birth certificate.

The next stop was at St. Vinnie's Thrift Store. The sign said it opened at ten, so she scrolled through her Facebook account while she waited. Inside, she found a used highchair and crib. The clerk who helped her carry the items to the car saw that she had a toddler and a baby in the back seat. "We used to call those 'Irish twins,'" she joked as she helped load the furniture in the back of the SUV. Amanda didn't bother to correct her.

"One fifty for everything, Jacob," Amanda reported while he and Jeff carried the furniture from the car and hosed it off. "I guess we'll need to call this the nursery from now on," she joked as she wiped the surfaces with a spray bottle of disinfectant while they tightened the screws. Fortunately, Jules was thrilled at sharing her room.

"Good value, liebchen. Enough left over to spend on disposable diapers. Looks like you'll need them."

"Beth was using the natural method like her Amish people use," Jeff interjected. "Adam tells us when he needs to go."

"He's only seven months old!"

Jeff smiled. "He's never worn diapers. Trust me."

Amanda waited for the men to leave make their way to the barn before she googled "Natural Toileting." A home page for *Baby Elimination Communication* popped up. She spent the morning researching possibilities while Emily played on the floor with the toddlers. When her brother made a grunt, she informed Amanda that it was time.

Amanda was still dubious as she deposited him in a potty chair that her son had used. But Emily insisted. After a successful toilet break, Adam played contentedly until he indicated that he needed to pee again.

In late afternoon, when Jules informed her in an almost-perfect sentence that her diaper was dirty, Amanda threw up her hands. "All right, little miss. If Adam can do this, so can you."

The next day she spent the morning listening for Adam's signal. When it came, she was vociferous enough in her praise that, a few minutes later, she found Jules quietly sitting on the potty chair reading a picture book. By the next day, Jules had grasped the concept.

"So, problem solved? We have no need for diapers?" Jeff grinned when he and Jacob arrived for lunch.

"One problem anyway. But I'm hiring help. I think Imelda is back from Mexico by now. She might want her old job back."

⚓

Imelda stood in the kitchen, shaking her head as the two toddlers slung mush onto the floor. She reached to wipe the tile with a paper towel and straightened, holding her back. "I'm too old for this, señora. I ask my daughter if she wants to work."

Yolanda arrived the next morning. Amanda was on her way out the door to drop Noah off. Emily happily accompanied them, ready for her first day of school in a new pair of jeggings and a fuzzy pink top. Amanda carried copies of Emily's birth certificate and vaccination record in her purse.

At the school, the principal apologized. "I will need to see the legal parent," she explained. "It's regulation. I assumed you knew this."

Amanda's face burned with embarrassment. "I'm so sorry. Of course I knew this. It's just...I've been on damage control since the children arrived. Their father is...grieving. He's adjusting to a new job and—"

The principal nodded. "I understand. But the rules are the same. Have him take a moment tomorrow so we can chat." She reached to take Emily's documents and slipped them into a file. "I'll keep these." She smiled. "Tell him to arrive early. That will allow Emily to transition into her new classroom without disrupting the other children. I'm sure she'll appreciate that."

On the way home, Emily's chin trembled with disappointment while Amanda tried unsuccessfully to keep her spirits up. "Let's go home and play school. We can learn to write your name. We'll practice our ABCs and see how you do. Then we'll make mud balls with wildflower seeds inside and toss them out in the garden to wait for the rain."

Emily shook her head so violently that her braids slapped together. "I want to go to school like Noah. I want my mama. I want to go home."

Amanda watched from the car as Emily ran across the parking lot to her father's new office. When she peeked in a few minutes later, Emily was occupied with a yellow marker and a stapler. Jeff agreed to escort his daughter to school the next morning.

Amanda spent the rest of the morning washing and folding clothes while Yolanda scoured the kitchen of sticky fingers and spilled food. "You running a day care center, señora. You should maybe get a state license," she joked as she unloaded the dishwasher of a dozen new sippy cups and plastic toddler trays.

"Good idea. Wanna go into partnership?"

Yolanda slipped a handful of colored spoons into a cup and set it on the counter. "I think maybe we call our day care, *Dos Crazy Women!*"

Amanda laughed. "Maybe we *are* crazy. At least it feels like that some days."

"Give it time, señora. You find your rhythm."

Jeff pulled into the driveway the next morning without Emily. He stopped by the house on his way to his office to ask if Amanda could pick her up at 2:45.

"Let's see, Noah's class lets out at noon. The little ones have their naps around that time and Yolanda's only here until noon. How's this going to work?"

Yolanda stood silently, looking thoughtful. "Maybe my mother can come and sit with the babies until you get home. Or one of the fathers? I'm sorry, I cannot help."

In the bedroom, Adam had woken from his nap and was ready for his snack. Jules wandered in with the end of a roll of toilet paper in her hand. The other end trailed down the hall, into the bathroom. Amanda picked up her phone and made a call to the principal. "Do you have any openings for after-kindergarten school care? It would only be for two hours. Temporary. Until the end of the semester." She waited with fingers crossed. "Maybe next month?"

Chapter Twenty-Four

✿

In the kitchen, Yolanda put the finishing touches on an enchilada casserole with rice and refried beans that filled the kitchen with heartrending aromas. Amanda gave a silent prayer of thanksgiving as she set Adam in his highchair. Afterward, she sliced an avocado and fed slices to him and Jules.

At supper, Emily fought with Noah about where they would sit. Amanda settled the dispute by making construction place cards in their favorite colors and placing them on opposite sides of the table.

Jeff was engrossed in his phone and didn't notice that supper was ready until she called him a second time. He carried the phone to the table and set it beside his plate. In the middle of dinner, its vibrating caused him to check the caller ID. Amanda sent a pointed look at Jacob before she picked up her knife to cut up the children's food. By the time she finished feeding Adam, her plate was cold, and everyone else was nearly ready for ice cream.

"I like Jeff," she complained to Jacob that night,

"but it's been a month. He needs to step it up for his kids' sake. I told him about Parent's Night next week, but I'm not sure he heard me. Or even cares."

"He's pretty stressed with everything. Give him some time." Jacob sounded reluctant to broach the problem.

"Great. So he works eight hours at a desk and he comes home too tired to be a parent. That wasn't our deal, Jacob."

"No...I hear you, liebchen. I'll talk to him." Jacob rolled to face the wall, his signal that the conversation was ended.

Amanda spent the next half hour trying to calm herself enough to sleep. When Adam woke in the middle of the night, she waited to see if his father was going to get him. When the baby's wailing threatened to wake the house, she slipped out of bed and padded down the hall to take him to the bathroom.

Emily was in tears the next morning because her project for Parent Night wasn't finished. She refused to eat her oatmeal and threw her lunchbox on the floor when Amanda handed it to her. She glanced over to see how Jeff intended to handle it, but he was engaged on his phone playing a game. Sudoku.

Amanda picked up the lunchbox and tucked it into Emily's backpack. "You tell your teacher that your daddy didn't have time to help you this time, Emily. Your teacher can explain how important it is when your daddy comes to Parent Night."

Jeff looked up when he noticed Amanda glaring at him. "What? Did I miss something?"

Amanda handed Adam to his father and picked up her car keys. "I'm driving the kids to school. Adam needs to go potty and get dressed. If you need to know where his clothes are kept, ask Yolanda." She scooted the two older ones out of the door without waiting for a reply.

When she returned, Jeff was on his phone while Adam was trying to pry a kidlock off an electrical socket in the den. He looked up sheepishly and jumped to his feet while she walked over, picked his son up, and carried him into the kitchen to wash the smeared cookie from his hands.

The week dragged by in an endless ritual of feed, wipe, potty, nap, read and repeat. Amanda spent her day with the little ones to stimulate their hands and brains, praising them for every small accomplishment. By the end of each day, she was covered in poster paint and Play Doh, exhausted from monitoring spats and from handing out nutritious snacks and cutting fruit into bite-sized pieces.

"I need a vacation," she complained to Jacob one night. "It's like I have two sets of twins."

He looked puzzled. "I don't understand. You have Yolanda. Doesn't she help?"

"Yeah, for three hours a day. I'm grateful, but still, it's a lot."

"We can pay her to stay a few hours longer. Is that what you need?"

She massaged her aching neck and considered what she was about to say. Jacob wouldn't understand, but she needed to be honest. "She has her own family. We're lucky to get her at all. What I need is for Jeff to step up and be a father." She lifted her chin defiantly. "And you, too, while we're on the subject."

Jacob nodded, his face flushed with guilt. "I guess maybe this is my fault, too. I can talk to him."

"I'll believe it when I see it."

"Maybe it's you who needs to show compassion. Not him. Pray on it, okay?"

That night, Amanda waited in vain for Jacob to broach the subject. When she finished putting the children to bed, she returned to the living room and collapsed into her chair with a bottle of wine. Jeff looked up from his phone and she managed a smile. "How's everything going, Jeff? I mean really. Are you adjusting to Oregon okay?"

He looked up again, his eyes ringed in dark circles. "I guess so. Thanks for asking."

"I know this is hard. But your children need you. They ask why you don't tuck them in, and I don't know what to tell them."

He shifted and his sockets filled with tears. "It's great here. But I miss her so much—" His voice broke. He glanced at the floor while he covered his mouth with fingers that shook. After a moment he continued. "I look at the kids, and I see her. I know I've checked out, but I can't help myself. I look for distractions, so I don't have to face them."

Amanda felt her belly contract as she pressed her hand on his. "You don't need to explain. I saw you that day in Ohio. The way you looked when you came to pick her up. The lengths you went to so she could see her mother one final time." Her voice choked. "I...I looked up your route. You drove all day and night to get Beth home again. I could see in your face...you felt so powerless. I'll never forget that look. You were haunted.

Broken." She swiped at her tears, not caring. "I saw your love for Beth. And so did she."

Jeff broke down, his sobs loud in the sleeping house. Amanda heard Jacob in the garage, but for the moment it was only her and Jeff, trying to make sense of the unexplainable. She sat quietly while he wept with the abandon of a child, releasing his sorrow without caring who saw. She picked up a box of tissues and set it nearby without drawing attention to herself as his pain ripped open the scars he was trying to heal. He murmured disjointed phrases as though his thoughts penetrated his grief. She glanced at the door, wondering if she should leave, but fearing that any movement would interrupt his process.

A shudder of pain rippled through his body, and he was still, his shoulders bent over, and his head hidden. When he finally looked up, his eyes were swollen and his face ruddy with emotion, but he seemed at peace. Amanda poured him a glass of wine. He drank it without seeming to notice the alcohol. When he finished and set the glass down, he ran a hand through his hair and looked up.

She reached to move the glass away from the edge of the table, a flimsy stall for time while he collected himself. The guise worked. He straightened and took a deep, cleansing breath. "I'm so sorry you had to see that."

"You needed it, Jeff. To release all that stuff. You've been strong for everyone. For your kids, for Beth, I'll bet even for your parents. But now you need to take care of *you*." She heard herself murmuring trite adages that people had used on her, and she heard the wisdom in the words. "We're here to keep Beth alive for her children. You can help by recalling the good times. They need you, especially Emily. She needs to know her mother—every detail. The way she smiled, and sang, and smelled, and made Christmas special. Her favorite foods and the times when she got stung by a bee and got mad. Emily will grow in the image of her mother, and you'll help her be the best version of herself. Show her how much you loved her mother."

Jeff stared at the floor. When he looked up, his eyes indicated a new resolve. He nodded and his face took on new character, his lost look replaced by purpose. "When she died, I felt like I died, too. When she left, I figured I'd come out here and drop the kids off, and then I'd just disappear. They'd be better without me." He kept his face lowered as shame crept across his cheeks.

Amanda smiled. "And yet, here you are."

He nodded woodenly. "Emily needs to know how lovely she is. How blown away her mother was by her. She's the best of us, and Beth still lives through her children. We both do." His eyes filled with tears. "I can do this. You guys made me see a way forward when you offered me a job. The timing...even the position was perfect. I think Beth helped it to happen."

Amanda smiled. "I think so, too." She reached for a box of tissues and took one. "She called me, you know. We spoke for hours about her hopes and dreams for all of you. She asked me to help her family."

Jacob entered and glanced from one to the other, clearly confused until Amanda gave him a quick look that convinced him to detour to the kitchen for a long drink of water.

Jeff rose from the chair. "I have a lot to think about."

He gave a wry, guilty look on his way out of the room. "I should tuck my kids in. And tomorrow night, I'll read to them. I'll say good night." He gave a feeble wave and disappeared.

Later, in bed, Amanda explained, "He's going to be okay. He turned a corner tonight."

Jacob nuzzled her. "I hope so. He's been sleepwalking. Truth be told, I was worried."

"I think he's back. And looking forward to being a father." She sighed with pleasure as Jacob kneaded her back. "He understands you haven't given him a pity position with the business. He'll earn his keep. Probably save you tons of money. You should discuss your ideas and ask him to make a revised business plan. I think he's up to the challenge. Hard work will keep him occupied."

"I agree. The old manager was your father's hire. She was still too loyal to him to take my ideas seriously. That's why she left."

"Jeff will have your back, Jacob." She passed her hand across his shoulders, massaging the area where he held his stress.

"Hmmm, I like the way you have *my* back. A little to the right?"

❧

The next morning, she handed Jeff his son's bowl of oatmeal and a spoon. "He can eat it by himself, but he needs encouragement."

He smiled. "Point taken, Amanda. Thanks." His phone was in his pocket, silent for once.

She bent to wipe Adam's spilled food off the floor.

"Parent Night is on Tuesday. Emily might enjoy a father-daughter pizza beforehand."

That night, after Jules was asleep, she invited Noah to sit with her in the rocking chair while she read his favorite book. He snuggled against her and sounded out the words he knew, matching them to the pictures. She watched as he concentrated with his tongue against the inside of his cheek, like his father. "Look at you, Noah, reading already. Who will I read to when you're too big?"

He shook his head in pleasure. "I won't ever be too big, Mama. I like sitting here, just the two of us. It's special."

She finger-combed his hair and noticed it was getting thicker; he was losing his baby-fine curls. "You're growing up so quickly, Noah. Not my baby anymore." She picked up his hand and examined his fingers, growing long and straight like his father's. She realized he'd been spending more time with his father since Beth's family had arrived. "How's Yankee doing these days? Have you and Daddy been riding him?"

Noah nodded. "Daddy gives me chores. I brush my horse after school. Like Silas."

She pressed her lips against his crown and inhaled, dreading the day when she wouldn't be permitted such liberties. One day soon he would insist on bathing himself. In a few years he would retreat into his room with his door closed, and then one day, he'd be gone. Her heart sang when he accepted her kiss and reached for a hug with a look of childish contentment. "How does your tummy feel these days?" she asked. "Do you get thirsty at school? Or get a headache? You need to tell me if you start feeling silly. Promise?"

Noah nodded, but his attention was captured by a word in the book. He sounded it out and looked up, pleased. She wrapped him in a hug and felt him squirm free.

A moment later, Emily appeared in her PJs to get her goodnight kiss. "Daddy read to me. So now you can read to Noah by yourself, okay?"

Chapter Twenty-Five

A manda picked up her phone on its second ring. The HR person on the other end spent a moment in small talk before she got to the point of her call. "Mrs. Ruth, we have an opening for a primary teacher, and I notice that your certificate is still current. Would you be interested in a temporary position while one of our teachers is out on family leave? Your name was suggested by several of the faculty. You did such a wonderful job last time."

Amanda reached to help Adam, who was trying to stand against a chair that threatened to overturn. In the den, Jules had climbed onto the sofa and was reaching for the lamp. She rushed to extricate her daughter, setting her back on the floor with her phone in one hand and Adam in the other.

"How nice of them. Tell everyone hello. And thank them for thinking of me." As silence grew on the other end of the line, she handed each of the toddlers a cracker bribe. Without conscious thought, she glanced in the mirror over the fireplace and noticed the new frown lines at the corner of her eyes that had taken residence in the past few weeks, despite the frownie strip she was now wearing for her crow's feet. On the other hand, another wrinkle would be worth it. *Carol isn't going to believe this!*

On the other end, the HR woman coughed discreetly, a hint that she was waiting for a response. Amanda blinked her daydream back into reality. "I'm afraid I must decline your offer. My circumstances have changed rather dramatically, and I need you to take me off the list. But I do appreciate the call." She managed to extricate herself without going into too much personal detail. *No point in torpedoing my career forever.*

She waited until after lunch, when Jeff was in the nursery tucking Adam in for his nap, before she told Jacob about her morning. "It felt so good, honey. They offered me a position in the classroom again."

Jacob's face took on an ashen hue as he leaned closer, trying to discern her mood. She almost giggled at the fear forming behind his eyes. "What did you tell them?" His voice sounded tense.

"Great question. Thanks for not jumping to the mansplaining part. I'm impressed." She leaned forward to wrap her arms around his neck. "We should do this more often."

"You're killing me. What did you tell them?"

She laughed. "What do you think? I told them I'm outrageously fulfilled, with a handsome husband and four great kids, and a houseful of chaos and a not-very clean kitchen, and five beds that need changing and a stack of dirty clothes that could fill a moving van." She released him and shifted in his arms. "Actually, I told them I'm immensely satisfied with my life, and I wouldn't change a thing. Not for all the classrooms in the world."

"Liebchen, what am I to do with you? You drive me crazy!" He laughed, and his voice sounded relieved.

Jeff returned from the nursery. "Don't forget, we have a meeting with the County in half an hour. You want me to go over there alone?"

Jacob rose from his chair and led the way to the door with a last, relieved glance at Amanda. When they left a few minutes later to drive into town, she found herself humming.

As soon as she finished loading the lunch dishes into the dishwasher, she called Carol. "I have a minute if you do. My toddlers are asleep, and we can talk until they wake up. Then I need to run to pick up Noah."

Her martyrdom sounded terrific to her ears, but Carol laughed. "When your spare family came to live with you, I told Rennie Jacob was going to need a robo-maid. But now I realize he has one. It's you!"

"Carol, you won't believe my morning! Someone from Planet Earth just attempted to communicate with me. It was awesome. We exchanged what is commonly known as 'adult conversation.' A live person asked me intelligent questions and waited for me to answer. It's a concept I'm unfamiliar with these days."

"What happened? Someone offer you a job?"

Amanda punched her fist into the air. "Yes! At my old school. I'm thrilled. It feels good to know my hard work was recognized. I have some good friends at that school, and they came through for me. I'd almost forgotten that I exist."

"You need to stay in touch with them, girl! Even if

it's only a phone call." Carol hesitated. "You told them 'no' of course. There's no way you'd choose career over those darling babies."

"I *did* tell them no."

"Do you regret your decision?"

"You know what, Carol? I really don't. It feels so good to say that. I'd forgotten how happy I am being home. I love every second of my life. Dirty dishes, sour clothes, and all."

"Keep that thought, Amanda. Take a deep breath. Close your eyes and remember how this feels. Perfect contentment. You'll need it the next time Jules wets her bed and you're out of clean clothes."

Amanda sobered at the thought. "True. But for now, in this moment, I love motherhood in all its glory. I'm very, very happy."

"Attagirl. That's my bestie. Now go start a load of whites and enjoy a nice glass of tea while the kids sleep." Carol laughed. "Just stay away from the cookie jar. Stress eating will kill your girlish figure. Trust me, I know."

"Sugar is my crack cocaine."

"Whoa there, Mama. How long's it been since you and Jacob had a date night?" When Amanda didn't answer, she persisted. "You take care of your marriage, hear me, girl?"

The washer was on its fill cycle when Amanda hung up. A few minutes later, her toddlers woke from their naps and came running down the hall. She finished giving them juice and a snack in time to load them into the car to collect Noah. Most days Jeff arrived to keep an eye on the little ones so she could run into town, a small concession, but it saved her from having to strap two children into car seats for a fifteen-minute run across town. Small steps. Emily had signed up to ride the bus to school, and she was happy and proud of her independence.

That night Amanda broached the subject of a date night with Jacob as Jeff walked into the kitchen and set his phone next to his plate. "Jeff, do you think you can handle all four of them for a few hours?" She'd given the idea some thought. Jacob's quick look told her he shared her apprehension, but she persisted. "It's been a long time, Jacob. We need to do this."

Jeff glanced up uncertainly. "I guess we'll find out. Sure. I got this."

She glanced over to see Jacob frown, and she hesitated. When she'd formed the idea in her mind, the plan had seemed stronger. "Maybe I can hire one of Imelda's granddaughters. They're good with kids."

"How hard can it be? I can give them baths, a snack. Read a couple of books. We'll have a great time. When are you planning to go?" Despite his confidence, Jeff's face looked shiny. A moment later he shrugged and straightened. "I need to do this. I'm so obligated to you guys that I'm drowning here. Guilt makes it easier to ignore the decisions. I pretend it's not my job to parent. But I know I've been sluffing. Beth would be the first to call me on it." The room resounded with the sound of a deep breath. "I got this, Amanda. Go have yourself a night on the town."

Jacob's thoughtful nod from across the table settled the matter. She directed her question to him. "How about Thursday night? I'll make a reservation at that place we went to on your birthday last year. I remember we loved the food." *Has it been that long since we went out alone?*

"Sounds good. So this is settled, ja?"

"I'll feed the kids before we leave. Spaghetti, so they'll have something to scrub off in the bathtub," she teased.

"Nice." Jeff smiled and picked up his fork. "Emily, you'll help me, won't you?"

Across the table, Emily nodded enthusiastically.

Date night began with Emily helping her to pick out a necklace and earrings that matched her favorite dress. She preferred to wear jeans, but Emily insisted on pumps and a spangly belt she found in the closet. Jules perched on the bed while Emily rooted through her jewelry box searching for the perfect accessory. She pulled out an amethyst bracelet and hooked the clasp with a look of awe in her eyes.

Amanda stood and shook the folds of her dress. "Do I look okay?"

"Oh, Amanda, you look beautiful. Like a queen, only you don't have a crown." Emily danced across to the closet and returned with a hat box. "Do you have a tiara? Elsa wears a tiara. I saw her in *Frozen*. You need one, too."

Amanda laughed. "Sorry. No tiara, but I have this jeweled hairband. It was my mother's. Will it do?" Emily's eyes gleamed as she combed out the curls Amanda had carefully crafted. Afterward, she placed the hairband and tilted Amanda's head to assess the effect before squealing in triumph. Jules joined her, clapping and screaming in excitement.

Amanda dipped into a low curtsy and hugged

Emily. "You're my fairy godmother. Look how pretty you made me look. Now I need a handsome prince."

"It's Uncle Jacob, silly!"

"Daddy!"

As she kissed the children, she whispered in Emily's ear, "One day I'll do the same for you. When a handsome boy takes you to your school dance."

"Promise?" Emily's eyes shone with excitement.

When they entered the restaurant, Amanda laughed off Jacob's suggestion that she remove the hairband. "Emily says I need to look girly tonight. I'll send her a photo."

"Then you'll take it off?"

She finished sending the selfie and set her phone back in her purse. "You still have a touch of Plain in you, honey. No matter what you say."

He laughed and took a sip from the beer the waitress brought. "Yeah, some ways. But I think you're pretty the way you are. Beautiful, in fact. Perfect."

She slipped her hand in his and the touch caused her heart to race. "I've missed this."

"Yeah. Me too. Our lives are filled with noise and dirty noses," he teased.

"But I wouldn't trade it for anything, would you?"

"I'd trade maybe for a day on the beach, under our sea shack I built for you when we visited the ocean for the first time together. Remember?" He brought her fingers to his lips. "Our lives are full. When I am working in the greenhouse, I look over at you working in the kitchen window, and my heart races. We have a good life, liebchen."

"You don't regret leaving?"

His eyes were twin pools of passion. "I have more

than enough. You've seen to that. Even the things I think to leave behind, you didn't allow me to leave. You brought me back to my family. They are there, still. I don't lack for anything."

She smiled. "Not even noise?"

"Especially that!"

They arrived home to find that Jeff had left a single light on. Inside, the house was quiet, and the kitchen had been cleaned. Amanda glanced at the dishtowel and saw that it was still damp. "He must have worked all night," she whispered.

"It will do him good," Jacob whispered. "Now let's go to bed before one of the children hears that we're home. You are not a mother until morning."

Chapter Twenty-Six

J acob spun his pickup into the yard and braked in a hail of dust. He leaped from the truck and set his western hat back on his head while he wiped the toes of his boots on his Wranglers. When he reached the back door, he tossed his hat on a hook and grabbed Amanda to swing her around.

"You won't believe today. Me and Charlie won the team roping event." He reached into his jacket and pulled out a shiny belt buckle. "I been wanting one of those since I started."

Amanda felt the buckle's weight in her fingers and her mind recalled one she'd won on a similar day. The triumph of winning was still fresh in her mind, along with the sound of applause when the winner was announced. "I should have been there." For a moment she wondered how she'd let her dream slip away. Until she shook herself with the reminder that this was his triumph. "You worked hard for this and I'm so proud of you." She saw the pride in his eyes and teased, "Does this mean you're trading your red suspenders for a new belt?"

He grinned, and his face flooded with embarrassment. "Maybe. Why not?"

She lifted her arms as he swept her into a kiss that left her breathless. "No reason."

He gave the buckle to Noah to carry into the living room while he downed a glass of water. "We stopped by Bronco's to celebrate," he admitted.

"I'm surprised Charlie's new wife allows it." She smiled. "How's he doing?"

"Charlie? He's looking for another job. The rancher he's working for is calling it quits. Selling to the Land Conservancy."

"What's he going to do?"

Jacob set his glass on the counter and walked over to stare out the window. In the distance, Yankee raced along the fence line, all legs and arched pride, a thoroughbred to his last years. He squinted and turned, his expression troubled. "Horses is all he knows. Ranching, cattle, cowboying. He doesn't want to grow shrubs for the city market like me."

She snorted. "Maybe he can drive a truck. That's the last frontier."

"Maybe. He has a while to think about it. Something will come up for him."

"Hopefully." She returned to her task. "We'll send out feelers. You want to start the barbecue for supper? We're having burgers tonight."

❦

Rosie phoned two days later. "I think I'm ready to dust my feet of this place for a while. You folks looking for company?"

"Always. Are you flying or taking the train?" Amanda pressed her hand over the phone. "Rosie's coming for a visit!"

The voice on the other end sounded energized. "Hells bells, I'll take the train. See what I'm missing in life. Maybe there's some bison hanging out on the prairie I can shoot, just like Buffalo Bill."

"Those hunters almost decimated our bison," Amanda reminded her.

"Yeah, and I'm a better shot than most of them were. I'd be dynamite. But I love those critters. Wouldn't harm a hair on their heads."

"So when can we expect you?"

"I dunno for sure. I got to find someone who'll caretake this place while I'm gone. I'm running some feeder calves here, help pay off the taxes. Figured with all the meadow grass, I'd be a fool not to." She laughed. "But it's proving to be more than I bargained for, fences breaking and all. I'll need to keep them grazing for another year or more until I sell them off. Depends on prices. I get enough per head, I might stay in the business permanently."

The unasked question in her tone made Amanda sit up and listen. "You need us to come up and give you a hand with the roundup?"

Rosie's hesitation spoke louder than her protest. "Nah. Not really. Handful of neighbors said they'd help when the time comes for roundup. But I gotta feed those critters and see to their creature comfort." Amanda heard the frustration in her voice.

"Trust Rosie to get herself into a jam," she told Jacob later. "She just didn't think it through."

Jacob smiled. "That lady is nobody's fool. She knows exactly what she's doing. She wants me to run up there, take charge and prove myself. She wants to satisfy herself that I'll take over when the time comes. She's forcing my hand."

"Is that what you want? To take over the ranch? We've been over this before and you never give me a straight answer." She knew better than to jump to conclusions. Motorcycle aside, Jacob was a considerate man. He wouldn't do anything without her agreement. She glanced again at his new roping buckle and wondered what it would be like living on a secluded ranch in Wyoming. "We need to do what works for us."

A sigh hinted at his frustration. "Liebchen, let it go. We don't need to make a decision right now. We have enough on our platter."

Rosie called again, a week later. "Got a line on a cowboy who'll come live at the ranch. Work for room and board and a little walking around money. Maybe take one of Tibb's old saddles in the bargain."

Amanda held her hand over the phone to mask her audible relief. "Well, then that's settled. You'll get help, and the cowboy'll have a roof over his head."

"Yep." Rosie was quiet. When she started up again, she sounded miffed. "But it's not a done deal. Friend of mine, knows this fellow, says he's fond of the bottle. So there's that to consider. All things considered, I might not make it down there this year. I'll need to stick around. Keep an eye on this fellow, see how he works out."

"He can't cook for himself?"

"'Spose he could, but I wouldn't feel right leaving the place with a drinker. He needs to earn my trust. If he can stay off the bottle."

"So you're not coming? Noah will be disappointed."

"Yer house must be straining at the seams with all the folks living there. I better stay put." Rosie's tone indicated that she wouldn't be talked out of her decision.

Amanda tried to end the call on a positive note. She described the clear Oregon coastline and the crabbing they planned to do from the Bandon wharf when they visited at the end of the week. She talked up the way the kids were growing, and the new words Noah had learned to read. "He wants to show you his new motorcycle. He and Jacob have been taking it out on Sundays to the sand dunes. He's getting pretty good on it."

"What that boy needs is a horse," Rosie snapped. "Do him a heap more good. Teach him people-handling skills."

Amanda hung up a few minutes later with a feeling that something was wrong. Rosie didn't seem as chipper as usual. And what was that anger all about? She confided her fears to Jacob when they were getting ready for bed. "I wonder if she's ill. Maybe her heart? Or a small stroke? She seemed distracted, irritable."

"Maybe she's worried about the fellow she thinks to hire." Jacob paused to watch her brushing her hair. "Although she has a knack for hiring good help. She hired me."

"Yeah, and look where that got her," Amanda teased. "You lit out of there like your tail was on fire."

"What else could I do?" He lifted her hair and

pressed a kiss on her neck. "You wouldn't leave me at peace. I had to come."

Charlie dropped by one afternoon while Jacob was still at the kitchen table. With a beer already in his hand, he dropped into a chair without taking his hat off, a sure sign that he was worried. "I just don't know what to do, Jacob. This sale is going through quicker than we thought. Three weeks, I'm done." He dragged his fingers through his shaggy hair. "Carrie-Anne is pregnant." He looked up, his face shamed. "I haven't told her yet. I feel like a failure."

Amanda raised her head from the refrigerator where she was digging in the vegetable bins for apples. "She doesn't think you're a failure. You're smart, Charlie. You always have been. Maybe it's time to consider another line of work. Go online to the Unemployment Office. File a claim."

He looked up, visibly annoyed. "You don't expect I already thought of that. You know how much I'd be getting? That and food stamps won't keep us in beans. Carrie-Anne can't work. Who'll hire her with a bun in the oven?"

Jacob looked up from his beer. He tapped his fingers on the tabletop as he considered. "How do you feel about moving out of state?"

Charlie's beer halted midway to his mouth. "Depends. Where you got in mind?"

Jacob glanced at Amanda, waiting for her nod before he continued. "How does Wyoming sound? I got a friend up there needs a cowboy. She's a widow, likes to keep a milk cow, and has a fireplace that eats through cords of firewood."

"Jacob...." Amanda broke into the conversation with a look directed at Jacob. His enthusiasm seemed to be contagious but possibly short-sighted.

Jacob ignored her with a grin at Charlie's avid concentration. "She wouldn't mind having a baby around, either. Might turn into a permanent situation."

"Whereabouts in Wyoming?"

"Why? You afraid it's sheep country?" Jacob laughed. "There's a few of those. A fellow could make something of the ranch if he put his mind to it."

Charlie crumpled his empty beer can and tossed it aside without seeming to notice. He pushed the chair back and clambered to his feet, pacing from one end of the kitchen to the other like a coiled spring ready to fly. He raked his fingers through his hair, spun around to give Jacob a look of jubilation, and thrust his hand out for a handshake. "Cripes almighty, friend. A dream come true." He looked up, frowning. "This better not be some prank you're pulling. I know I got you bad when I set you on that bald-faced nag that was born deaf. But that was a long time ago. You proved yourself a hundred times since then."

Jacob grinned. "This is no prank. I'll call Rosie and set it up. She'll agree if I make the recommendation." He sobered and gave Charlie a searching look. "She's in trouble out there. Has a lot of pride, but she needs some help. And she has a big heart for babies. You'll be doing her a favor."

Charlie looked down at his boots and his face reddened. "I'd like to think so. Makes me think I can provide for my family without selling out my dream."

Jacob pulled out his phone and made the call on speaker. "Rosie? You still in need of a cowboy?"

"What's that? Who is this?" On the other end, the crackle of static gave way to a whoop of relief as Rosie put down whatever she was holding and held the phone closer. Her voice grew louder. "Jacob-boy? You bet I am. The fellow I had in mind won't be working out. Wrecked his pickup truck on the way home from a bar, and I saw no sense in hiring Trouble."

The next few minutes were spent ironing out details. Rosie spoke to Charlie over the phone, peppering him with questions until she was satisfied. "Say, weren't you the one was teaching Jacob to rope? I like the cut of your saddle, young man. And now you say you're married and expecting a little one? Well, I got a partiality for sweet things under my roof. We got a Jim Dandy baby doc up here, and a pregnancy center that'll help with the expenses."

"How soon do you need me?" Charlie paced, his breath sounded like he'd been running.

"Come on up soon as you're able. I can't pay much till we sell the cattle, you understand. But maybe we can work out shares. That'll incentivize you into keeping the wolves in check. And if you're off some-where on the ranch, I'll be here to drive your missus to the doctor, something comes up."

"That would take a load off, that's for sure." Charlie had lost his attempt to remain calm. His face was the color of rose wine in a bottle. "I can start next week if you need me."

"Next week would be fine. I'll make a trip to town and stock the freezer. A pregnant gal needs her nutrition."

When he hung up, Charlie stuck his hand out to wring Jacob's again. He inhaled and gave a short chuckle in a visible effort to steady himself.

Amanda smiled as she sliced another apple on the cutting board for the children. Trying not to intrude, she slipped the slices onto a plate and carried them into the den.

⁂

They invited Charlie and Carrie-Anne over for dinner the night before they left. Carrie-Anne was shy until Amanda began asking her questions about the pregnancy. She ventured quick, frequent glances at Charlie and blushed at his obvious adoration. Charlie brought a six-pack, Jacob barbecued tri-tips, and Amanda made her aunt Lydia's twice-baked potatoes and copper penny carrots. Carrie-Anne made the salad with quick, efficient steps that showed her love of cooking. When Amanda saw how ill-at-ease she was, with a house full of people she hardly knew, she asked her to help with the children's meals while she put together the apple crisp. By the time they sat down to eat, the young woman was laughing along with the men.

When it was time for them to say goodbye, Jacob slipped Charlie a thick envelope with a wad of $50 bills inside. "Just take it," he ordered when Charlie's face flooded with embarrassment. "Our baby gift. You'll need it for extras." Amanda smiled as she watched her husband handle the transaction with sensitivity. Service to others—his Amish creed.

After their guests left, Jacob swept the floor while she filled the dishwasher. Jeff scraped the grill clean and carried the trash out before he left to put his kids to bed.

"This was a good night." Amanda followed Jacob outside to hang the mop over the fence. "You know, Rosie's going to fall in love with their baby and forget all about ours."

Jacob reached for her. "I suspect Rosie holds enough love for everybody's kids. She will fill her house with laughter. Who could want less?"

"You're right. I was just being silly."

"But, you're right about one thing. Maybe this is the answer to our problem. Partnership with Charlie. He could work the ranch, and we could remain here, like we planned."

"And visit Wyoming when it's roundup time?"

Jacob's eyes flashed with amusement. "And when it's time to inoculate and worm. When it's time to shoe the horses—"

"Okay, I get your point. You want to be a cowboy." Amanda slipped her hand in his as they walked to where a spotted owl hooted from the small, forested area across the pasture. Jacob stood in silence, listening to the night sounds along the creek.

Overhead in the darkness, the new moon lent the suggestion of light on the horizon. "Look, Jacob. It's the aurora borealis. This is just crazy! I've never seen it like this." They watched the purple violet haze creeping across the dark sky, low along the tree line. "Conditions have to be perfect for this."

He wrapped his arm around her. "Conditions are perfect tonight, liebchen."

Chapter Twenty-Seven

Rosie's voice rang over the phone, trilling in highs and lows like a bird's song. Background noises hinted that she was walking around the house looking for something—or someone.

"Hello, Ruth Family! Hadn't heard from you for a spell so I thought I'd better check in. Time flies. You know, it's been a minute since we seen each other." She laughed and her voice sounded younger, less stressed. "That cowboy you sent my way is crackerjack. He's out there today bringing the cattle to close pasture. I can't say I miss the saddle sores. Getting older. I'm happy to stay inside where it's warm." Her voice cut out, and her breath came harder.

"Rosie, what are you doing? You sound winded." Amanda waited for the connection to clear up while Rosie's voice cut in and out in a static monologue. "You're sweeping under the beds so the baby won't get exposed to dust mites? I never took you for a housekeeper."

"Don't laugh, Amanda Ruth! We got a baby here,

and I don't want her getting croupy on my account. Anyway, I'm not outside, feeding and doctoring, so I need to keep myself busy."

"How's Carrie-Anne doing?" Amanda could hear clanking in the background.

"That gal's a marvel. She's making up a stew out of last summer's carrots and parsnips. Charlie had to put down one of the steers, and we butchered it out on the counter here. Carrie-Anne made room in the freezer for every bit of it."

Amanda heard the praise in Rosie's voice. "Well, you're set then. Got all the help you need. No reason for us to hurry up your way."

Rosie turned from the phone and her voice lowered. "Amanda, you just simmer down. I recognize that tone. No reason to feel pushed out of shape by the green-eyed monster!" Her voice tightened into a lecture. "She's a great little gal, but some of her ways is strange." She coughed and lowered her voice to a whisper. "She leaves her Bible where I can find it, and I think that's presumptuous. Like I don't have one of my own?"

Amanda laughed. "I know you do. I saw it on the shelf gathering dust. Why don't you get it down and set it by your chair. That's all she wants."

"Harumph." Rosie ignored the point as though she hadn't heard. "How's that big strapping man of yours?"

"Jacob's fine. He's in Portland today on business. He took Noah with him."

"Noah didn't have school?" Rosie sounded like she disapproved.

"Well, technically. But Jacob thought he needed some daddy-son time. It's a bit much with the four kids, you know. He gets overlooked sometimes. Emily is so outgoing and a year older, so she takes a lot of the air in the room, you know?"

Rosie laughed. "Amanda, you sound like a damned mother bear."

Amanda started to protest and ended up laughing with Rosie. "Don't I though? I love Emily, but Noah's my son. I love him differently."

"Touché!" Rosie paused to let her words sink in. "There's room for all kinds of love in this world. Don't think there ain't."

Amanda heard the regret tinging Rosie's voice, despite her attempt to hide it. "You're thinking of your son, Steve today, aren't you?"

Rosie's voice softened. "I found a box of his baby clothes under the bed when I was sweeping. Took me by surprise. I remember when I got those things. Good friends had a shower for me and gave me practically everything I needed. We were dirt poor and proud, and it was a godsend."

"What are you going to do with them?"

Rosie's volume lifted and she laughed. "Heck, I wiped my tears and tossed the whole lot into the washing machine. By tomorrow they'll be keeping Carrie-Anne's baby warm till we sell the cows and she can afford a few things of her own."

Amanda heard the joy in Rosie's voice from sacrificing her precious items, something she never expected to part with. *Better to give than to receive.* "I have a lot of Adam's old things. I'll batch up a box and send them. What else does she need?"

"Need? I expect she could use just about anything. Baby's sleeping in a dresser drawer, but that'll change in another month or two. She's a tiny little thing, but she's active."

They talked for another few minutes before Amanda hung up. She walked through the house looking for Jules's outgrown Exersaucer and bouncer. Rosie didn't have room for a lot of stuff in her little farmhouse, but the baby needed to occupy herself through the long winter months.

She packed a carton with clothes, bedding, and the portable bouncer. By the time she taped the lid on the box, she'd emptied one drawer of Adam's dresser of outgrown baby clothes. *Charlie's kid is going to be a handful. She might as well start getting used to boy's britches. They'll keep her warm.*

Noah was ecstatic when he arrived home with his father. "We saw the big trucks, Mama. And we ate french fries at *Five Boys*. And Daddy said I could have some hamburger. And we went to a store and Daddy looked at a little motorcycle for me, and he said if I'm good, maybe I can get it for Christmas."

Amanda continued cutting potatoes without looking up. When she glanced over at Jacob, his face was apprehensive. "We talked about this, liebchen." She nodded and reached for a bowl from the cabinet while she counted to ten. "I know." She bent to give Noah a kiss. "So you and Daddy had a good time?"

Noah's joy was priceless. He pulled up a stool, washed his hands without prodding, and took his place at the table. When Emily came in with her father, fresh from a game of checkers, she seemed subdued by Noah's newfound importance.

At bedtime, Noah described his day in such detail that she was struck with the realization that Jacob had been right in insisting he pull their son out of school for the day. She fluffed Noah's curls until he shrugged her hand away in protest. "Mama, don't do that. I'm big now. Can I get my hair cut like Daddy's?"

"Daddy's? His hair is straight."

He shook his head emphatically. "The kids at school think I look like a girl."

"Oh. Well, we can't have that." She saw his pink cheeks and his fine, strong chin. He was nearly six years old. "Why don't you ask Daddy to take you to the barbershop? You two can have another guy day. Would you like that?" She stopped herself from ruffling his hair again and leaned to give him a goodnight kiss with a silent prayer that he wasn't ready to give up her kisses yet.

On Saturday, he burst into the kitchen, calling for her as he ran through the house. When he bounced into his bedroom where she was folding freshly laundered clothing, she had to catch her breath. Standing in her little boy's place was a young man with close-cut hair, proudly grinning at her as he rocked back and forth in a new pair of black and gray slip-on sneakers. Gone were his favorite lace-ups with their ethnic elephant design—the ones he'd begged her for because his best friend had a pair.

She lifted her hand like a sunshade and pretended to search the room. "Young man, have you seen my son, Noah? I think he's around here somewhere, but I don't see him."

He laughed and his ears reddened. "It's me, Mama. I'm your kid, Noah."

She flattened her palms against her cheeks and pretended to be shocked. "No! You can't be! You're all grown up. My Noah has curly hair and..." Abandoning their game, she placed her hands on his shoulders and leaned closer. "Noah, when did you get so handsome? You look like your daddy."

He beamed, obviously wanting her to continue. She tried to think of something to mark the occasion and her gaze landed on a jumble of orangutans, elephants, and tigers on his bed, the objects of his obsession for the past two years. "Do you think you're ready to change your bedroom now? Get a big boy room?" His eyes flickered around the room. "You don't need to decide today, but we can do it when you're ready. It's your choice."

She finished laying his fresh clothing in his dresser while he bounded down the hall to show Emily. A moment later, they were running out of the house toward the stables, arguing about which of them got to ride Yankee first.

That evening, Emily slipped into her room. Amanda sat at her dressing table, wiping avocado facial mask from her face while Emily tiptoed around the room, picked up a book from the night table, and set it down. She picked up Amanda's perfume bottle, sprayed a mist into the air and walked through it before placing it back on the table. On the high dresser, she found a pair of earrings and held them up to her ears.

She walked over to watch Amanda putting the finishing touches on her face. "Whatcha doing?"

The last smudges of mask slid onto a tissue, allowing Amanda to blink several times. "Just trying to chase my wrinkles away. I want to stay as beautiful as your mama." She glanced up, encouraged at the pride in Emily's eyes. "But that's impossible. No one's as pretty as Beth."

Emily nodded and traced her finger along the edge of the vanity. "Do you think I look like her?"

Oh, so that's what this is about. Second grade anxiety. Amanda hid her smile and searched for words. "You have her eyes. You know what they say, 'eyes are the window to the soul.' Well, you have a beautiful soul."

"But my teeth are too big. And I look dorky."

"Says who?"

Emily's eyes teared up. "One of the boys in my class says I have horse teeth."

Amanda pulled her into a hug. "Oh, honey. He doesn't think you're a dork. He likes you. That's what little boys do when they think a girl's cute. They say things to see how she'll react. They think it's a compliment, I suppose."

"Did anyone ever call you a dork?"

Amanda hedged. "They didn't use that word back then. I think they said we had cooties."

Emily shook her head. "You know what I mean. Did they make fun of you?"

Amanda hesitated as she recalled her own years of taunts and schoolyard bullying. She recalled the boy who taunted her with a sing-song chorus of "step on a crack, break your mama's back," after the accident, when her mother lay paralyzed in her bed with an uncertain future. She saw Emily blinking back tears. "Some of them. It hurts, doesn't it?"

Emily nodded again, clenching her fists. "I told him to stop, but he won't."

I'll deck the little creep. "Can you talk to your teacher? Maybe the three of you can sit down, and you can tell him how it makes you feel. He may think he's being funny."

"Do my teeth look like a horse?"

Amanda shook her head as she checked out Emily's buck teeth. "Your face is in-between. Your body is in the process of changing. Some of your parts will grow a little faster than the others, and one day you'll look like your mama. You'll start to feel different, and your breasts will grow." She laughed when Emily's eyes widened. "Maybe that boy is jealous because you're starting to look older, and he isn't."

Emily looked dubious. "You think so?"

"I know so. Why don't we ask Jacob what he used to think about girls when he was in school? I'll bet he had a crush on a girl when he was your age."

"Did you have a crush?"

She thought back to her second-grade days when the only boy in the world was Charlie Rivers. But she wasn't about to admit that to either Emily or Jacob. "I don't remember anybody special," she hedged. "But I remember how mean the kids could be and how hurt I was by their name-calling. Don't let anyone bully you. It's cruel. You don't need to come home every day feeling sad. That's not fair to you."

Emily tried on some lipstick and added a pair of dangly, clip-on earrings before she found a musty mink stole in the closet. "Was this your mother's? I'll bet she was pretty, too." Amanda bit her lip and admitted that her mother had worn it in the early years. Emily draped it over her shoulders and slipped on a pair of high heels while Amanda added a wide-brimmed hat and a pair of sunglasses.

"Can I get a selfie with us?" Emily asked.

"Absolutely." Amanda fastened a fascinator hat on her head and made a silly pose. The photo looked like two sisters playing around in their mother's clothes.

Emily regarded her with awe. "Amanda, I hope I look as pretty as you do when I'm old."

Amanda laughed and dropped her phone back in her purse. "Hey, I'm not that old! I'm only thirty. And you're going to be eight on your next birthday. Have you thought about what kind of party you want?"

"Did you have a special birthday when you were eight?"

Amanda blinked rapidly. "I remember the year I turned ten."

"What happened?"

The question caught her off-guard. She shared about how her aunt Lydia had arrived to make her a special cake, right after the ambulance brought her mother home from the rehab hospital. The birthday memory had stuck after all the others had faded. "We left the window open, and the cat ate most of my cake," she fibbed. At the look of disbelief in Emily's eyes, she made a quick decision. "Let's have a girl's day out. Just the two of us. Whatyasay?"

Amanda arranged appointments for pedicures at her favorite shop. Emily chose a neon purple polish and got a "thumbs-up" from one of the nail techs. Afterward, they shared hot fudge sundaes and laughed about eating dessert first. At the mall, Emily bought stickers at a kiosk. A few stalls further, she insisted they count all the flavors of jelly beans the shop sold before she spent her allowance on a Jelly Belly poster for her wall. At the food mall they settled on Chinese food and lemonade. When they passed a jewelry store, Amanda led the way inside and asked what kind of earrings she'd buy. Emily's gaze lingered on a pair of pretty butterflies. "Would you like to have your ears pierced, Emily?"

They emerged from the shop an hour later with Emily proudly wearing a pair of gold posts and carrying a sheet of care instructions. She slowed to check herself out in the store window. "That was fun, Amanda. It only hurt for a minute. Can we do it again sometime? Go shopping, I mean?" She sucked in her breath and remembered to pull her fingers away from her earlobes. "I'm happy I got my ears pierced, but I was scared at first."

For a moment Amanda was eight again, getting her ears pierced with Lydia—and feeling like a butterfly herself. She reached for a jellybean and popped it into her mouth. "Emily, we need to do this more often, not just once. Let's choose our next adventure right now, okay? So we won't forget."

Emily glanced down at her fingers. "Can we go visit the aquarium? Some of the kids were talking about it."

"The one in Newport? How about inviting a few friends? We could drive over to the coast and make a day of it. Maybe have a slumber party afterward?"

Emily looked up, her face transformed by joy and possibility. "Could we? I mean, it wouldn't cost too much?"

Amanda reached for Emily's hand and squeezed it. "Come here, sweetie. Mind if I give you a hug right here? You deserve to be happy, and I'm the lucky lady who gets to make that happen. I promised your mama you'd have a great life, and I wasn't lying." She waited for Emily's face to light up at the mention of her mother. "Now, no worries about money. Your job is to be a great kid. And to do your chores," she joked.

As they drove home, Emily rotated her new ear posts like the paper instructed. When she looked up, her face was convoluted in misery. "Amanda, I don't remember my mama. When I close my eyes, I don't see anybody but you. Do you think she'd be mad at me?"

Amanda found a parking spot in front of the Town Square Park and cut the engine. "Let's take a walk, Em." She captured Emily's hand in hers and pointed out the prolific foliage that created a fairyland in the middle of town. They made their way from one planting to another, watching bees pollinating the blossoms, and butterflies lifting from one plant to another along, until their path led them to the footbridge where, on the other side, people were sitting outside enjoying coffees and pastries. By mutual agreement they halted in the middle of the footbridge, Amanda to lean on the wrought iron fence that overlooked the creek, while Emily searched for something to test the waters. She found a pebble and tossed it into the slow drifting water. Not satisfied by the puny splash, she looked around for a larger stone. Finally, she ceased her exploration and stood silently eyeing the water,

Amanda took a breath. "Em, none of us remember everything about our childhood. A lot of our memories are just feelings that remain with us. My mother was paralyzed from her neck down when I was your age. She couldn't bathe me, or play with me, or even drive me to school. But I remember her doing those things, even if it doesn't make sense." When Emily nodded, she continued. "I have photos of her doing all sorts of things with me when I was younger. My memories are a jumble of things that happened and things that maybe I just wished we could have done. But it doesn't matter, because in my mind, we did them all."

Emily turned from studying the water and her body language shifted to avid interest.

"Our memories won't fade; in fact, they will get stronger as we grow older. Trust me on this. You won't forget your mother, you'll become her. When I need to remember mine, I just look in the mirror. She's up there, watching. She's all around me." Emily's forgotten pebble dropped to the concrete as she contemplated what Amanda was saying. "Emily, carry your mother inside. She won't leave you. She'll help you to be a good person. Does this make sense?"

Emily nodded and her tears welled up. "I think so."

"It took me a long time to understand. And you will, too. I promise. Your mama will be with you."

"What about my grandma? Mama said Grandma wouldn't come to see her."

"Your Grandmother Emma is a wonderful woman. One day we're going to drive back to visit her, and you're going to find this out for yourself. Do you remember when she visited your mama? The day I showed you the farm?" When Emily nodded, she continued. "She was sad that day. But she had to follow her community's rules."

"Why?"

Amanda hesitated. "She lives by a strict code of rules that everyone must follow. Your mama turned away from that code, so your grandma needed to be strict."

"Do you think that?" Emily's eyes were wide.

"I think God wants us to love each other, no matter

what." A couple of kayakers glided past and disappeared. "That's what your mama thought, too. She forgave your grandma. And you need to, too."

Emily nodded. "Can we get a soda before we go home? Then I want to hang up my poster."

Chapter Twenty-Eight

❦

"Jacob, did I say the right thing? I never asked Jeff what he wants me to tell Emily about God, or her Amish relatives, or any of it."

Jacob rolled over, irritation tingeing his voice. "You women worry too much. You told Emily to put love at the center, not fear. How can you go wrong with that?" He reached to run his hand along her arm. "Turn off the light, it's late. Let's get some sleep and see what problems the new day brings us."

❦

Jeff surprised them the next day by announcing that he was taking his kids to the coast. He packed a lunch and carried camp chairs and sand pails to the trunk. "I'll be happy to take your kids, too."

Jacob glanced at his small back seat and the two car seats already installed. "Thanks, but no. Noah's going to help me out at the roping arena, aren't you, bud?"

Noah looked up and his face broke into a grin. "Can I?"

Jacob reached to rub his hand over his son's newly cut hair. "You betcha. Right as rain. Get your jacket and tell Mama we'll be back by supper."

Amanda stuck her head out the door and gave Noah a buzz on the cheek. "Grab a bite before you come home. Your sister and I are going to the city."

Jacob drove with a Johnny Cash country western song filling the cab with guitar strings and bass vocals while Noah bobbed his head in rhythm, his face so proud and fierce that Jacob had to turn away to avoid embarrassing him. "Hey, bud, let's stop off at the western store and see if they have a hat that'll fit you. Mom won't want you coming home with a sunburn."

At the store, the clerk produced a stack of kid-sized straw hats, some with chin strings attached. Noah chose one and adjusted the tilt. When he was satisfied, he took a last look in the mirror and hooked a thumb at the clerk. "I'm just a kid. My dad's paying."

At the arena, Jacob showed him how to swing the gate closed. "Hop up on the top rung and watch how I do it. When you get the hang of it, you can take a turn."

Noah climbed to the top of the fence and sat with an older cowboy who explained how the ropers worked. Finally, he jumped off and helped with the gate until he was covered in fine-churned dust and grime.

On the way home, Jacob listened to his son describing how he'd kept a steer from escaping, his voice filled with satisfaction. *My daed understood that I needed to feel this pride. We didn't call it by the same name, but I learned that my efforts mattered. My father's guidance. This is what made me the man I am today.* He thought of his younger brothers, Samuel and Young Levi, pushing the cows into the barn before the sun rose, and he understood that discipline led them into manhood. "How about we stop for a root beer?"

"That sounds good, Dad. And some french fries." Noah flicked a glance at his father.

So, no more "daddy." Jacob reached over and gave Noah's hat a tug. "Think root beer will hurt your tummy?" He winked at his son's protest. "We'll order small mugs."

"I can't have ice cream. I have to be careful, or I'll get sick, and then I can't work the gates."

"You've come a long way, son, taking charge of your situation. That's a relief to your mama. She worries, you know."

"She still thinks it's her fault. Anyway, I don't like ice cream—much."

Jacob hesitated. "What about meat? You miss that?"

Noah studied the dials on the control panel behind the steering wheel and shrugged. "I guess." He reached for the radio and turned the dial louder. "If I say 'yes,' will you feel bad and teach me how to drive?"

Jacob shrugged at his son's impish grin. "Let's start with the tractor. I guess you're old enough to take it out across the field. What do you say?"

"Yes!" A moment later, Noah slid his hand along the seat belt harness and leaned in to make his pitch. "Will I get paid? I'm saving my money for a horse."

"A horse? I thought you wanted a bigger motorcycle."

"Yeah, that too. But I want to learn to rope, so I can help Charlie herd his cattle when we go visit."

"We planning on going up there soon?"

Noah nodded. "I heard Mama on the phone with Rosie. She and Charlie are selling their steers. A buyer's coming in a big truck next month, and they need to have all the cows counted and penned before the truck gets there. Charlie can't do it all by himself, so Mama said she'd talk to you about it."

He pulled into the café and cut the engine. "Then we'll do it. Talk to Mama, I mean. Let's have that root beer and head on home. We got a lot to do if we're going to be cowboys."

Later, high on root beer and corny knock-knock jokes, Jacob pulled into the driveway. He glanced around for Amanda's car while Noah jumped out and started toward the house. "Not so fast, bud. We got a horse to feed and water. Chores come first."

By the time they finished, his stomach was ready for some real food. He led the way into the house and snapped on the overhead light in the empty kitchen. "Where's Mom? I don't smell supper, do you?"

Noah shook his head. "I forgot. Mama said to eat before we came home. She was going to Eugene."

"Now you tell me? We could have eaten at the café." When Noah's hurt look threatened to unravel their day, he backtracked. "Okay, bud, wash up. You and I are responsible for our own supper."

Noah smiled. "What are we having?"

Jacob considered. "Chuckwagon grub, son. We're cooking like the cowboys tonight." He pulled out a cast-iron pan and set it on the stove while he directed Noah to get two russet potatoes from the pantry. He handed his son a potato peeler and dropped a couple of soy breakfast patties into the cold pan. When the potatoes were peeled, he showed Noah how to grate them into hash browns and squeeze the starch out before he added them to the hot oil. He searched the refrigerator for Noah's container of egg substitute while Noah mixed his drink.

"I think I need another name for my swiftie." Noah measured water into the mix and added half a banana and a handful of blueberries. "Swiftie is a baby name."

"You have one in mind?" Jacob flipped the potatoes and rescued the slightly burned patties. With a quick glance at Noah, he added three slices of bacon to the empty space where the patties had been and popped a lid on the skillet.

"Nah. I'll just call it my supplement like Dr. Washington does. She treats me like a big kid, you know?

"And we don't?"

Noah shook his head as he tightened the lid on the blender. "Not like Mama treats Emily. She thinks Emily's big, but sometimes at night, she cries."

Jacob paused with one hand on his spatula. "Have you told Mama about this?"

Noah looked up and his face reddened. "Emily deserves it. She's bossy."

Jacob plated the meals and set them on the table while Noah poured his supplement into a glass. "Emily misses her mama." He waited for his son's tentative nod before he continued. "Would you miss your mama if she didn't come home tonight?" He felt a stab of guilt at the worried look his son darted at the door. "Noah, your mama will be home soon, but Emily's mother won't. She's in Heaven. Emily needs to feel like she's your new sister. Do you think you can do that?"

Noah looked uncertain. "Sometimes she's mean."

"Sometimes my sister was mean to me. And I was

mean to her. But we loved each other, and we forgave each other." He pushed Noah's plate closer and picked up his own fork. "We need to help Emily. And we need to eat this before it gets cold."

They were in the middle of washing dishes when Amanda drove in. Jacob met her at the door to take a sleeping Jules from her arms. He carried her to her bedroom while Noah showed his mother his new hat. When he returned to the kitchen, Noah was telling her about his day.

She managed to run his bath water while his son talked non-stop. He heard Noah protest. "I don't need all those things in my bath. I'm a cowboy now. I need room to stretch out."

Amanda returned to the kitchen with a barely suppressed smile. She poured a cup of coffee for herself and leaned close for a kiss. "Noah had a good day. He wants to be like you now. No more bath toys."

"Apparently no more swifties, either." He interlaced their fingers and felt her wedding ring. "It's *supplement* now. Like Dr. Washington calls it."

"Noted!" She tilted her ear at the sound of the bathroom door opening. "I'll be right there."

"I got it. Mama." Noah's voice trailed off toward his room. "I can read my book tonight. Talk to Daddy about Emily."

"Emily?" When Noah's bedroom door snapped shut, Jacob explained the situation in Noah's words without adding anything to the story. Amanda looked up with a wounded expression. "Why didn't he feel he could tell me about this? I'm his mother."

"I guess it's my turn. Happens with boys. But don't

worry, he'll come around again when he's twenty-five. Then he'll be yours again."

"Jacob, you're killing me. I'm not ready for him to grow up."

He laughed at the misery in her tone, most of it exaggerated for his benefit. "I'll be his hero for a week or two, then I suspect he'll want his bath toys back."

Amanda wasn't giving it up. "I didn't mean to favor Emily. She thinks I favor Noah." She laughed. "But if the kids are complaining, that means we're doing something right."

He rose to his feet and pulled her to her feet. "Enough family talk. I got a country western song stuck in my head, and I still remember how to two-step. I want to hold you."

They were in a slow dance when the lights from Jeff's car flitted across the living room windows and the sound of his engine cut to silence. "Poor timing. I was just about to make my move," Jacob whispered.

The door opened with his sleeping son on Jeff's shoulder and Emily dragging sleepily behind, her face sticky and pink from the smudge of cotton candy stuck to her hair.

Amanda started toward the three, but Jacob's touch on her shoulder stopped her. Instead, she waved goodnight and closed the door to the living room.

"Let him enjoy the fruits of fatherhood," he whispered. "It's good for him." He pulled her into his arms as the music shifted to another slow dance. The mood was ruined by a scratching at the door. "Shhh, liebchen, what is that sound?"

Chapter Twenty-Nine

A lab puppy sat whining at the back door when Amanda opened it to investigate. A moment later Emily raced past, her sleepiness forgotten as she scooped the pup into her arms and buried her sticky face in its fur. "Look what we found, Amanda. A coyote chased it across the road in front of us. The puppy was so scared she was shaking. I held her all the way home."

"It must belong to someone. Did you drive back and check?"

Emily nodded. "Dad made us leave a note at the laundromat when we came to the next town. And a note at the post office. He says we can keep it until someone claims it."

"We'll need to notify the pet rescues from here to the coast. Someone must be out searching for this fur baby." The puppy scratched itself. "She has fleas. Where is she going to sleep?"

"With me. Daddy says she'll whine otherwise."

Amanda darted a look at Jacob, expecting something other than a grinning man making cow's eyes at the puppy. *Men!* She held her tongue, despite the effort it took to do so. "My dad stored his dog dishes on the back porch. I'll find a water dish."

She returned with an unused bag of kibble and showed Emily how to soften the dry dog food with a bit of water. The pup frantically lapped water from a dish, spilling half of it on the newspaper she laid on her spotless floor. When the puppy finished, it bounded over to inspect the room, its tail wagging with happiness.

"Let's wash her feet before you take her into your r —" Too late. Emily was already down the hall with the pup secure in her arms.

She stooped to clean up the mess and thought better of it. *Emily's dog, Emily's mess.* She straightened to find Jacob watching from the doorway and shrugged. "You started it." He turned and disappeared into the living room to turn off the Allen Jackson song still playing in the background.

She woke several times during the night when a puppy's whining broke through her REM sleep, as she preferred to think of the precious hours of rest she might have gotten if she hadn't needed to wake Emily each time her puppy needed to go outside. On her last trip she decided to stay awake; the sky was lightening in the east, beyond the line of trees where she'd buried her own dog when they were both fourteen. With a cup of coffee, she found a seat on the porch swing and watched the sky meld into a blaze of rose-orange. She'd read once that there were sixteen shades of sunrise, depending on the amount of dust in the air.

Emily came dragging from the kitchen with the puppy tagging behind. She sank into an Adirondack chair and held her head in her hand. Amanda smiled and offered her a sympathetic pat. "Rough night?"

"I think I'll name her Luna. That means 'moon' in Spanish. She likes to stay up at night."

"Where are you planning to keep her while you're at school today?"

Emily's eyes widened. "Amanda, I can't go to school. Luna needs me."

Amanda summoned her best mean-teacher look. "You're going, no question about that! I saw a portable kennel in the storage room. I'll get it out. When you get home, you can take Luna for a walk before you start your assignments. She'll be twice as glad to see you."

"No animals in the house." Jacob stood in the doorway watching Luna drink from her water dish. "The watering and feeding will be done outside." He glared at Emily and shook his head to ward off her protest. "I will not bend in this decision. No animals in my house."

Emily carried the puppy and the dish to the mud room and closed the door before she fled into her room to get ready for school. When she returned, her eyes were swollen from crying.

Amanda paused with a plate of pancakes, already wavering in her resolve, but Jacob beat her to a response. "Where's your father? What does he say about all of this?"

"He's in the shower. He'll say it's okay for me to keep Luna in my room at night." Emily stood glaring at Jacob.

Amanda tried to warn Jacob to use a softer tone, but he deliberately avoided her gaze. "Enough. Sit and eat your breakfast. We'll figure something out." He picked up his mug of coffee and leaned forward to attack his stack of pancakes while Emily picked at her own.

"It's my turn to drive you children to school," she said. "Your puppy will be safe in the mud room. Adam and Jules will be thrilled to help me take her for a walk." She retreated to the hallway. "Noah? Your pancake's getting cold."

She returned from school drop-off to find Jacob and Jeff still at the table. Without speaking, she dropped her purse on the counter and poured herself a cup of coffee. Adam was finished with his breakfast, and Jules was making airplanes out of her pancake, flying it over her head instead of eating it. Amanda slathered almond butter on the remaining cake and started to eat, trying to ignore the puppy scratching the other side of the door.

"Jeff? What are your plans for the puppy today?"

Jeff looked up with an expression of surprise. "The puppy? Oh, the rescue pup. I don't know. Guess we'll need to contact someone. Maybe if you have a minute..."

"We can divide the calls, but you have to tell Emily if someone claims her pup. And while you're at it, explain the house rules. No sneaking her into the bed after we're asleep. Doesn't matter how much she complains, that's how it has to be." She heard the scratching again. "And you take it to your office today. See how that works out."

She watched Jeff walk across the parking lot to his office, his arms filled with puppy kennel and a water bowl, with Luna trailing behind him. Adam and Jules settled in front of the TV to watch *Sesame Street*, a good time to call the animal rescue facility. She texted

Jeff to take a photo of the puppy and waited until it came through before she attached the image to the email she sent out. She paused with her finger on the 'send' button. *You're a heartbreaker, for sure. People will be coming out of the woodwork for you. I hope no one claims you. The kids need a puppy.* It felt strange, having no dogs around. Jacob had taken two strays to the animal rescue after her father picked them up on one of his last driving excursions. And his faithful old lab had passed just before they left for Ohio—a blessing at the time. Amanda opened the file and studied the quizzical expression on Luna's headshot and remembered how Emily's face shone every time she looked at the puppy.

She picked up her mop and wiped the pawprints tracked around the kitchen. When she finished, the floor shined like a laboratory. *Where's the character? It looked better before.* In the den, *Sesame Street* had ended, and the credits were rolling on the letter M. "No more television, kids. We need to walk Luna."

Adam and Jules took turns with the leash until the walk across the pasture turned into a free-for-all. Luna lunged at a flock of Canadian geese near the creek. She dragged Adam toward a gray squirrel barking from an oak tree, but he hung on until Jules rushed to help him. In the frenzy, the puppy pulled free and made a mad dash toward the creek.

Amanda gave chase. Behind her, the kids were crying, and Adam lay covered in mud. The puppy disappeared in the tree cover and yipped at something too far away to see. Standing undecided in the middle of the pasture, Amanda considered the futility of her chase, until an image of Emily's heartbreak forced her to reconsider. Suddenly, the puppy was running back toward them, its hind legs tangled in the leash. She crouched, holding out her hands while the puppy inched close enough for her to reach the leash and untangle it. When she lifted the pup against her, Luna's heart thumped like a wild thing.

Against her better judgment, she allowed the puppy to spend the morning in the kitchen with Adam and Jules. At lunchtime, when Jacob and Jeff arrived for sandwiches, the puppy was asleep on a blanket in the mud room. Jacob opened the kitchen door, looked around and wrinkled his nose, before he shot a suspicious look at Amanda. "Smells like dog in here."

She smiled and bent to pull a tomato from the refrigerator. "I wasn't aware that puppies had a smell." She sliced the tomato and set it on the table. "I'll google it after we eat."

At three-thirty, Emily ran from the bus stop and dropped her backpack at the door, scarcely breaking her pace before she pulled Luna into her arms and buried her face in fur. She lifted her puppy and danced around in a circle, almost breathless. "I waited for you, Luna. I knew you'd be here when I got home."

While Emily coaxed the puppy across the parking lot to her father's office to retrieve the kennel, Amanda walked out to where Jacob was driving the forklift. He saw her and cut the motor, waiting for her to speak.

"Jacob, we need to talk." She smiled as his concentration changed to wariness. "It's nothing bad. I just need you to know how important this puppy is to Emily. I think we need to stay out of it and let Jeff handle it. Technically, it's his decision. He made promises to her, and we can't overstep his authority."

"What do you suggest? You know him, he'll keep his nose stuck in his computer, and you'll do the work."

She watched Emily racing around in circles with a plastic bag, teasing Luna each time it filled with air. "I remember that happiness when my father brought Ginger home for me. My mother was in the rehab hospital, and I was so lonely. He carried this fur bundle into the house, and I saw those brown eyes begging me to love her, and suddenly I had something to worry about besides my own misery."

She reached for his sleeve. "Jacob, it's different for you. You had a farm filled with animals, and you didn't allow yourselves to bond with them. Maybe you named your cows. Remember how you came home that first day and told me that some of them still remembered you?" She waited for his tentative nod. "Jacob, she's lost her mother. She needs this. She needs Luna."

Jacob's gaze swept the yard where the children laughed and ran in circles, and he bit his lip. "I leave this to you and Jeff. You're right, it's his problem. But," he gave her a glare, "...no sleeping in the bedrooms. On this I don't budge. The pup sleeps in the kennel. On the porch, ja?"

"We may need to move a bed out there for Emily."

He turned back to his forklift and raised his arm in farewell. "That can easily be done."

In the office, Jeff watched the children from his window with an expression of joy. When he saw her approaching, he opened the door and waited for her to enter. "Jacob has an objection?"

Amanda heard the curtness in his tone. "No, he says this is your decision. Emily's your daughter, and you know her better than anyone else."

"Jacob said that?" He took his seat and glanced at the spreadsheet on the screen while his face flushed. "I'm surprised. I thought he didn't want the dog."

She smiled at his relief, not so different from her own a few minutes earlier. "He didn't say that, exactly. He said no dog sleeping in the bedroom." She let the words settle before she continued. "You know Emily. That's a rule she's going to fight. But she needs to respect Jacob. To understand she has to compromise. This is a lesson that is bigger than just a puppy, and it's better she learns it while she's young."

Jeff nodded.

"It won't be forever. One day you'll probably buy a house, and you can set your own rules."

"You wouldn't mind if I moved out one day and took the kids with me?" His intensity told her that he'd been considering it.

She leaned to pick up a pen that was threatening to roll into her lap and set it in a chipped mug that read *World's Most Wonderful Husband*. "When you're ready to move on, we'll support your decision. But one problem at a time." She stood and turned toward the door. "Luna is going to be a good puppy. But I think we're going to need a companion for Noah or we'll never see another day of peace around here. I talked to the rescue kennel today, and they have some great dogs."

She waved herself off and closed the door to the office while Jeff returned to his spreadsheet. When he came in at quitting time, he asked Emily if he could help take Luna for a walk. They returned just as Amanda was putting supper on the table. She heard the scrape of the kennel door being closed and the dog settling in. Luna didn't even whine.

For the next two days, Amanda worked with half an ear cocked to the phone, waiting for someone to call to say they'd lost a puppy. When the call finally came, she took a seat at the table while the woman on the other end expressed her gratitude. Chalk it up to wistful thinking, but something didn't seem sincere. The woman's teary, grating voice struck her as disingenuous. When the woman asked for her address, she interrupted to ask, "What color is your puppy?" She waited while the woman considered.

"A yellow lab, just like the picture, of course. Why, you think I'd want to steal a puppy from a kid?" The woman's defensiveness triggered her suspicions.

"Does your puppy have any distinguishing marks?"

"Oh, 'course not, it's a purebred yellow lab. We paid a fortune for it."

"Then why was it running loose on Ryder Road?" Amanda asked.

"It got out of our yard. We live on the road, and it was only out for a few minutes. You people must have picked it up right after it escaped. Caused us a lot of trouble. We've been frantic."

Amanda crossed her fingers and mouthed a quick *thank you, Jesus.* "So you live right there on Ryder?"

"I just said that. It's our dog!"

It's? What dog lover calls their dog 'it'? "I'm sorry, did you say your dog was male or female?" She'd intentionally omitted the detail in the "Pet Found" notice. A small point and the woman had a fifty-fifty chance of guessing right.

"It's a...male...I mean a female."

She heard the uncertainty and gripped the phone closer. "Sorry, whoever you are, but I don't even know a Ryder Road. I made the name up. Shame on you!" She slammed the phone down and stood glaring at it until she was satisfied the woman didn't intend to call back.

Jules looked up from where she was cradling the puppy like it was one of her dolls. "That lady sounded mean, Mama."

"You heard that, did you, sweetie? Well, she's not going to get our dog, after all."

Emily flew into the house from the bus stop, not stopping for her milk and cookies, not even complaining when Amanda handed her a list of duties she'd be expected to do if she wanted to be a responsible dog owner. "I'll clean out her kennel right now. And I'll save my allowance so we can pay for her vaccinations. My teacher says she needs puppy shots."

Amanda smiled. "I imagine she's already had some of those, but we can call a veterinarian to schedule a visit. I'll make it for after school. You'll want to meet your dog's doctor." *What am I doing? There's a good chance someone will claim the dog, and she'll be heart-broken. Or maybe it's microchipped. We didn't think of that.* She looked at Emily's face as she happily tended to the kennel. *She may get her heart broken, but not by me.*

When the next few days passed without a call, Amanda began to relax. On the day of the appointment, she drove to school and waited while Emily introduced her puppy to three girls who were waiting for their bus. When Emily returned beaming with the puppy in her arms, Amanda didn't have the heart to ask her to kennel it; she asked Noah to sit in the back seat with the younger kids and drove to the vet's with the girl crooning to her puppy on her lap. She met Noah's gaze through the rearview mirror and saw him scowling. *And so it begins.*

Luna passed her exam with colors. The vet administered a DHPP shot and explained that she'd need to return in two months for a booster and a rabies shot. The best news: no microchip.

Noah rode home in silence. That night, he picked at his dinner and refused to help walk Luna after dinner with the other children.

"What's the matter, bud? Something bothers you?" Jacob asked. "Let's go milk the cow and have some quiet time, just us men."

Jacob carried the bucket back into the house later and set it on the counter while the sounds of the younger ones grew louder where they were playing in the yard. "Noah wants to go to the shelter and pick out a dog that no one wants."

"Noah said that?" Amanda paused as she wiped away the last of the crumbs from the table. "That sounds like him."

"I was watching my horse today. Yankee's getting on. I don't think the kids should be riding him anymore."

"So, a second dog and a couple of younger horses for the kids? With the chickens and rabbits we already have, we're going to end up with a zoo."

"Don't forget the cow. Is it bad that we have a zoo?" Jacob laughed and reached for the cheesecloth to strain the milk into a gallon jar. "Livestock provides for our needs. Keeps the kids busy. Build good habits now, so they will be productive adults."

"You get no argument from me." Amanda opened

the door to admit Emily and the younger kids, each of them fighting to see who would take the leash off Luna. She glanced over at Jacob and mouthed, *We need another dog.*

Jacob waited for the noise to quiet before he asked, "Noah, what do you say you and your sister go with me to find a rescue dog? Maybe Mama wants to help. What do you say?"

"Without Emily?" Noah's eyes lit with excitement.

"Not this time. You and Jules need to pick out a dog that will suit you. That will be your best friend." Jacob stood at the door, jingling his keys like they were a cache of gold and he was the pirate king. Noah led his family out to the car and climbed in.

Two hours later, he held tight to the leash of a mixed-breed mutt that strained to greet Luna. With Jacob's help, the two dogs met each other and began rolling around in the dirt.

Chapter Thirty

❧

"Noah and I are thinking about going camping for a couple of days. We're taking our bikes over to the sand dunes. Would you girls like to come?" Jacob stood in the living room holding a gigantic tent that Amanda remembered from her childhood.

She wrinkled her nose when she caught a whiff of musty mildew. "That's disgusting, Jacob! That thing hasn't been aired out since I was twelve years old. You'll come home with a rash if you sleep in that thing!"

He gave it a shake and jumped back when a layer of white powder filtered out. "You're right, liebchen. We will sleep outside under the stars."

"The stars, Jacob, really? Go down to REI and get a real tent. And some sleeping bags while you're at it. We probably need them anyway if we plan to go to Rosie's for the roundup."

Jacob grinned. "So Noah told you, did he? I was waiting to hear from Charlie before I got everyone's hopes up."

Amanda helped him carry the tent outside before she ran the vacuum over the carpet. Adam and Jules were old enough that she no longer needed to keep the floors clean for toddlers, but kids still got sick from stuff they picked up off mildewy carpets. When she finished putting the vacuum away, Jacob was piling their camping equipment on the kitchen table. "We didn't use it much." She picked up a dented cook pan and tried to match it with a bent lid. "Dad used to go elk hunting before Mom's accident."

Jacob tossed a skein of rope into the heap and stood evaluating the mess. "We need to get away for the weekends, Amanda, or we will be like your father, with the stories of his life all happening in the past."

She picked up a box of safety matches, rendered worthless from years in the damp storage. "I agree. Let's drive over to Pendleton and buy a travel trailer."

"Pendleton? My Amish friends worked at the RV factories in Indiana. They were no lax hands when it came to craftsmanship. We make a list of what we need in our vacation home, and then we go shopping for the best deal."

"Bunkbeds!" Noah shouted. "I get my own because I'm the boy."

Amanda gave Emily a sympathetic look before she could protest that she was a year older. "Let's work together to clean up the dishes before we sit down and make a list." She peeked outside where Jeff was cleaning the fish he'd just brought home. "How about it, Jeff? Are you in?"

"A camp trailer? Yeah! I saw one tonight at the lake that looked sweet. If I wasn't saving for a house, I'd get one myself." He flipped the fish over and started scraping. "Our children won't be young forever. We need to make some memories." He looked up with a look of chagrin. "I asked Emily if she wanted to go fishing, but she said she wanted to stay home with her dog. She doesn't seem up for anything I'm interested in."

Amanda smiled. "Ummm, Jeff, that's not how this works. Kids want you to share what *they're* interested in. Em's a girl, but she has a lot of varied interests. She wants to ride motorcycles like Noah. I think she'd love camping if we get her into it. Jacob's bringing home a couple of beginner horses for the kids to learn on. Emily's already told me she wants to join 4-H and get into a horse project."

"Why doesn't she talk to me about that stuff? I'm her father." Jeff rinsed the scales off his knife and cleaned out the sink. "I'm doing okay with Adam. He likes to tag along with me. I told him I'd take him fishing next time. After I checked out the lake and everything." He looked up with a penetrating look that indicated he'd been doing some thinking on his fishing trip. "Emily's more like her mother. Beth never liked the farm. She wanted to see the city. She loved shopping for food instead of growing it herself, but she had guilt that she was shirking her duty, not passing on what she knew to her children. When she was dying, she thought maybe she got the cancer from eating fruits and vegetables that had been sprayed."

"Jeff, there's no telling why she got sick, it could have been anything. Placing blame on yourself, or her, isn't helpful. Emily's artistic, like Jacob. She's filling a sketchbook with her drawings. And she wants a Tablet for her birthday."

"Yeah, she told me. I worry that she'll get sucked

into the internet. She tends to go all in on everything she does."

Amanda smiled. "Like you?"

He thought for a minute and grinned. "Point taken. It's not a trait that'll make her friends. I'll need to help her manage her obsession, won't I?" He wasn't really asking the question but reaffirming himself.

"Would you like to tag along and help us find a family-friendly travel trailer?" She laughed. "Wow, that was a mouthful."

"I feel like I do a lot of 'tagging along.' You guys can't be thrilled having me in the house all this time." He glanced at the fish and grinned. "You know what they say about houseguests and..."

"Jeff, you're not a guest. You're family. We wouldn't have the kids in our lives without you. This is for them, so they'll have a childhood they will remember with fondness. Once they're launched, you can buy your own house or move to Timbuktu, it won't matter. But this arrangement is working, don't you think?"

He looked up with a lost expression as his face flooded with gratitude. "I don't know how we would have survived without you and Jacob. Beth understood what her family needed. I thank her every day for what she did for us, asking you to take us in."

"Yeah, sometimes I think she's with us here in the house, just watching. It has to feel good, wherever she is, knowing she doesn't have to worry. I'd want someone to do the same for me, if our fates were reversed." In the kitchen, the kids were clamoring for their supper. "We better get started. Want me to fry up those things?"

"Nah, I got them."

Jacob pulled into the yard with a thirty-six-foot trailer hooked behind his Chevy Duramax. The trailer had a bunkroom at one end with slide-outs on either side, a real mattress with a door on the bedroom for Amanda, and a full-size bathtub for the younger two. Noah and Emily called dibs for the top bunks, and the younger two chose the bottom ones. Amanda made a trip to Ikea and came home with plastic totes for everyone's stuff.

When Jeff walked through the space and saw the arrangement, he made a trip to REI and bought a three-man tent. "I'll eat with you guys, but that's close enough for me." He chuckled and then patted his son's head. "You can sleep out here with me if you want. I don't snore."

Their first trip to the coast was made in two vehicles, Jeff driving his family and the two dogs while Jacob towed the trailer. Amanda protested that she wasn't ready for sand camping, but everyone outvoted her choice of full hookups in an RV park. "It's all or nothing, bud," Jacob assured Noah as they rolled their bikes down the ramp from the pickup and set them on their kickstands.

Jacob stood in the middle of a sandy circle and coached Noah until he could shift and brake without hesitating. He suited up in his protective leather clothing and nodded in deep concentration at everything his father was saying. When Amanda realized she was making him nervous, she walked out along the water with the dogs. "Leashes, my furry friends. The signs say there are plover nests around here. So, no barking!"

She returned to find Emily driving in circles in the sand on Noah's bike, her helmeted face wreathed in a grin. When she saw Amanda, she gassed the throttle and pulled ahead, the tilt of her head indicating that she was fighting to get the bike back under control while Jacob watched with an air of nonchalance that must have taken all his effort to pull off. When Emily finally braked to a stop, he was filled with praise.

Jeff surprised everyone by taking a turn. He eased into the first turn and circled back in graceful figure eights. When he grew tired of the single track, he revved the engine and raced up the nearest dune. When he returned, Emily's proud hug nearly knocked him off the seat. His grin was nearly as wide as his daughter's. "Your turn, Amanda."

Amanda accepted the helmet with trembling hands. Without looking around to see who was watching, she slung her leg across the seat while her head rang with Jacob's riding advice, hard-earned during their driveway practice sessions in the evenings, with the children asleep in their beds. A compromise in the hope that she could understand his obsession with speed and danger.

She put the bike in gear and headed for an empty dune with a dozen serpentine tracks leading to the top. *Definitely doable.* She hit the incline with her hand on the throttle and her legs clenched against the gas tank as though she were sitting in a saddle again. Suddenly she was racing the clock with the roar of a crowd in the background. Instinct kicked in, but this time a race up the dune, the bike blasting upward with sand flying off her rear wheel. She felt the tires dig in. She gassed the throttle, felt the bike buckle, and held on, her only thought the single track leading to the top. Once there, she waved to her family and started back down.

Noah's eyes were huge and disbelieving when she pulled up and cut the engine. Everyone started laughing at once. "You fooled me, Mama. I thought you didn't like my motorcycle. But you do."

"I wouldn't go that far, kiddo, but at least I get what all the excitement's about. It's fun, isn't it?" When he nodded, she admitted, "I like riding out here on the sand, but not on the roads." She glanced at Jacob. *Our deal, the sand.*

Their first meal in the trailer was a triumph of macaroni salad and grilled hot dogs, with plenty of carrot sticks and cucumber dip for Noah. Amanda insisted that everyone crowd around the dinette while she prepared the meal.

Noah claimed the prep area to prepare his supplement. He set it on the table, his triumph complete when Adam reached for the cup and begged for a sip. As Adam licked his lips in appreciation, Noah looked up to see everyone watching. "Chocolate with bananas," he explained proudly. "Sometimes I put coffee in it, too, 'cause I can have coffee anytime I want."

After supper dishes were finished, he led a hike down to the beach to search the low tide for crustaceans and seashells in the moonlight. He carried the flashlight to the beach, and reluctantly relinquished it to Emily.

When it was her turn, Emily ran ahead, spotlighting crabs disappearing into the wet sand as the moon rippled off the water's surface, shimmying in the faint glow of dying light in the west. Waves tiptoed to shore in whispers and slips, and the gentle slurp of retreating water felt safe and kind after the noise of the motorcycles and the raucous noise of riders trying to outdo each other on the dunes. Here, the sea whispered, and the children responded, creeping barefoot as if their voices would chase the sea creatures back into their nooks.

When Jules and Adam were wet and their bodies chilled, Amanda announced it was time to hike back to the trailer. Adam and Jules tussled for control of the flashlight until Jeff lifted his son onto his shoulders and commandeered the light in the interest of safety.

"We'll get flashlights at the hardware store tomorrow. Then you can each have one," he promised.

Back at the trailer, the children were too keyed up to sleep. Over the older two's protests, Amanda pulled out a battered board game, *Candyland,* and set out a bowl of microwave popcorn. By the time Jules reached the Peppermint Forest, she was yawning. Adam joined her and they slipped into their beds without protest, their whispers drifting back to the table. "She forgot our story."

"Yeah, but we didn't have to take a bath."

Their giggles dissolved into quiet snores before the older two decided to join them and Jeff left to climb into his tent.

Later, in their own bed, Amanda rolled over to face Jacob. "I love that we're here. And I love you."

"Enough to ride my bike tomorrow?"

She smiled against his cheek. "Don't think I won't."

"Yeah, liebchen. You did good today! A surprise always."

Amanda waited to see if the moment was right. "I

was thinking about something Rosie told me once. She said not to cut ourselves short. Jacob, she was talking about babies. She said we'd regret it if we don't have another one while the kids are little. Do you think she's right?"

He turned to study her in the moonlight streaming through the open window. "You wish to have another baby?"

The words spoken aloud held power that she hadn't considered. "I don't know. Maybe. Why not? We love ours, and we're good parents. The world could use another kid with our genes. After all, what have we got to lose?"

"You're raising four already, and the world is different from the one in which the Amish raise theirs. At home, the older ones help to raise the younger. Work is a discipline, and everyone grows closer because they do it together. There is no carpooling, no soccer, no 4-H meetings—all the things that you fit into your day. There, responsibility is the center of the family. Here, it seems that recreation and busyness set the tone."

"We're not like everyone else. We spend a lot of time talking around our table."

Jacob's chuckle vibrated against her cheek. "Well, maybe. Yeah." He nipped at her ear. "Growing up, the table was for sure the center of our home. I miss that old table. John has it now."

"And you think our children won't know our values?"

He considered her question while the softness of their breathing absorbed the silence. "It won't be the same. They will have free will and more options. This will be both good and bad for them."

Good and bad. So judgmental. Words filled with fear. "Our kids will be fine. Look at all the fun we had tonight, laughing and eating popcorn. We can do this every weekend if we want. We can take the kids traveling, and teach them what a wonderful country we live in. Let's do it, Jacob."

He laughed. "And who will mind the business?"

She spoke before she thought. "Jeff can. He knows as much by now as we do. He reads everything he can get his hands on." She laughed and corrected herself. "Maybe not actual books, but he reads everything he finds on the internet, and he retains it. He talks to the workers from his heart, and they respect him."

"Working in the nursery? I think of him in the office. Behind the desk."

"Give him the responsibility, and I think he'll surprise you. Maybe a trial run? Let's see if he'll let us take the kids to Wyoming and help with the roundup. Then we'll take off for Ohio...and see the Grand Canyon, and all the National Parks. Jacob, maybe he'll agree to let us take them for the summer. He needs some time to develop his interests. He's dying to explore the art museums in Portland and go backpacking and bicycling with some friends he met at a beer garden in Silverton a while back. Think about it, Jacob. He married Beth when they were so young, and they were only married for five years. He lost her when Adam was a tiny baby and he's been keeping everything together since then."

"The children would miss their father." Jacob kept his voice controlled with Jeff sleeping in the tent only a few feet away.

"We'll leave that up to Jeff. He can drive out to

meet us or fly out for a few days. We can Zoom every day or two. I think he needs this. He needs something besides living under our shadow for the next ten years. He says he loves living here with us, but..."

"Let's sleep on this, liebchen. This could be a good plan, we see."

The next morning, Emily helped prepare pancakes and bacon while Noah assisted Jules with setting the table under the awning. He set rocks on the napkins to keep them from blowing away, while Jules collected sticks and stones to make a table arrangement.

By the time Amanda finished eating, Jeff was collecting his fishing pole. "He craves solitude," Amanda admitted to Jacob as they watched him leave a few minutes later. "He's in a position where he can't win. He tries, I know he does, but he's not a natural parent." In the kitchen, Noah ran dish water into the sink while Emily cautioned him about emptying too much gray water in the holding tank. *Emily is like her mother. She has everything under control.*

"Let's take the little ones down to the beach," she suggested.

Jacob set Adam on his shoulders and Jules picked up the end of the leash that was attached to Ruby, their new rescue dog Noah had chosen when it sat up and begged for him the first time he saw her. He had taught her a handful of new tricks, even if house training was proving to be one of the hardest.

"Ruby, Luna—what is it with the pets' names?" Amanda joked. "Too much *Sesame Street*. 'Today, the Miller family is brought to you by the letter 'U.'" She laughed. "Even Jules."

Jacob tugged her hastily-braided pigtail and bent to

claim a kiss. "Liebchen, do I ever tell you you're crazy-beautiful?"

Adam giggled and clapped his hands. "Uncle Jacob, you're kissing Aunt Amanda."

He straightened and set Adam back on the sand with a grin. "Yep. One day you're going to have a pretty wife, and you're going to kiss her, too."

"I'm going to marry Amanda."

Jacob reached to tickle Adam's toes. "We'll see about that, bud."

Jules spent the rest of the walk trying to perfect her cartwheels while Noah struggled with the leash, thinking he was leading the dogs when clearly they were leading him. At the water's edge he released the leashes and ran after Jules in circles, as they chased each other with seaweed whips and jumped from drift-wood logs.

Finally, wet and tired, they headed back toward the trailer. Noah stood on his tiptoes, trying to string a clothesline, and Emily hung the damp beach towels to dry.

"Look at you two! We need to do this more often," Amanda couldn't stop smiling as the older ones led the younger children to their bunks to read. "This deserves cocoa."

Later, Jacob got the bikes out and Noah offered to show Emily how to ride up the dune on his motorcycle. She shook her head. "I'd rather take the dogs for a walk. See if I can get Luna to come to my voice command." When she returned, laughing and splattered with sand, she seemed happier than she'd looked in weeks. Amanda slipped her arm around her shoulder and pulled her close. "You're not the same girl anymore, Em. You're growing up."

Emily nodded. "I think I want to be a vet. After high school, I mean. I like animals better than people, and they really like me, too."

Amanda nodded. "Have you talked to your teacher about this? You'll need to take a lot of AP math and science classes. We can get an appointment with her and see what she recommends."

"Amanda, I'm only in third grade."

"True that, but it's never too early to start. I know one of the counselors at the junior high. I can talk to her, if you want."

Emily hesitated. "Not to hurt your feelings, Amanda, but I got this. I'm really used to doing things for myself. Besides, you have the other kids to worry about." She stood rigidly, letting the stiff ocean breeze toss her sandy blonde hair into her face until she reached and clipped a loose strand back where it belonged. Her eyes seemed focused on something far out in the waves, a buoy or a porpoise, it bobbed on the surface before disappearing into the waves. "Look, it's a seal. It's looking for something to eat. I'm reading about them. If we see a baby seal on the beach, we need to leave it alone because it's waiting for its mother to return." She turned toward the grassy strip of sand, as if searching for a lone seal pup on the sand. "I wish I had a pair of binoculars. I could sit on the bluff and take field notes like a scientist."

Amanda shared the request with Emily's father when Jeff returned from the lake with enough trout for dinner. He knelt on the sand and placed the fish on a bundle of newspapers while he cleaned them. "That's a good idea. I'll pick up a pair for her. Maybe we can go birdwatching sometime."

"She's interested in seal watching right now, Jeff. That's what she wants to do with you."

He looked up, blushing. "Oh yeah, right. Sorry."

Amanda left him to his work and climbed into the trailer to start a pan of potatoes. When he returned with the trout ready for the pan, she heard him asking Emily if she wanted to show him where the seals were nesting. They walked off out of hearing range sharing a story that required Emily to use her hands a lot.

By Sunday night the kids were sunburned and ecstatic from three nights without a bath. The dogs had slept on their own beds on the floor of the bunkroom. Jacob hadn't objected when he saw that they didn't make a mess. *Small steps.*

❦

Back home again, Emily staggered out on Monday morning, carrying her backpack and an empty leash. "I need to walk Luna. I can eat my toast while I do it." Her eyes were dull with exhaustion, but she didn't complain.

Amanda took the leash and set it on the counter. "We'll take care of Luna today. You sit down and eat." She brushed Emily's hair back and finger-braided it. When she finished, she pulled out a hair band she kept in the junk drawer while Emily finished eating her poached egg and drinking her cocoa. She stood to check herself out in the mirror. "Cool, thanks, Mom." She stopped and turned, her face blazing. "I don't know why I said that. It just slipped out. I'm sorry, I didn't mean anything by it." She looked like she wanted to say more, but Amanda slipped her arms around her.

"I don't mind. And I get it. You can call me 'Mom' if you want to. I understand that I'm your earthly mom, and Beth is your heavenly mom. We share you, and it's okay to do that." She pressed a kiss on Emily's cheek. "Do what comes naturally, Emily. Don't overthink it. Just trust your instincts, okay?"

Emily's look of relief spoke for her. Outside, the bus pulled up, so she grabbed her bag and ran down the driveway while Noah rushed past with a piece of toast in his mouth. When the bus pulled away, Amanda shut the door and turned to prepare the younger children's breakfast. When she sat their plates in front of them, she pulled out a chair to join them, but the idea of a poached egg didn't settle right this morning.

"What's wrong, Mama? You look like Dr. Seuss's green eggs and fried ham." Jules pointed her fork, laughing.

"Maybe I had too much beach camping. We sure had fun, didn't we?" When Adam nodded, she asked, "What was your favorite thing?"

Jules stared at Adam, thinking. "My bestest thing was when Luna made Adam fall into the water and he got all wet and it was silly. And I liked walking in the water and having the waves chase me. And I liked at night, when we played games, all of us, even Uncle Jeff."

Adam giggled. "I beat my daddy in *Candyland*. And then he looked silly 'cause he was the *Old Maid*."

"It was fun, wasn't it." Amanda listened to them retelling the parts of the trip that already left an impression, even the rare trip to DQ for soft serve ice cream on the trip over. She ran water into the sink and washed dishes, filled with satisfaction. *When we nail it, we nail it.* "Let's get dressed and take the dogs for a walk. See how Yankee's doing this morning. I'll bet he missed your brushings while we were gone."

Chapter Thirty-One

"The whole summer?" Jeff's face flooded with surprise as he stared from Jacob to Amanda. "What would I do without the children?"

Amanda explained their plan. "We'll take them back to Wyoming, and Emily can help round up the cattle. They're ready for market, and they need the extra help. She's a really good rider now, and Jacob and Charlie won't let anything happen to her."

"And after that?" Jeff's eyes still held uncertainty.

Jacob picked up a map and unfolded it on the table. "Here's the route we plan to take. Over to Yellowstone, then to Cody to see the Pow-wow and the Buffalo Bill Museum." He laughed. "You could fly up and join us for the weekend. They have a pretty decent prime rib at Buffalo Bill's old saloon. I've had it, myself."

Amanda picked up the map. "We'll hit the National Parks in Utah. Drive through some of the Indian reservations. Emily's studying Native Americans in school next year. This would give her a real advantage."

"And Adam? He's only three. He'll miss his father."

She smiled. "We thought of that. We'll Zoom you. He can talk to you anytime he wants."

Jeff sat on the sofa, his eyes wide and uncertain as he tried to absorb everything he was hearing. "Two months? That's all summer."

Amanda nodded. Not quite. We'll have them back in time for school."

"They'll miss Father's Day. We always done something special."

Amanda heard the panic in his voice at the idea of losing one of their last connections to their mother. "We celebrate Father's Day. Jeff, we want to take Emily back to meet her grandmother." When Jeff jumped to his feet in surprise, she waved him back down. "Your children need to know their family. We can stop in Chicago and meet your sister, and you can fly out and meet us, but Emily has another aunt, and a grandmother she doesn't even know. We can change that."

Jeff glanced down at the carpet while the grandfather clock ticked from the hallway. He looked up again. "I feel so obligated. It's tough, you know, being here under your roof, working at your business, having you looking after my kids." He gave a short grunt of embarrassment. "Heck, who are we kidding, you're raising them. You're the mother they no longer have."

"Jeff, don't do this. Let's just figure out what's best for them, okay?" Amanda stood and collected their coffee cups. "If it makes a difference, we're taking our own kids, no matter what. We'll wait to tell them until you decide."

"It will break my kids' hearts to get left behind..." He smiled ruefully.

"Jeff, this is an opportunity to finally heal. You've been treading water since Beth's death. You haven't had a chance to deal with your feelings, or your anger. Someone once said, 'If nothing changes, nothing changes.'" Amanda paused for good effect. "If you keep doing what you're doing, you're going to keep getting what you're getting."

Jeff smiled. *"The Lies about Truth?* I read it."

"Well, then, if you want change, create it."

He hesitated. "You think I'm making this about myself?" His eyes widened as he heard his own words. "You're saying my head's not on right, and I need to take care of it." He glanced around the room until he summoned the nerve to look at them directly. "You take the kids. But I'll fly to Chicago and travel with you. I need to face the grandparents and my sister together. It's the right thing to do."

Relief escaped in her pent-up breath. "Then let's make this a family vacation. We'll ask Emily and Noah what they want to see. They can do some research and come up with a plan. I remember Mom telling me about a place they visited on their honeymoon called Bubblegum Alley." She smiled. "They each left a wad of bubblegum on the brick walls in the alley, and they took a picture. It's famous now, but the walls were pretty sparse back then."

Jeff grinned. "Right, so...Bubblegum Alley in San Luis Obispo? I've heard of it. How about The Paper House? Or the biggest ball of string in Minnesota. Is that really a thing?"

"I think it's twine. We certainly won't want to miss *that*! If it exists." She laughed.

At supper, Emily and Noah jumped up and down

in excitement while the younger ones joined in. "Can we bring our dogs?" Emily asked.

Jacob shot her a mock warning. She smiled sweetly until he nodded—and the kids erupted in cheers.

"What else could we do with those dogs?" she asked him later. "Jeff can't take them on the plane."

"It's going to be a long trip," Jacob grumbled. "But we'll find a way."

⚜

A few days later, Noah asked to speak to them after supper. "Mama...Daddy...my dog Ruby is old, and she doesn't like traveling. She sleeps a lot, and she gets tired of Luna always playing with her. Maybe she can stay here on the farm and have a vacation, too. Jeff and the guys can look after her."

Jacob swung Noah up in the air. "That's very kind, Noah. You put Ruby's needs before your own. Your grandmother will say 'you did a good turn.'"

"I'd like to see Grossmummi Emma again. And I want to show Silas I can still push the cows into the barn."

"He'll be glad to see you, that's for certain," Jacob assured him.

Noah beamed. "I'll tell Emily she can use the dog bed this time. She'll be glad."

"We'll need to get our chores caught up so we can leave as soon as school is out."

⚜

Amanda glanced out the kitchen window into the noontime sunshine, past the rose garden just beginning to bud. "Jacob, someone just pulled up. Are you expecting a new employee?" A hitchhiker in plain brown trousers and a tee shirt climbed from the passenger seat and stood uncertainly, his form shadowed by the row of maples in full leaf lining her driveway. "Whoever it is has arrived by Uber. I know that driver." She opened the door to let Ruby outside and stood with the door cracked. "Jacob, come quick. I think you should see this."

The new arrival's shaggy hair was covered by a straw hat and his red suspenders matched the ones that Jacob pulled over his shoulders as he strode to the door and pushed it open. He let out a shout of surprise, and the boy dropped his knapsack and thrust his hand out.

Jacob gripped his brother's hand and then reached to pound his shoulder. "Samuel! What are you doing here? I thought you'd be back home, helping our brother get his crops planted."

"Nei. I decided I would spend my rumspringa sorting myself out. I saw you did such a good *wunderbaar gute* job of it, I thought to see how you turned out." Samuel looked around at the forklift shutting down for the lunch break, as Jacob's workers moved to open their lunchboxes. "This is yours?"

Jacob ignored the question. "How did you find me?"

"I copy the address from a letter your wife sends my mother. A whole stack of them she has in a drawer, tied with twine. Then I catch a ride like you did, with a trucker." Samuel grinned and tugged at his brother's suspenders. "What is this, some of the old ways still stick?"

Jacob grinned and thrust his arm over his brother's muscular shoulder. "Come on in the house. My wife prepares the midday meal. She will put together a plate for you, as well. Pork chops and potatoes. You look like you could eat the whole package of chops."

"Package? You don't be butchering out your own hogs?"

"Nah, I have better things to do with my time. Hogs aren't allowed around here. We're not zoned for it."

Samuel raised his eyebrows in surprise. "You bow to the Englisch rules now, bruder? The Jacob I knew would stand up for his beliefs. What else has changed since you left?"

Jacob put his head down and began eating to avoid the questions he couldn't answer. He recalled himself at Samuel's age, raw and questioning everything. When he cleaned his plate and started on a second cup of coffee, he leaned back in his chair and contemplated the changes in his brother since the last time they'd seen each other, "You've grown to the height of Daed's Belgians."

"One of the draft horses took sick last winter—Fiddler. John's wife talked to an Englisch family that runs a rescue, but the horse was old and sick. John sold him to the slaughterhouse for a few hundred. Too bad, he was a faithful friend. Dad said it was the first team he bought, back when he and Mamm were starting out."

"I practiced my harnessing on him. I came about to his knees first time I tried." Jacob toyed with the salt shaker as he recalled the big draft horse.

Amanda sat at the table with her coffee, listening.

When they slipped into their dialect, Jacob looked up and reddened. "Sorry, liebchen. I forget myself. We will speak in English only from now on." He grinned at Samuel. "Sometimes I forget that I am not married to a Plain woman. Amanda is a *wunderbaar gute* mother. And a fine cook."

She almost choked on her coffee. "Samuel, don't believe him! We fuss about whether the dog will be inside the house or out, about whether I will be home from town in time to cook him another enormous meal. When we got married, he could eat his weight every day, it seemed. Now, since he relies on the tractors and pickups, he is easier to cook for. I tell him he will get fat like that Amos Byler everyone laughs about."

"Ja, Oncle Amos. He died last year, after suffering much from the gout. His wife told how she soaked his feet in cabbage leaves and left it overnight for relief. Every time we saw Old Amos, it was another remedy." Samuel turned serious. "He suffered greatly, wearing those old black leather shoes, but the elders didn't budge." He looked down at his own shoes, a pair of electric blue flip-flops, and grinned. "I will hate giving these up if I decide to go back."

"If?" Amanda decided to face the elephant in the room.

Samuel directed his words to his brother. "I was hoping that you might have an answer. I know horses. If I wanted to work in a factory, there are plenty of those back home. I was hoping for something different."

Jacob glanced at Amanda. "We will put our heads together. But first, we get you settled. Drop your things in the den and my wife will find a place for you to sleep. I take and show you how we grow our shrubs."

That night, after she made up the sofa bed in the den for Samuel, Amanda wandered through the house, tucking small bodies in. Emily and Jules shared a room. Noah and Adam, as well. Jeff had his own room. Noah might not mind sharing a room with his uncle, but the same might not be said for Samuel. A four-bedroom house, and they were out of space.

She rinsed the cleanser from her face as Jacob came to bed, his face hinting that he shared the same concern. "I am racking my brain for where my bruder might fit in," he grumbled. "Ja, his coming is a surprise, for sure,"

She smiled at how quickly he had resumed his old speech patterns with the coming of his brother. "You sound like the Amishman I fell in love with, with your 'ja's' and 'bruder's'," she teased.

He looked up, surprised. "Ja...yes. I suppose you're right. It's nice, using the old language. Like when I dream, I suppose."

"Jacob?" Amanda paused with her washcloth midway to her face. "Your brother knows horses. Can he ride?"

"I suppose he could learn. There's not much to it once you know the animal's mind."

"True." She caught his reflection in the lamplight and saw him smiling. "Who do we know that needs a hired hand?"

Jacob straightened from his pillow and nodded thoughtfully. "He can ride out to Wyoming with us in two weeks and meet Charlie and Rosie. If they like him, he can stay."

"Rosie will think it's old times with another handsome Ruth under her roof. I wonder if she has any of Tibbs' boots left in her closet."

"I'll give Charlie a call. Tell him we got the roundup covered."

৩৯৩

Samuel was up before the sun; she heard him opening drawers and clinking cups, trying to make coffee. When her conscience wouldn't allow her to fall back asleep, she pulled on her robe and walked to the kitchen. "Morning, Samuel. You're up early."

"Ja, force of habit. I thought ta be of help, but I think it'll take some practice." He grinned. "I don't see where ya put the coffee pot."

"It's a coffee maker." She lifted the lid and added six scoops of coffee, filled the pot, and replaced the lid. "I don't know how you like yours, but Jacob likes it strong. If you want, you can add water and heat yours up in here."

Samuel followed her to where she was pointing and studied the buttons on the microwave without comment. When the coffee was ready, he watched as she poured two cups and added some of Jacob's fresh cream from a pint jar.

"This is how we do it. Lots of electric gizmos to get used to, I suppose." She laughed and pointed to the pitcher of milk from an earlier milking. "You're lucky we have a cow. Jacob insisted. He hated the powdered creamer from a box."

"I am not so fussy. Mamm was tired by the time I

came along. She had to take special care with what Young Levi eats, but me, I don't complain much. Anything is good." He took a sip and his blue eyes shone with contentment.

"I remember you were always the happy boy, Samuel. But now you come to see what you like and don't like?"

He shrugged. "I don't do too much thinking until I see if I go back or not. If I fill myself with new ideas, maybe I won't be able to live under the restraints my community puts on me." He looked up, his eyes conflicted. "Jacob says, better I find out now than later."

Like he did. And your sister, Beth.

In the hall, Emily emerged from her room dressed in a pair of jeans and a sweatshirt to stare at the stranger sitting at her father's place.

Amanda rose and poured her a glass of orange juice. "Emily, I have someone I'd like you to meet. This is your uncle Samuel. He is your mother's younger brother."

Emily stared, trying to make a connection between her mother's light hair and his thick, sandy curls. "Did you know my mother?"

"I was only seven when she left. I remember her because she was always laughing, and my daed didn't like it. She was in her rumspringa and running around with some of the girls from our community. She had a lot of friends, and she loved to tell stories to me when I went to bed. I remember how her imagination seemed to be bigger than the things most of us knew. I think she spent a lot of time in the library, reading." He hesitated. "I was surprised when she agreed to baptism. But that was before she met your father."

"Did you miss her when she left?" Emily's eyes were guarded as though his answer was more important than the question seemed.

"Yes."

"Then why didn't you write her?"

Samuel's face flooded. "She was shunned. I remember the day the deacon came and told us. She'd already packed her things and moved out. For a while we saw her in town, working in a restaurant. We weren't supposed to talk to her, but sometimes she slipped me notes to give to Jacob. And they met sometimes, so he could tell her about the family. Then she and your father moved away, and nobody knew where she went."

Emily listened with wide eyes, making the connection to what she knew and what she was hearing for the first time. "Daddy drove us back one day, when I was little. We came to Amanda's house, and she drove down and got my grandmother, and brought her to see us. I remember her. She had sad, beautiful eyes that looked like she was usually happy—except when she looked at my mama—and brown hair with specks of gray in it. And a plain blue dress with a black apron. And a cap on her head."

He smiled. "All the women wear the same thing. It's our custom."

"Why didn't she want to see us? I thought she'd come when my mama was sick, or to the funeral. But she didn't come. Daddy said we weren't to bother ourselves with Mama's side. But we don't have anyone else."

Samuel fiddled with his fork. Amanda stepped in to spare him further embarrassment. "Emily, there will be time for more questions, but you need to get ready for school." She turned to Samuel. "Emily has high honors in her math classes. She wants to be a veterinarian." Too late, she saw the confusion on his face. "Emily, make your lunch while I check on Noah."

"He's always late."

She laughed. "True that!"

When the bus pulled away, Amanda poured another cup of coffee when Jacob pulled out a chair and sat down.

"Any more men eating at my table, and I'll put out a *boarder's welcome* shingle," she joked as she opened a carton of eggs and broke eight of them into a bowl. "Pancakes and bacon coming up."

Jeff arrived and poured three glasses of juice for himself and the two little ones who arrived with sleep still in their eyes. He pulled down plates and buttered toast before he poured himself a cup of coffee and sat down. Glancing from one brother to the other, he extended his hand. "I'm Jeff, Beth's husband."

Samuel's face flooded with embarrassment. When Adam approached and tugged at his leg to show him his Lego airplane, he bent over and gave the toy more attention that it probably deserved, postponing the moment when he might have to face his brother-in-law. But Jeff seemed as embarrassed by the encounter as he was. Jacob turned the talk to fishing and hunting, and the moment of tension passed.

"So you are the man in charge of the books?" Samuel directed his question to Jeff and listened to his reply with a look of concentration.

Later, he followed Jeff to the office and studied the computer and printer with the same intensity. Amanda accompanied them, partially out of curiosity and partially in an attempt to ease Samuel into what must seem like a foreign culture. But she realized she need have no fear for his adaptability. Apparently he had picked up computer knowledge at the library or at one of his English friend's houses, because he seemed unfazed.

"Next we visit the workings of the farm, the greenhouses?" When Amanda nodded, he followed her across the yard to where Jacob was talking to two employees about the day's work. "It must be *wunderbarr gute* to sit in the boss's seat and have the work done to your satisfaction," he joked when Jacob left the men to join him.

Jacob blushed and ventured a glance at Amanda. "My father-in-law set this all up. I inherited a well-run farm, and I consider myself blessed."

Samuel brightened when he saw the cow chewing hay in the barn. "If you show me where the bucket hangs, I will do the milking." He looked up at Yankee, grazing in the field, the horse's ribs marking the effects of worn teeth and long years. "So the old horse still stands. Daed was set on selling off our horses when they were no longer useful, no matter that they were like pets to us *kind*. But I remember you set a great store by your driving horse."

Jacob pulled an apple from his pocket and used his Leatherman to cut it in quarters. Yankee ground the pieces in his mouth. "I have to make a run into Oregon City for a couple of hours, want to ride along?"

Samuel grinned. "Sure. I like to see the countryside. It reminds me of home."

When they returned that evening, Jacob had

explained the plan for Wyoming, judging from their conversation as they walked in for supper. He dropped a box of apples on the counter for her. "From one of my suppliers. I'm told they make good applesauce."

Amanda saw Samuel's look of surprise that she would make applesauce for her family. "When I was a girl, I used to watch daytime TV with my mother, after her accident. And I used to think everyone but us was rich and sat around in their best clothes, talking about each other." She poured a pan of hot gravy into its serving bowl and set it on the table. "I was under a false impression. And so are you, Samuel. I work hard. Here, take this platter of meat and set it on the table. And take your hat off, you're not in the barn."

Samuel gulped and did as he was told while Jacob watched with a half-hidden smile. They sat for supper and Jacob led them in a blessing that he made up on the spot. His brother looked up with surprise when he finished, probably expecting a moment of silent prayer. Jacob smiled. "I said what I needed to say. No need to let the roast get cold."

After supper, Samuel practiced with Noah in the yard, bunting the ball while Noah tried to get the soccer ball around his quick legs.

"I'm glad Uncle Samuel's here," he told Amanda that night when they were reading an adventure book together. "He said he'll help me make a tree fort, down by the creek, with boards we found in a pile behind the shop. Daddy said it was okay because Samuel was helping."

"I'll miss Samuel when he leaves."

"Maybe he won't go. Maybe he'll stay here and live with us."

Amanda smiled. "We better ask Samuel what he wants to do."

Chapter Thirty-Two

❧

Jacob pulled the trailer up against a stand of aspen, leaving just enough room for the pull-outs. He cut the engine, and a blue-eyed Border Collie ran up, snapping and snarling.

The barn door opened, and Charlie stalked out. He put his fingers to his mouth and gave a shrill whistle. "Sit, Dingo." When he reached the dog, he bent to pat its head. "Give him a minute to get acquainted. He's not used to strangers."

Jacob glanced at Emily as she clutched Luna inside the car. "We brought a dog with us. How's that gonna work out?"

"Let's introduce them. See what happens." Charlie kept a grip on his Collie while Emily gingerly snapped a leash on her dog and set her on the ground near Dingo. The two of them circled each other until Luna gave a yip and leaped up to cuff the other dog's face. They tumbled over each other in the dirt. Jacob reached to unsnap the leash and the dogs took off.

Charlie grinned. "Well, I'll be. My dog's found

himself a friend." Amanda climbed out of the SUV and stretched her legs, followed by the younger children just as Dingo circled back around. "Let him get a sniff of you," he advised, "so he'll recognize you next time you're outside. If he bothers you, be firm with him. Tell him to sit. Or ignore him. He's territorial and pretty protective, but he likes kids."

Rosie ran out with flour spackled on her cheek and her arms open wide. "Somebody come here and give old Rosie some sugar." Jules laughed and ran to throw her arms around her.

She waited until Jules untangled herself and turned to Noah. "Come here, you handsome thing!" She gave him a hug and laughed when he backed away, livid with embarrassment. When Amanda pushed the last two children forward, Rosie squatted to their level. "Adam, hello there, son. Welcome. And this must be Emily, the niece who's going to help us bring in the herd. Let's see your roping hands, young lady. Nice. You'll do."

Emily blushed and accepted Rosie's hug with a fierceness that surprised Amanda. Rosie bent down and scooped Luna up into her thin arms. "What we got here? A charmer, that's for sure. She's got Charlie's dog pure discombobulated. That ornery dog doesn't usually take to strangers—dogs or people."

"Luna's not afraid of anyone. She chases coyotes for fun," Emily bragged.

"Way I heard it, the coyote was chasing her, the time you found her. But she'll be safe around here with Dingo. He'll bark at anything that moves!"

From the house, Carrie-Anne approached with a new baby in her arms and another little girl at her side. Emily left her dog to run over to see. She grazed the baby with the tip of her finger and giggled when it laughed. "She's beautiful. What's her name?"

"We call her Alice, after Charlie's grandmother," Carrie-Anne said. "It's an old-fashioned name." She indicated the pig-tailed two-year-old at her side. "This is Jetta. She's Charlie's helper."

"Hi Jetta. I like your name." Emily hesitated. "Can I hold the baby?" When she finally returned the baby to its mother, her eyes glowed with happiness.

"That one has a way with little ones," Rosie murmured in a stage whisper. Emily overheard and ducked her head in embarrassment. Rosie chuckled when she darted a look of gratitude at her and ran off to see what the other children were doing. "She's a beauty. Her mother was Jacob's sister, you said?"

"His older sister. His best friend, too, until she left the community to marry Jeff. He stayed in Oregon, handling the business."

Rosie nodded as she surveyed the activity in the yard. "Look at us, two orphans with more love than we know what to do with."

"We brought you another." Amanda pointed out Samuel, who was giving Adam a ride in a wheelbarrow partially filled with straw. He looked young and happy, gripping the handles with muscled arms that reminded her of the time Jacob wheeled a load of straw home for her. She looked up and saw Jacob watching her with an expression that said he was remembering, too.

"We done good, child. Building us a clan to keep us from getting lonesome." Rosie leaned in and whispered, "You give any more thought to what we talked about?"

"About having more babies?" Amanda glanced at

her hands to hide her blush. "Well, I guess I'm going to have to tell Jacob one of these days."

"Well, good for you!" They watched Emily pulling the baby in a homemade wagon. "Lucky you, you're going to have a built-in babysitter this time."

Across the yard, Charlie was telling Jacob and Samuel a story that elicited whoops of laughter. Charlie's face radiated happiness. Gone, the guy who had spent his weekends partying. His eyes filled with pride when he glanced over to see where his wife stood. When she smiled back, he returned to his story with a lightness that told its own sweet story.

Amanda heard the aspen leaves rustling. Beyond, a doe and her fawns crossed the hillside on their way to the creek they had hiked to on their first visit to the ranch. Jules had been a baby back then, and now she was ready to begin kindergarten. Adam would join her as well, and the house would be empty. She didn't realize she was patting her stomach until Jacob looked over with a question in his eyes. He stood for a minute before his face lit into a smile.

Rosie watched with a look of smugness as though she were somehow responsible. "I told him, you go get that gal," she confided in a whisper loud enough that Jacob heard.

He doffed his hat and started toward them, his sandy hair catching the setting sun until he looked like he was wearing a halo. "You ladies talking about what I think you are? Is it true?" His eyes addressed Amanda, but it was Rosie who answered.

"That's for your wife to say." She grinned. "But we may need to add another wing to the old farmhouse, you intend on bringing more Ruths to stay."

Jacob turned to where his brother was helping Charlie hook up lights for the campfire later that night. "Bruder, come meet a good friend. She's been a mother to me when I needed one, and now I'm thinking she'll do the same for you. Samuel, meet my English friend and the best outsider you'll ever meet."

Rosie included him in a hug. "Some kind of strong family resemblance, son. Welcome to the ranch. We got a great need for you if you're up to filling your brother's boots."

"Yes, ma'am." Samuel shuffled the toe of his boot in the sand. "I am."

A string of lights twinkled in the yard where the kids were taking turns on a rope swing Charlie had hung in the huge maple tree. He'd trimmed the limbs back from the house and added the swing for his own daughters.

Amanda grabbed a sweater for the early June evening and started toward the corral to give herself a moment away from the commotion. From the trailer, Jacob started toward her, his gait loose and relaxed against the backdrop of laughing children and barking dogs. "I love it here." She tucked her arm under his.

"This is where I realized I couldn't live without you." Jacob's voice resonated with conviction, inches from her ear.

Amanda closed her eyes and breathed in the sound of his voice. It was the thing she associated with him when his image crossed her mind. Not his looks, although he had the power to stop her heart with a glance, but the certainty with which he faced every problem.

"And now I see in my wife's face that I am to be a

father again. What a wonder! Another feisty little girl like my Jules or a thoughtful, caring boy like Noah?" He hesitated and his eyes filled with mischief. "Or maybe this time twins?" He bent for a long kiss. "I am blessed, liebchen."

She remained against him, feeling his heartbeat, slow and dependable for another fifty years or more. "Know what I love about you, Jacob?"

"Hmmm, you be wanting a list, liebchen? That's a tall order. How long do I have?"

"Not your modesty," she teased. "I love that when you're faced with a problem, you just *know*!"

"A Godly man lives in certainty. Our path stays consistent. It's the 'making it up as we go' that leads to problems." He bent to pull a blade of grass and slipped it between his teeth. "We are not lost. Even if we do not always walk in tandem."

"I sometimes choose a different path," she teased. "But we are a good team."

"Not unevenly yoked?"

"Nei, husband, never that." She watched him swirl the grass between his lips. His arm reached to bring her against him. In the west, the sun was on its way to meet the mountains, and inside, Rosie's pie bubbled in the oven. "The tandem harness may need to be adjusted now and again, but I promise, our lives won't be boring." She drew a satisfied breath at the tableau she saw before her. A moment to capture in a photograph or a journal, but words seemed inadequate to express what she felt. She inhaled fresh Wyoming air and exhaled again.

Jacob's arm brushed against her. "Happy, wife?"

She swayed against him, reluctant to break the

spell. "Jacob, since I was a little girl, my greatest fear was to be alone. But look at us. We have this strange, wonderful family. Everyone's here because you've given them something they need. That we need!" She eased against him when a gust of cold air hit. "Look at us. Our lives are full." She pressed his hand on her belly and chuckled. "And soon to be even fuller."

Jacob smiled, intent on the shadows enfolding the distant mountains in patches of gray and cobalt while clouds puffed the sky in orbs of waning light. She saw the sun's effect reflected against his ruddy skin. His robin's egg-blue eyes seemed backlit with contentment.

She reached to squeeze his hand. "We're blessed, husband."

About the Author

A fifth-generation Californian, Anne Schroeder's love of the West was fueled by stories of bandits and hangings, her great-grandfather and his neighbors working together to blast the Norwegian Grade in Southern California out of solid rock, Indian caves, and women who made their own way. She worked her way through Cal Poly University with a variety of odd jobs that included waitressing at a truck stop cafe in Cholame—near the spot where James Dean died.

She recently served as President of Women Writing the West, and her short stories and essays have appeared in print and online magazines. She has also been awarded several Will Rogers Medallion Awards and LAURA Short Fiction Literary Awards for western and inspirational fiction.

Anne lives in Southern Oregon with her husband, dogs, and free-range chickens where she volunteers regularly for the St. Vincent de Paul soup kitchen.